(r?)**EVO**lution…

Copyright 2020
Glen Albert Phillips
Library & Archives Canada ISBN 978-0-9782694-4-9

I would like to dedicate this novel to the special people in my life. This includes my dear friend Chris Kay and his mother, as well as my mother, father, and sister Nicole.

Date – Friday May 1ˢᵗ, 2020

Introduction

In the early 22nd Century the United States is overwhelmed by a violent socio-economic crisis, which threatens to tear the country apart, further destabilizing a world disrupted by climate change, wide spread conflict, pandemics, and multiple new technologies.

Central to the crisis is a genetically engineered elite who control America's economy and its institutions. Enjoying unparalleled wealth and opportunity, they live in a world where AI, genetic medicine, and reproductive technologies have pushed the frontiers of their existence far beyond what was once imaginable. For them, cancers, neurodegenerative diseases, epidemics, and physical and mental imperfections have all but vanished. They are the most perfect iteration of the human species to have ever walked the planet, free to pursue pleasure, vanity, and social status, oblivious to the masses of ordinary naturally conceived Americans struggling in a corporatist system designed to lock them out.

Realizing the existential threat to the future of the American Republic, a progressive alliance narrowly elects a new President who promises to resolve the crisis by nationalizing access to human genetic engineering and medicine, emulating other developed economies who implemented these changes decades earlier to prevent collapse. With time of the essence, the nascent Administration quickly hires a team of experts to devise a path to bring the President's promise to fruition. Part of the team is Zane Fischer, a young and brilliant mathematician working for Syllabus, a prestigious consulting firm located in Salish City, far from the political and economic epicentre of the United States.

The path forward for the President's plan is far from certain, with many entrenched and powerful forces opposing the new Administration, ruthlessly willing to use everything at their disposal to protect their interests, and not hesitating to destroy anything in their path.

Release

Date – Thursday October 31st, 2120

The air in the room was warm and humid, laced with scents of lavender, jasmine, and the sweet acrid smell of sweat. There was barely a sound to be heard, other than the steady pitter-pattering of rain droplets splashing against the awning outside. He lay still, not moving a muscle, his heart thumping slowly and steadily, as his breath washed back and forth over his sweaty body like waves against a shoreline.

Gently, almost imperceptibly, the silence faded, surrendering to the sounds of trees swaying in a late springtime breeze, sprinkled with the tweeting of birds fluttering about in the air. He could hear the sounds of bells ringing in the distance, their chimes drifting in and out with the direction of the wind.

Suddenly a deep powerful voice filled the room, *"inhale to the count of five. One…two…three…four…five. Wait and hold your breath. Now slowly exhale, to the count of six. One…two…three…four…five…six. Hold your breath again for five. One…two…three…four…five. Now let the breath slowly fill your lungs, your heart, your chest, and spread out across your body like a wave of energy."*

The voice repeated the instructions several times more, as the room filled with the steady rise and fall of human breath. Then after a few minutes the voice said, *"find release, move those beautiful fingers and toes, flutter your lips, and reach your legs and arms as far as you can."*

"Stand up and open your eyes."

Zane stood up and opened his eyes, looking through the soft humid din at his reflection in the mirrors on the wall. His body was covered in a sheen of salty sweat, running in rivulets down his face, his torso, his arms, and his legs, pooling on the mat at his feet. As he gazed at himself and the other bodies in the room, he noticed the chimes and bird calls had vanished, replaced by chanting voices accompanied by sitars, harps, tambourines, and a constant drum beat.

The voice barreled out, *"become the rhythm! Become the voice! Submit to your desires!"*

The room slowly came alive as the mass of naked sweaty bodies began moving to the rhythm of the music, mindlessly repeating the chant. As the drum beat tempo subtly increased, the forms in the dimly lit room began twisting and turning with more energy and intensity. Suddenly, he felt a ripple of energy pulsate across the surface of his skin, as one hand, then two, three, and more touched him. He responded, touching others around him, as he was pulled to the sticky humid floor, his body intertwined with dozens of others, gyrating in a heaving, groaning, sweaty mass of ecstasy. The climax came, rushing like a bright light down a narrow tunnel, as every fibre in his being writhed in one final burst of absolute uninhibited pleasure.

Release.

Thirty minutes later he stood in the shower, completely relaxed, a cool jet of water running down his back. He looked over at some of his classmates, most of them regulars, there was one particularly attractive ballet dancer by the name of Shana, she had beautiful coffee coloured skin, was about a 1.80m tall, with thick long braided hair and intoxicating blue green eyes. Apparently she was born in Colombia to a rich family, or maybe it was Antigua or Surinam, definitely Caribbean, anyway not too important.

"That was another perfect yoga session wasn't it?" Zane said, as he looked over at Shana, her beautiful round breasts dripping with sweat as she stepped into the showers.

She looked at him and said, "yes it was decent, though I could have done with less of the music. I mean, what the fuck, you're all relaxed, and then there's this retarded chanting drumming music that is so loud you feel like it's going to blow your brains out, and you can't leave the room until it stops."

"Sometimes I think we should just go straight from *shevosana* to ending the class, the old-fashioned way. It would get us back to the roots of yoga, right?" another student added sarcastically from the other side of the locker room.

"Yeah, but that would defeat the purpose of the class, wouldn't it?" Shana laughed mischievously, as she smiled at Zane and the other classmates in the shower.

"I totally agree, isn't sex yoga all about finding release?" said a very muscular blond-haired white dude standing in the shower beside Zane.

"Exactly," everyone answered.

Zane finished his shower and slipped past the dude to grab a towel from the rack, sauntering across the heated tiled floor to the back of the change room, where his gym bag sat on a bench. He finished drying himself and then tossed the towel aside, opening the bag to pull out a black coloured thermal regulating body suit and a pair of black ankle height boots. The skin-tight suit slid on easily, its soft elastic material cooling quickly as it adjusted to his body temperature. He stepped into his boots, slipped his bag over his left shoulder, and walked over to the mirrors to fix his hair. Instantly the lighting adjusted to his skin tone, providing the perfect frequency to accentuate his dark olive features.

"Looking good bro!"

Zane looked over and smiled, it was the blond-haired white dude from the showers.

"You too man! Got to like the auto adjust lighting, I wish they had it everywhere."

"Well bro, to be honest, you probably look good under almost any lighting!"

There was an awkward silence, as Zane gave himself one final look in the mirror, "well have a good night, and see you around."

"Definitely bro, hope to see you too."

Zane headed to the reception and walked through the automated exit gates. *"Zane, your yoga workout session was 1 hour and 45 minutes, would you like me to do a calorie estimate?"*

"No EVO this is not necessary, but you can order me dinner, I'm famished."

"I can order for pick up en route, or I can have it delivered to your apartment."

"Apartment please."

"My pleasure Zane, I am placing your order now. Based on my calculations your meal will arrive 5 minutes, 28 seconds prior to your arrival."

Renfrew Plaza outside the yoga studio was wet and slick from a light rain that had been falling non-stop since earlier in the day. Despite the late hour, there were still large numbers of commuters, many of them probably only leaving work, or maybe heading to and from dinner meetings or workout sessions like his. Besides the commuters there were the usual street cleaning robots rolling across the plaza, sweeping and collecting autumn leaves and polishing the concrete pavers. Within a couple of minutes he reached Renfrew SkyTrain station, his eyes adjusting to the lights of the entrance, as he bolted up the stairs to the platform.

The platform area was brightly lit and the walls covered with real and virtual murals and floating holograms. Like every other SkyTrain station, it was separated from the train tracks by a glass safety barrier allowing more people to squeeze in during peak commute times. Besides running a steady jumble of advertisements, the murals and holograms also reflected some of the history of the neighbourhood, which once was home to colourful carnivals, exhibitions, and theme parks – a history long since erased by sleek office towers and residences of the city's upper middle-class technology workers.

"Attention, the next train approaching the platform is for Lake Douglas with connections to the Cassiar Connector and the Docklands LRT Loop. Please stand clear of the opening doors to allow passengers to exit first."

The train pulled into the station and the glass safety doors slid open. About a dozen people exited before Zane stepped inside. There were no open seats, so he stood and held the hand rail as the doors closed and the train glided out of the station.

"Passengers are reminded to be alert for any suspicious objects and report them to the authorities. This is a six-car train for Lake Douglas and the next station is Gilmore, with connections to the Docklands LRT Loop and the Cassiar Connector."

The train floated along the elevated tracks, snaking past clusters of sleek glass towers rising forty and fifty floors into the dark cloudy sky. On clear summer evenings one had views of Hastings Park and the shipyards down at the port; however, on a late autumn night, all he could see in the glass were reflections of the interior of the train, catching glimpses of the people around him. Everyone looked different, but oddly the same, an army of urban technocrats who lived in the dense clusters of hundreds of towers built around the sprawling SkyTrain network.

Bored of staring at nothing, Zane logged into Teva, the latest and most popular virtual real estate game sweeping the planet. He was addicted, spending any fleeting moment he had on it. There were some real success stories on Teva, people who had built vast virtual empires collecting commissions from the transactions of hundreds of millions of followers. Zane followed dozens of these Teva celebrities; however, his favourite was a brilliantly handsome Danish architect by the name of Simon Bjorg, who had several hundred million followers and assets in virtual farms, cybernetic bazaars, and electronic entertainment, collectively worth hundreds of millions of universal dollars. On rainy weekends, when there was nothing to do in the real world, Zane spent hours in some of Bjorg's elaborate public markets, trading in computer-generated assets and playing interactive cybernetic sports.

Games like Teva were so sophisticated they even impacted the real world. The sums of money invested in the virtual realm was so large, that whenever a popular game experienced a spike, a crash, or a failure, the real economy was also impacted. History was littered with the stories of failed games that wiped out celebrities and bankrupted millions of people who gambled too much of their real savings on a bubble they believed would never burst.

EVO interrupted his thoughts, *"Zane, your station is next. I would suggest disconnecting from Teva and moving closer to doors. For your information your dinner has just been delivered."*

Zane refocused his attention away from the game, his retina eye screen clearing, revealing the interior of the train as they pulled into Lougheed City. The doors slid open and moments later he was engulfed in throngs of late evening commuters filling the vast Lougheed City Station complex. About five minutes later he was outside on the street, following the familiar path from the station to the small plaza between his building and four other large towers. The plaza was oval shaped, with scattered low-level lighting illuminating the assortment of bubbling water features and ornamental vegetation of differing varieties planted along the perimetre. Crossing the open space, he heard a SkyTrain rumble by on the overhead tracks, its noise briefly blocking out the constant buzz of air drones and the pitter-patter of rain hitting the pavement. There was a "whoosh" as the glass lobby doors slid open in front of him, and he walked quickly through the foyer to the elevators.

Zane stepped out the elevator and walked down the carpeted hallway to his apartment, passing dozens of studios and one-bedroom flats occupied mostly by younger professionals like himself. The front door unlocked as he arrived, closing softly behind him as he kicked off his shoes and walked into the kitchen. He popped open the delivery docks, pulling out a dinner box consisting of a meatless burger, fries, a smoothie, and a large house salad. Clearing the kitchen counter, he sat down on a bar stool as EVO illuminated the wall screen, connecting to the endless chatter of network news.

"For those of you just joining us now, this campaign is down to its final weekend, as the three leading candidates spend all their energies on the key swing states of California, Florida, and Texas. These states will decide the race for the next president of the United States, a battle between three very different directions for America. Economic inequality has as usual been an important issue, with the Social Democrats campaigning on higher taxation of wealthy Americans, while the Libertarians and Republicans have campaigned to lower taxes in an effort to stimulate economic activity to help raise the wages of lower income Americans. Medicare has played a central role in this campaign, as Americans will be asked to decide the future of access to genetic and reproductive medical technologies, better known as gentech. Will they choose the Social Democrats who want to nationalize it under Medicare, or will they pick the Libertarians, who want to roll back Medicare and restrict access to gentech to just private clinics? The Republicans have avoided this debate and campaigned strongly on the Climate Crisis, hoping they can be the senior partners in a potential coalition presidency with the Social Democrats to bring in an urgent Climate Infrastructure New Deal. We'll see where all of this goes this coming Tuesday night on November fifth."

"Thanks Joe, look forward to watching you guys on Tuesday on our network's special twenty-four-hour election day coverage. In other news, continued conflict on the Indian subcontinent between Muslim and Hindi extremists. Russian, Chinese, American, and EU military forces have launched coordinated air operations over the region, bombing strategic military targets in an effort to ensure the now seventy-five-year conflict remains as contained as possible to the region. China has also stepped up border management along the Tibetan plateau, adding additional landmine and drone monitoring technology to ensure no refugees or insurgents can attempt crossing into Chinese controlled Tibet. China's totalitarian regime is also continuing their widely condemned ethnic cleansing of non-Chinese populations on the Himalayan plateau, as it seeks to reinforce a buffer zone along its western border with nuclear contaminated former Pakistan and India. Liberal states, along with a number of states from the Non-Aligned Bloc attempted yet again to sanction China at the UN yesterday; however, Russia and other Totalitarian Bloc allies ensured the UN measure did not have the votes to pass at the General Assembly."

"In economic news, South American members of the Non-Aligned Bloc have signed a landmark agreement to reforest up to seventy percent of the seven million square kilometre Amazon basin by the middle of this century. It is hoped future revenues from carbon capture markets will eventually replace income from the livestock sector, which has been decimated by the synthetic meat industry."

"In Climate Crisis news, the UN reports ocean and rainfall flooding in Bangladesh has made much of the country uninhabitable. Unfortunately the country's more than two hundred million inhabitants have no escape and their government is completely overwhelmed by the crisis. It is estimated lifespan in the country has fallen to just thirty-two years of age, as many Bangladeshis face the onslaught of monsoons, regional epidemics, and continued low-level nuclear contamination from the Pakistan-India Small Nuclear War in 2062..."

13

The news made him feel anxious, it was always the same incessant chatter about the US election and gentech, the climate crisis, the fallout from the 2062 Pakistani-Indian Nuclear War, and the endless brinkmanship between the Totalitarian, Liberal, and Non-Aligned Blocs. He sipped his smoothie, trying to imagine the miserable existence for those millions of people in Bangladesh, and indeed the millions more who were trapped in the global periphery, brutally quarantined in perpetuity to suffer the worst manifestations of the climate crisis.

"Zane, may I propose chatting to some of your friends to get your mind off the news, or perhaps checking up on the status of your Teva holdings?"

"No EVO, I don't feel like doing that."

"In that case, may I suggest that episode of late 20th Century Star Trek, which you had just started watching yesterday."

"Oh yes, what was it about again?"

"The episode is called 'The Trouble with the Tribbles'. It's about small furry critters called Tribbles, who exist only to eat and reproduce."

"Ah yes, I remember now. Bring it up."

Zane returned his attention to the screen, mindlessly chewing his fries and burger as images of a toxic dust storm in northeast India switched to a mixture of ads for virtual games, sex toys, and popular narcotics. After a few minutes the show appeared, starting at the point he had left off the night before. He was addicted to Star Trek, the popular cult fictional space travel series he had been watching over the past few months. It was about the Enterprise, a roving spaceship travelling the galaxy, searching for new life, led by an emotive maverick by the name of Captain Kirk, who was accompanied by a team of scientists that included Spock, a humanoid Vulcan with superior intellect and logical reasoning. In this episode the Starship Enterprise had been invaded by some mysterious furry animals, who were reproducing at an exponential rate, threatening the ship with catastrophe as they consumed all of the resources on board.

He sat mesmerized watching Kirk, Spock, and the crew battle the invasion of the furry creatures, as they eventually devised some ingenious way to rid the Enterprise of the infestation and save themselves. The show ended and Zane snapped the connection off, sitting for a moment in silence. The Tribbles, they were like a deadly virus consuming a host, geometrically reproducing in numbers until the entire system collapsed. Human history was filled with Tribbles – diseases, pandemics, cancers, plagues, and wars; however, the worst of them all was man, he had inflicted more damage on himself and the natural world than any of those "Tribbles". He sighed and stood up, pushing his bar stool in against the kitchen counter, and walking over to the incinerator chute to dispose of the dinner containers.

The lights in the rest of the apartment automatically turned off as he entered the bathroom. He stood in front of the sink, briefly looking at his reflection in the mirror, before turning on the faucet to wash his face with some cool water and mint soap. When he was done, he wiped himself dry with a towel and took a swig of dental solution, gargling it around in his mouth for a minute, before spitting it out in the sink. The solution had a horrid taste, barely disguised by the mint flavouring. It was part of an anticavity vaccine his doctor had prescribed to replace the costly 21st Century exercise of tooth brushing, flossing, and dental visits.

Zane pulled off his clothes and tossed them to the floor, walking into the softly lit bedroom. Straight opposite the doorway behind the bed was a large floor to ceiling window, with a view of countless towers stretching for kilometres from Lougheed City towards New Westminster, Brentwood City, and Metrotown. He leaned forward and pressed his naked body against the cool glass, gazing down at the stream of traffic on the streets fifty-five stories below. There was a whirring noise to his left, he looked over and saw a small drone dock with one of the ports of an adjacent apartment. He wondered what it was delivering. Food? Drugs? Sex toys? A missing part for some device?

Suddenly there was a bright flash from a window in the building across the plaza. Zane eyes darted to where he thought it came from, catching the figure of a beautiful Asian woman standing in an apartment directly across from his. She was wearing a loose-fitting white dress and had the body of a ballet dancer, with long svelte black hair flowing past her shoulders. He was about to wave to her, but before he could, her window abruptly plunged into darkness and she vanished from view. He wondered who she may be, what was she doing, what was she looking at?

He thought about the woman, as he stood silently staring through the glass at the endless glittering window panes filling the view from his bedroom window. Perhaps she would reappear, so he could look at her again and maybe catch her eye. His thoughts were interrupted by a high-pitched buzz from the façade of the condominium beside him. It was the delivery drone, its rotors increasing in frequency as it undocked from the delivery port and

16

momentarily hovered near his window, before dissolving into the mass of drones swarming like hornets in the narrow airspace between the towers.

He looked away from the drones and noticed the lights in the apartment with the beautiful woman were on. She reappeared in the window, gazing at him with a sensual smile. They stared each other, then suddenly she lifted her white lace dress over her head and tossed it to the floor. He let out a gasp of surprise, hypnotized by the perfect naked form before him. She smiled again, slowly and tantalizing moving her hips, mesmerizing him as she ran her hands through her hair and over her body. The spectacle lasted a couple of minutes, then in a flash she vanished, her apartment plunging into darkness.

"Zane, sorry to interrupt, but would you like me to dim the lights?"

He let out a wistful sigh, realizing she probably wouldn't return. *"Yes EVO, I should get to sleep."*

"Lights dimming. I will also lower the shades. Sleep well Zane."

"Good morning Zane, did you sleep well?"

He rubbed his eyes as he sat up in bed, pushing the duvet off his body.

"I imagine you did, since you had your weekly release session last night. For your information the refrigerator dock is sufficiently stocked for breakfast; however, I would recommend placing an order for vegetable and fruit replenishment. Do I have authorization?"

"Authorization granted EVO."

"Thank you Zane. Shopping for you now. Shopping completed. I have arranged delivery via the refrigerated kitchen port for 10:42 this morning."

"May I open the shades?"

"Yes EVO."

"Shades opening Zane."

He lay still in bed looking out the window at the dark sky outside, watching as a slick acid rain fell, coating the glass in an oily sheen of dust, water, and pollution. Despite the rain the morning air outside had that familiar smoky texture to it, layered with a deep carpet of dense brown fumes that hung over the city skyline, obscuring views to the distantly lit mountain tops. Winter was finally on its way, a welcome reprieve from months of intolerably hot temperatures and smog from bush fires. According to the MetService it was going be short, but colder than normal, with the possibility of snow on the streets. Zane doubted that would happen, MetService cloud seeding rarely failed in diverting storms, and the road heating grid was always there as a backup.

"Zane, sorry to interrupt, but it is 5:45 am and you need to be at the gym no later 6:00 am to be on time for work."

He sighed and rolled out of bed, pulling on some gym clothes and shuffling reluctantly out the front door. A minute later he stepped out the elevator on the forty-sixth floor, walking quickly past the gym gates and one of the annoying droid attendants offering training advice. Ignoring the bot, he went straight to an empty bike, connecting it to his EVO and logging into his Teva game. In moments he was on a virtual reality ride on a near-empty road running through one of his latest Teva acquisitions: a share in a vast swath of virtual reality real estate called Lalalandia, running for kilometres along an exquisite, yet to be developed coastline. The bike ride lasted twenty-five minutes, then he disconnected from Teva and did thirty minutes of weights and light stretching. Once he was finished, he ducked through the gates and ran the staircase back up to his floor to get showered and changed.

A half an hour later he was outside crossing the oval plaza in front of his building, gritty acidic raindrops hitting his face as he zigzagged through the crowd of morning commuters. Most of the people were on foot clutching dripping umbrellas, but a few were on electric scooters and bikes with their heads buried inside soggy raincoats. He reached the far end of the plaza and entered the familiar winding footpath to the SkyTrain station, the trees overhead filled with vibrant red, yellow, and orange coloured leaves, their colourful hues announcing the definitive arrival of autumn. Surprisingly, a few wet leaves lay strewn on the footpath, somehow missed by the army of cleaning droids that swept, collected, and incinerated waste twenty-four hours a day, methodically ensuring the city remained sterilized and clean at all times.

Lougheed City Station was packed with its usual morning bustle, no surprise given it was one of the region's most important transit hubs. Shuffling in the crowd, he slowly passed through the crowded gates located beside the entrance to the commuter rail and trolley connectors, and then jogged up the stairs to the SkyTrain platform above. He reached the platform edge and waited in the crowd behind the glass barrier for the next train to arrive.

"The next train departing at Lougheed Station is for UBC."

The train glided slowly into the station, coming to a halt behind the glass safety barrier running the length the platform. The doors slid open and commuters spilled out like ants, pushing past Zane and the other people waiting to board. Once they were all out, he joined the push and shuffle of people cramming into the train, soon finding himself squashed up against a window several metres from the doors. He briefly looked at the people standing around him, listening as the train intercom made its familiar safety announcement before the doors slammed shut and they began moving. Everyone was staring vacantly into space, their eyes and senses entirely plugged into the Internet, watching shows, communicating with friends and colleagues, shopping, and playing virtual reality games. It was curious watching people plugged in, they looked like zombies; however, with a closer look, one could see their tiny retina screens flashing with micro-electric currents projecting images and data across their eyes balls.

Bored of looking around him, Zane activated Teva and switched off into his virtual world to hunt for more assets and followers. Unlike previous games, where he had lost more money than he liked to think about, Teva continued experiencing remarkable geometric growth in new players. From experience he knew it was critical the game kept growing geometrically for as long as possible, as growth was the fundamental source of new revenues. If growth slowed, the game could collapse, as users lost confidence and began rushing in panic for the exits, hoping to cash out in time to still make a profit to transfer to the next big game.

A critical element of any game was to follow the actions of celebrity players such as Simon Bjorg, who played a key role in influencing the game's activity. Unlike the masses, celebrity players were always given advance cues as to when the bubble was about to burst; however, sometimes they failed to act in time, and were wiped out financially. Nothing could beat the gossip about a failed celebrity, their downfall usually tragically ending in drug addiction, homelessness, and occasionally suicide.

EVO suddenly interrupted his thoughts, *"Zane, Memorial Plaza Station is the next stop. I would suggest moving closer to the doors, as the network indicates forty percent of riders will not be exiting here."*

He cleared his retina screen and dropped out of Teva, just as the train intercom announced, *"Memorial Plaza Station is the next station, passengers exiting here please prepare to disembark."*

Shortly afterwards they came to a stop in a glass tunnel, and the train and platform doors slid open. Zane joined the masses of well-dressed office workers pushing out the SkyTrain door, swarming for the station exit. It was Friday morning, 8:45, which meant there was just enough time to stop at Prado and pick up one of their new designer lattes. Anticipating his craving, EVO whispered, *"Zane your favourite Prado is nearby, I will place an order for you now."*

"Locating. Ordering. Order has been placed. Would you like directions to the store?"

"No thanks EVO."

His latte was ready by the time he reached the station exit at the conveniently located coffee house. Coffee, cream, and sugar in a perfect blend, with a hot crispy sugar doughnut on the side. He elected to have it in, savouring the last few minutes before it was back to the non-stop intensity of his work place. The coffee had a rich and creamy texture to it, the result of blending, roasting, and filtering some of the finest African coffee beans, and then adding full synthetic dairy cream to the mix. The doughnut crunched and melted in his mouth, sending bursts of sugar, cinnamon, cardamom, and vanilla across his tongue. If there was heaven, it was in this tiny coffee shop tucked in beside the station exit to Memorial Plaza.

Coffee and doughnut consumed, Zane walked past the doors and across the vast plaza. The square was enclosed by three large office buildings and a squat glass and steel-framed shopping complex, which sat to the east of the SkyTrain station. The first tower was city hall, an Art Deco design soaring sixty stories above the SkyTrain station. On the west side of the plaza stood a fifty-story rhombus shaped building, home to the head offices of the Chinese Imperial Bank of Canada, one of the country's largest financial institutions. Lastly, directly across the plaza in front of him, standing like a shard of glass breaking though the concrete, was the one hundred and one floor global head office of his employer, Syllabus Corporation.

Syllabus

Date - Friday November 1st, 2120

Walking through the company doors, he was immediately hit by a flood of messages and alerts as EVO connected to SyNet. Glancing at the message headlines, he could quickly see there was an unfolding crisis involving the restructuring project he was working on for a large biotechnology firm based in Stockholm. Among the first messages he saw were notes from the client threatening to take the deal elsewhere unless there was a significant rework of Syllabus' strategy.

"Zane, meeting in boardroom three in fifteen minutes, details to follow!"

Zane looked away from his retina screen and saw his team leader, Antonio Rubio standing in front of him.

"Hey, what the hell is happening with the client?" he asked.

"Zane, I'll fill you in at the meeting, no time now, got to speak to the rest of the team!"

With that his high energy project manager disappeared down the hall. Zane took a deep breath, it was a remarkable trait his project leader had, no matter the situation, he always took the time to speak to his colleagues directly rather than messaging through SyNet. It was an attribute well regarded by senior management, who appreciated Antonio's attention to detail and his willingness to put work ahead of personal considerations. Tall, dark, and handsome, Antonio was bred to lead - he born to a wealthy Sao

Paulo family, was educated in human genetics and management, and spoke Portuguese, Spanish, and English. Unsurprisingly the rumours were rampant that he was on the cusp of a promotion from consulting operations to a directorship, or possibly even a position as a junior vice-president.

"Hi Zane! Day-dreaming again?"

Zane jumped and sputtered in surprise, "oh hey Leyla!"

Standing in front of him was his eccentric bubbly co-worker Leyla Janssen, dressed in a perky knee-high pink dress with colourful polka dots, pink and yellow stockings, and a pair of bright candy yellow shoes with little pink butterflies printed on them. If that wasn't enough, her hair was tinted cloud blue, and a pair of large fake triangular glasses were perched on the end of her nose. Of course this was all for show, as Leyla was in fact a brilliant communications consultant, widely respected for her ability to match the perfect messaging strategy for any crisis at hand.

"Did you hear Zaney boy? Kay-Li is coming to town next month!!"

"Kay-Li, really!" Zane laughed, marvelling at his flamboyant colleague's excitement in the midst of what was obviously going to be an extremely challenging day at work.

Leyla smiled, ignoring Zane's obvious preoccupation for the state of his Friday, "I know, I can't beeelieve it, it's soo fucking kewl! So tickets go on sale tomorrow at 6:00 am, and I have trusty EVO programmed to bid on a pair for me and a special friend!"

She laughed, noticing Zane's clear lack of interest, "I know Kay-Li is not your thing Mr. 'I'm addicted to Teva', but at least humour me okay!"

Zane laughed as she added, "sooo, what are your plans tonight? It's Friday you know! Time to go out and partay!! Timothy Klein and I are going Downtown for TGIF after work, you gonna come?"

"Ah Timothy..."

"Yes Timothy, our favourite rich party animal!"

Zane laughed, "all depends how today's mess plays out."

"Ah don't worry about it, Antonio's a worry wart, he worries more than any project leader I've ever worked with. He's always thinking it's the end of the world, but we'll pull this one out of the bag. Trust me baby, I've been at Syllabus longer than you, and I've seen teams lose good deals. We are no nowhere near that situation!"

"Well I sure hope so, it's been a long week and I could really do with a chill weekend. If it doesn't rain, I was thinking of going up to Squamish on Sunday to do some solo e-biking."

"E-biking solo? Yuck, I can't stand that sort of thing, too weird for me! I'd much rather be out Sunday shopping with the girls, especially now that the new virtual China mall is open! Did you see it on the networks? It's -"

Leyla was cut off as Robbie, the team's sexy visual communications expert came sauntering over with a cup of coffee in hand. Robbie was a looker and an extrovert, who like Leyla loved conversation, especially if it was with a beautiful woman. He was in his late twenties, over two metres tall, with dark black skin, green eyes, and a thick mop of curly black hair. He also had brains to match his looks, educated at some of the world's top design schools in Rotterdam, London, and Barcelona, and already had a sizeable following of art connoisseurs, collectors, and agents who traded in his works.

"Hey guys!" he said, in his charming Oxfordshire accent.

"Oh hey Mr. British boy, how's it going? Did you hear about Kay-Li?"

"Of course I did! I've already got tickets!"

"What, how did you do that bitch? They're not on sale yet" Leyla asked, astounded.

"Ah my London and Rotterdam connections babe," he winked, with a big broad smile.

"Ah guys, sorry stop your very important discussion about Kay-Li, but we really should get moving. Meeting is coming up," Zane interjected, tapping at his wrist.

"Yeah, you're right Zaney, we should get to Antonio's big meeting. The poor boy is so stressed out about this project, which means he's almost certainly going to call another working lunch. Free food, yeah!" Leyla laughed as she flicked her hair.

The two of them walked off, leaving Zane shaking his head, staring out the window at the clouds. My god, at times it was hard to believe Leyla had a graduate degree in creative writing from Cambridge University, as well as an MBA in marketing from INSEAD in France. She really got off on playing bimbo; nevertheless, Zane knew it was a façade - in the months they had been working together on this project, he had seen how she was as sharp as a piece of glass, and if you got on her bad side she could cut you to shreds.

Aware of the time, he pulled off his jacket and tossed it on the hook inside his work cube. He then made a short detour to the washrooms to check himself over in the mirror and make sure everything was perfect, before stopping to pick up a coffee from the dispensing machine on the way to the meeting. When he walked into the meeting room everyone was already seated, leaving him the last spot, just to the right of Antonio. As he took his seat he could immediately sense the tension in the air, with everyone waiting for Antonio to say something.

Their project manager sat in silence for a few moments, relishing everyone's attention. "Okay everyone, you all look like you're about to give birth, which thank god no one has to do anymore!"

There was a bit of laughter as Antonio continued, "this is the situation folks. Contrary to all the hectic messages on SyNet and my demeanor this morning, this deal has not quite 'fallen through'. Rather the client in Stockholm is looking for more assurances with regards to the implementation of our strategic restructuring plan. In a nut shell, they are concerned that once they sign off on the deal they'll be stuck with less intelligent and less competent consultants on the implementation side of Syllabus' business."

Antonio paused, gazing around the table for effect, "to be honest we all know that is true!"

Everyone around the table chuckled with amusement.

"The implementation side of the company are just rule takers, not nearly as bright as us on the development side. So the client want assurances that everything will go smoothly, and have said they will only pay us based on the success of the restructuring."

Zane cleared his throat, "Antonio you've got to be kidding us, these people think the plan we've devised will fall short because of incompetence in other parts of our firm. We all know this plan is idiot proof, a naturally conceived dimwit could implement it."

There was more laughter, they all knew exactly what Zane meant.

"Okay everyone I'm sure you're all as annoyed as Zane and I, but this is not the first time a consulting firm has experienced this sort of predicament. What we need to do is get to work and revise the implementation schedule, establishing stepwise implementation metrics, which as they are met, will require the client to issue payments on agreed timelines. The challenge here will be to make them acceptable to the client, while not being overly onerous and costly for Syllabus."

Antonio continued, "I promised senior management we would deliver, and if need be we would work through the weekend to get this finished. This project is almost a done deal, and we can't afford to drop the ball now. Let's seal it and get it out of the door no later than Monday. Once it's signed we all get to move on to something new and hopefully more exciting. I for one am sick of this client, they're so fucking risk averse that I wonder why they even embarked on this restructuring to begin with."

Leyla suddenly interjected, giving Antonio a friendly wink, "baby I secretly don't want this lame arse project to end, because it means I won't get to see your handsome face every day!"

Antonio smiled, "don't worry honey, I'm not gonna let you go that easily! We've been on three straight projects together, and I have this funny little feeling we'll be together on the next one too!"

There was some more laughter before Antonio quietened them down, looking at everyone in the eyes, "guys we are counting on each other to deliver and get this updated plan to Stockholm by the end of the business day. None of us are to leave this office until I sign off on the final plan. Clear?"

"Clear."

"I didn't hear you all. Is it clear?"

"Yes!!" everyone shouted.

"Lastly, let's meet for lunch at 13:00 at the Syllabus Executive Café on the 101st floor. That's all for now, have a great and productive morning guys!"

Zane left the meeting already feeling exhausted, swigging back the rest of his coffee. For all of the joking around in the boardroom what needed to be done was no small task, especially given the timeline of just twelve hours. Revising the implementation plan and setting tighter metrics was not something one did with a jiffy marker and a cup a' tea, one needed to run simulations and confer with colleagues in the office and also in other offices in other time zones. It was only ten in the morning; however, it was more than likely SyNet was going to be alive and humming through the weekend and into the darkness of Saturday and Sunday night.

He sighed, standing in his immersive cubicle, which looked out through a bank of silvery grey windows on the eight-fifth floor, facing north towards False Creek and the old established downtown core on the city peninsula. The rain and clouds had parted, giving way to a smoke free crystal-clear view of the city below. Zane paused by the glass to admire the hundreds of skyscrapers packed in between the harbour and the mountains, boats and sea plans motoring in the bay, and helicopters and drones hovering amongst the sea of glass and concrete stretching up from the distant streets below.

In that sea of glass and cement, nearly every major international firm was visible. Logos from the world's leading energy and mining companies, manufacturers' head offices, accounting firms, consulting firms, big financial services firms, and even several of Syllabus' strategic consulting competitors. Salish City had it all, blessed to be located in a region relatively sheltered from the instability generated by the climate crisis. It was a place of opportunity that had experienced over one hundred years of population and economic growth, exploding into a diverse and international metropolis.

Syllabus' rise had followed that of Salish City, starting a hundred years before as a small local consulting outfit, to become the largest strategic consulting firm in the world. The firm's meteoric accent had been facilitated by its early expertise in helping governments and industry navigate the climate crisis, as well other major transformations such as social media, artificial intelligence, extraterrestrial mining, and genetic technology. Today Syllabus had nearly sixty thousand consultants and support staff in two hundred and fifty countries, hiring people just like Zane – young, attractive, high energy professionals, graduated from some of the most renowned business, engineering, and science schools in the Americas, Europe, and Pacific Asia.

His retina screens started to flicker, as EVO anxiously reminded him to stop daydreaming and get to work. Realizing the clock was ticking, he reluctantly put his thoughts aside and logged into SyNet through EVO. Instantly he could feel his heart rate accelerate as his retina screens lit up with a virtual immersive world of data, virtual screens, and chat rooms, access to which was controlled through complex levels of authorization to ensure information was only shared to the right people at the right time. In just moments the outside world ceased to exist, as he plunged into the tedious task of revising his restructuring model to meet the demands of the client.

The next hour flew by, and at around eleven he took a tea break in one of the reading rooms with Anita Wong, the team's Malleable Immersive Artificial Intelligence expert, or MIAI for short, to chat about the restructuring plan in person, as well as reflect on their future once the project was completed. Zane got along well with Anita, she had a cool and distant personality, and was definitely more comfortable with virtual AI bots and coding than speaking with people. She was Zane's closest work colleague, not just because they were the most introverted on the team, but also because she appreciated his expertise in mathematics and data analysis. Like Zane, she was raised in Salish City; however, had moved to Beijing in her late teens to study Mandarin and computer science at the University of Beijing, before relocating to Seoul to do a master's degree in applications development for deep data management. After graduate school she worked for a decade at two large data mining companies in the United States, before moving back to Salish City five years earlier to join Syllabus as a senior AI specialist.

After tea with Anita, Zane went back to work, not stopping until EVO messaged him with a reminder about the team lunch at the Syllabus Executive Café on the 101st floor of the building. Realizing he was already a bit late, he quickly wrapped up reviewing the output of the two restructuring simulations he, Miko, and Anita had completed that morning, and then dropped out of the SyNet, hustling to the elevators.

A minute later he stepped out of the lift into a large indoor Japanese garden, complete with bamboo and lush tropical vegetation, teak and stone floors, rock gardens, and a stream that flowed from a series of ponds containing varieties of Koi and rare amphibians. He walked through the gardens, passing the private entrance to the offices and suites of Syllabus' CEO and senior vice-presidents, arriving in front of the company's executive café.

A host greeted him at the entrance, guiding him past various tables interspersed amongst the lush vegetation. They arrived at the far side of the restaurant, which looked across the city through soaring panes of glass. Everyone was already at the table starting their mains as Zane took his seat.

"Late again Dr. Fischer!" whistled Robbie.

"Don't give him a hard time, he had been very productive this morning in saving our Stockholm deal, and maybe even your job mister artsy fartsy! Thanks to crazy Zaney, the numbers man, we may even have a half decent weekend!" Antonio smiled.

"Your lunch is arriving" whispered EVO, as a Mexican waitress slid his fusion Brazilian Japanese plate onto the glazed synthetic cherry countertop.

The lunch meeting got underway, each member of the team discussing their opinions of the project, and how much work they were able to produce over the course of the morning. Robbie explained how he had made some minor adjustments to the design aspects of the plan, making it more engaging for the client's employees and other stake holders.

"You guys may think I just spend all day drawing pictures, but my team and I are making sure all the design aspects of this restructuring are motivational and appealing for the client's stakeholders, no matter what culture they're from, or what work they do. A plan is bound to fail if it looks dull and doesn't catch the eyes. Everything has to match, from the new brand and logo, to the new company image. If it doesn't work, the client will reject it and go back to what they know."

Leyla nodded, adding how she and her remote writing team had adjusted the organizational restructuring plan for the client, while ensuring the new document was correctly translated into twenty-three different languages for the client's major operational zones.

Leyla added, "I tell you guys, Syllabus' AI linguistics service is nearly one hundred percent perfect, literally as we are producing the master documents in English, it is churning out the translated equivalents in the languages requested by the client. The human reviewers are doing less and less work, and in my opinion Syllabus should just have them terminated. In fact it is one of the recommendations I'm going to highlight in my final review of the project."

"Well you should be really proud of yourself Leyla, finding further efficiencies for Syllabus!" Robbie chuckled as he munched on his chips.

"So Zane, what can you tell us? What have you been up to, or have you just been staring out the window at the view?" asked Antonio. The whole table turned to look at Zane. He blushed, his mouth full of salad.

"Let the guy finish his salad Antonio!" Miko frowned at Antonio.

"Oh, wait a minute, Zane's off the hook, it looks like we have a dial in from one of our consultants in the Auckland office." Antonio smiled excitedly.

"Ooh let's guess, it's Sean Chan, Antonio's favourite organizational change expert!!" Robbie joked, as he winked mischievously at the rest of the team.

Everyone around the table burst into laughter at their manager's expense, as Antonio blushed crimson red, muttering, "thank you for the friendly banter Robbie, always appreciated."

As the project manager, Antonio had chosen all of the senior consultants on the project, including staff who were not based at head office in Salish City. Sean Chan, a tall swanky Asian Kiwi from Christchurch was one of Antonio's first picks, not surprising given his experience and training in organizational change. As the project grew in size, Antonio had him flown to Salish City and Stockholm several times to work directly with the main team and the client. Sean was the sort of character who connected well with everyone, and it wasn't long before everyone in the office had fallen for him.

"Hey Sean, just a moment while I get all of us on the call." Antonio said.

Zane's retina screen flashed for a moment, and then Sean's three-dimensional image appeared seated at the table with everyone else.

"Sean, how's it going? How the Kiwis?"

"Excellent bro, we're all doing good now that we finally got a handle on those bloody Australian possums! We sent them all packing back to Australia and things are much the better for it!" Sean laughed. "So I must say I'm very pleased to hear you guys are on top of the client's final laundry list of concerns. You guys don't mind if I listen in for a bit to get up to speed with what you've done?"

"No problem bro!" Antonio answered.

Antonio was of course always happy to have Sean jump in on meetings, and it was no secret they had a thing going. Leyla once even told Zane the company had deliberately set the two up as roommates at the last global meeting two years earlier to encourage bonding. As Leyla said, "Antonio may love his girlfriend Ocean, but he's always open to adventures on the side."

Leyla loved gossiping, to the point that at times her stories got a bit too personal, such as when she told him how thrilled Ocean was about Antonio sleeping around in the company with people like Sean Chan. Apparently Ocean believed one of the best ways to increase salary and status was to use all the assets one had, including sex. When Zane asked Leyla how she knew these things, she said Sean had spilled the beans to her on a one night stand the two of them had back in September.

"So we were just about to hear Zane fill us in about his data analysis updates, but the poor fellow had his mouth full with cabbage and lettuce. I mean do we have a math guy on the team, or a rabbit?"

Everyone burst into laughter at Antonio's joke, including some of the other Auckland crew who were logged in with Sean.

Zane went bright red, it seemed he often ended up being the object of office jokes, and today was no exception.

"Okay Antonio, stop being so cheeky and let Zane have his say," Anita said.

"Oooh, nice Anita, put the manager in his place," Miko winked.

37

Zane cleared his throat, placing his knife and fork on the empty plate. While he wasn't an extrovert, he did enjoy having the full attention of an audience as he wowed them with the complexity of what he did. Unlike everyone else on the team, his work was entirely theoretical, and required lots of computing power and the use of applications he developed himself. These tools were used to determine the probability of desired outcomes given certain inputs and variable changes. In the case of the organizational change project for their pharmaceutical client, Zane used elements such as budgets, timelines, organizational culture, and project objectives to determine the probability of a restructuring being successful.

"Guys I'll admit what I do looks complex, but it's actually not rocket science. The models I sent everyone this morning demonstrate there is a seventy three percent chance of our revised organizational restructuring plan being successful. This means we really don't need to make significant changes to what we developed."

"Isn't seventy three percent low?" Sean asked.

"Yes it could be better; however, the only way we could see a higher probability of successful implementation with the current objectives would be for the client increase their budget, or for us to cut our profit margins. Both are unlikely given they have no interest in spending more money and we don't want to work more for less."

"Hmm, hopefully the client will accept this level of risk," Sean added with some concern.

"You do have a good point. In fact, I decided to test on the probability of the client rejecting our proposal, and I determined there was only about a one in ten chance of that happening. The fact is they have invested so much time and resources with us, and they are so desperately in need of reorganizing their business, that I believe they will go ahead with this deal and throw their full energy behind it."

"Hmm, well thank you Zane for the update. I hope everyone has taken a moment to look at what he has put together, or will find the time do so after lunch," Antonio said.

"Hey guys, it's been fun hanging, but Auckland needs to logout here and get to work on our revisions."

"Cheers Sean," everyone waved.

Sean's image vanished as he logged out of the hologram chat, waving goodbye to the team and giving Antonio a sexy Kiwi wink. No one seemed to pay too much attention to the fact it was a Saturday morning in Auckland, it was Syllabus policy for all consultants to be on call at any moment, even if they were on a vacation or asleep.

Antonio turned to Zane and asked him if he had anything else to add, Zane shook his head. "Alright, I think we're done here, so let's get back to work. We need to have this thing nicely packaged for the Paris office to present to Stockholm on Europe's Sunday morning. From what I understand Singapore will be in charge of integrating all our updates and making everything look pretty. That said, Robbie, Leyla, since you guys are on visuals and communications, don't be surprised to be on call the whole weekend."

"Gotcha boss, I'll make sure I don't get too intoxicated on Saturday, just in case Michelle Lu starts calling me in the middle of the night to make some special updates!" Robbie winked.

"Michelle Lu from the Singapore office? She's still chasing you? I thought you'd told her it was just a one night stand," Anita laughed.

"Oh no, she wants to keep it virtual, something about how special our moment was at the conference in London, and how we should keep the flame alive."

"Oh my god, that's so pathetic!" everyone groaned in unison.

Antonio looked around with a hint of disapproval, "okay people the bill is paid and I'm out of here. No rush, you guys feel free to keep gossiping, but I have more important things to get done!"

Over the remaining hours of the afternoon Zane and the team finished putting final touches to the updated restructuring plan. They had cut out every aggressive change originally proposed, leaving only the bare minimum that needed to be restructured for the client to survive in the future. How ironic it was, after spending months and vast fortunes of money and resources, the client was only prepared to make the slightest of changes, a decision that not only risked their future, but also made him wonder why they had even decided to try restructuring in the first place. If there was one thing Zane had learnt in the two years he'd been in consulting, was how many clients were eager to make transformative changes at the start, and then did everything they possibly could to prevent those changes from being implemented.

By late afternoon he'd finished everything he could do on the Stockholm deal and logged out of SyNet, connecting to Teva to see how his virtual investments had performed over the course of the day. He was pleasantly surprised to find he had fifteen thousand more followers since the morning, pushing his total to just over ninety thousand. Gleaning over the data, he saw it was his investment in Lalalandia which was attracting most of his new followers, who were using his portal to invest in the Ponzi scheme's first waterfront developments. Zane was curious what those new developments would look like, making a mental note to take his next virtual reality bike ride there.

All this new growth did have some downsides. In particular the celebrity promoting Lalalandia was now pushing early investors like Zane to gamble more money, this time on a windfarm to power the development. Should he follow their call, or would it be wise to take some funds out of the game to reduce his real world debts? The reality was the game could collapse without warning, and the last thing he wanted was to be too invested when it happened.

He took a break from Teva and went to sit in the coffee room, where he ran into Leyla sitting at a table drinking an orange juice and munching on an apple.

"Aaarh, I wish it was Saturday already," he groaned.

"Why?" Leyla asked.

"I'm just sick of this project. It's so boring and this client is so risk averse. I just don't want to have to do another damn modification to the restructuring model."

"Ah count yourself lucky that you're basically done. Robbie and I have still have to rewrite the proposal file and update the communications materials with the team in Auckland."

"Yeah that sucks. You think you gonna make it out tonight with Timothy?"

"I don't know, sure hope I can, but who knows, we may get held up with Auckland and Singapore. You going?"

"Yeah I sent Timothy a message earlier. I'll probably head out in a bit, just procrastinating looking over my Teva profile."

"Your Teva profile? You making some big money on that game? How many followers do you have?" she asked curiously.

"I just checked now, I've hit ninety-thousand."

"Ninety-thousand! I've only got about two thousand followers; however, to be honest I'm way more invested in this game called Shop, the one where you build your own stores and try to get as many shoppers as possible. I've made a lot of money on that one, enough for me to let loose for a week in Puerto Vallarta this coming winter."

"Hmm, maybe I should do the same thing and cash out a ton of money to buy a vacation or pay down some debt."

"Tough call Zane, you never know when the bubble's gonna burst in these games."

Leyla got up and cleared the table, going back to her work cube and leaving Zane alone in the coffee room. He logged back into Teva, thought it over one last time and then transferred a chunk of funds from the game towards the debt on his Lougheed City condo. Instantly he lost fifteen thousand followers, and moments later received a torrent of messages from users asking if he had access to inside information about the game's stability.

Zane stood up and looked around the empty coffee room. Through the windows he could see most of the office floor had emptied out for the weekend. It was 18:30 and he felt it was time to call it a day. He walked to his work cube, slipped on his jacket and headed down the hallway to the elevators. At the exit he bumped into Antonio, who was just saying goodbye to the floor's night receptionist.

"Hey Zane, good work on wrapping up tonight, you heading down now?"

"Yeah I am."

"Mind if I join your bro?"

"Sure no problem."

Antonio turned to the receptionist and said, "okay Drew, have a good night."

"Goodnight gentlemen."

Antonio and Zane headed for the elevator lobby, engaging in some small talk. On the ride down Antonio spoke about his weekend plans, which included an invitation to an exclusive party put on by one of the city's biggest real estate developers at the penthouse of a newly completed one-hundred storey condo project out in Coquitlam. It was through his girlfriend Ocean's work – she was an interior decorator with lots of contacts in design, architecture, and construction.

The brief conversation also touched on news from senior level management. Antonio had received a message from their group's boss Jared Berg, VP Strategic Development, about a new mega deal coming down the pipeline from a major government health care sector client. Rumour was it would be the biggest strategic development project Syllabus had ever taken on.

The elevator glided slowly into the lobby and the doors slid open.

"Ok Zane, you have yourself an amazing weekend. I'll message you if anything comes up with the Stockholm deal."

The two colleagues nodded goodbye and Zane crossed the vast white marble Syllabus lobby to the front doors. He stepped outside, pausing to take in the flood of office commuters crisscrossing brightly lit Memorial Plaza on foot, scooters, bikes, and electric skate boards. Most of them were making their way towards the giant glass and tree covered shopping complex on the east side of the square, which was home to one of the city's largest shopping centres. On the north side of the plaza was the entry to the Memorial Plaza SkyTrain station, which sat underneath the enormous city hall complex and surrounding gardens. Memorial Plaza was the heart of Uptown, a space carved out of what was once a giant intersection of two major arterial streets, but which had undergone radical change following the natural disasters that struck the city in the 2040's.

Zane dove into the crowd, slowly weaving his way across the square to the northeast exit, gazing up from time to time at the holograms and three-dimensional advertisements floating in the cool misty sky above. The air buzzed with the constant humming of thousands of surveillance and delivery drones whirring in the sky overhead, a never-ending testimony to the power of 22nd Century corporatism.

He reached the far exit and joined the line of commuters at the Yellow Cabs taxi rank on Broadway and Cambie Streets. The queue was quite long, and it took about five minutes of shuffling in the soft cool drizzle to finally arrive at the front of the line-up. His cab door slid ajar and Zane slipped into the back seat, the door closing behind him as he said, "downtown please."

Timothy Klein

"Yes sir," answered the computer in a vaguely trans-Atlantic English accent. "If you could kindly please fasten your seat belt and I will be able to initiate the journey."

Zane clipped his belt into place, as his EVO whispered, *"you have been billed 125 universal dollars for a cab ride from Memorial Plaza to Downtown".*

They pulled away from the curb and were soon whirring through dense traffic under the shadow of an infinite sea of shimmering skyscrapers, screens, holograms, and brilliant street lights littering the side of the roadway. A couple of minutes later they ascended the access ramp onto Tsleil-Waututh Bridge, the taxi's near-silent electric motor humming as it weaved amongst hundreds of bright fluorescent scooters, bikes, driverless city buses, and other electric self-driving vehicles. The mist was now a steady downpour, rattling on the roof and lashing angrily against the glass in waves of water. The cab's windshield wipers battled against the deluge, flip-flopping furiously back and forth, as they tried in vain to keep the windows clear.

Zane was exhausted, Syllabus was a demanding high-pressure work place, whose prestigious reputation assured brilliant career opportunities for the future, but which at times left him so overwhelmed that he found himself questioning his decision to work there, and whether it would be better to consider a lower stress posting in academia.

"Zane you have a message from Timothy Klein. He would like you to send a location beacon."

Zane laughed, authorizing EVO to share his location. His friend was probably worried he was bailing out on the evening, which Zane was known to do from time to time when he had too much going on at work. His friend Timothy Klein was a remarkable man, the envy of many. Tall, handsome, athletic, late-forties, with a fortune worth billions held in real estate, MAIA, and genetic technologies. Timothy was always on the move, and it was a moment not to be missed when he was in Salish City. He was Zane's best friend, or the closest thing resembling friendship in the 22nd Century. They had known each other for over a decade, ever since Zane was starting out at Stanford at age twenty-one as a graduate student in mathematics. He remembered after their chance meeting on a dating application, Timothy jumped on a bullet train from Salish City and came down to San Francisco to visit Zane for a weekend. He recalled their awkward first night in Zane's tiny basement suite in Palo Alto, followed by two surreal nights in a mansion Timothy rented for them in Presidio Heights.

That was the start of a long relationship, an improbable friendship between two people from very different worlds. Timothy visited whenever he could, and occasionally paid a ticket for Zane to come up to Salish City to spend a few days at his fantastical apartment in the downtown district. In his mid-twenties, when Zane completed his doctoral defence, Timothy was quick to insist he do an MBA, to expand his horizons to better understand the workings of the world.

He took Timothy's advice and eventually settled on doing an MBA in Montreal, primarily for its reputation as a global knowledge centre, but also for the opportunity to live in a French speaking metropolis in North America. Montreal was a wonderful city, but like most urban centers on the eastern seaboard it was suffering from steadily worsening fallout from the climate crisis. The winters were intolerable, with highly unpredictable swings from giant ice storms and glacial cold, to metres of snow paralyzing everything in the city. The summers were even more destructive, with extended deadly heat waves punctuated with cloud bursts, floods, electric storms, and large tornadoes.

Over the two years of his MBA Zane lost contact with Timothy, but towards the end of his studies he reappeared on the scene, getting Zane in to have a meeting with a friend of his who worked at a large strategic management company based in Salish City. The company was called Syllabus, and Zane discovered Timothy's contact was in fact one of the company's vice-presidents, a man by the name of Jared Berg. Jared was an affable fellow, well-travelled, an AI wizard, and a passion for strategic thinking. He took an immediate liking to Zane, and encouraged him to come out to Salish City to meet with some of his top senior head office-based consultants. Zane took Jared up on the offer, and it was there he met with Antonio and Leyla, and shortly thereafter was offered a job.

EVO interrupted, *"we are arriving at your destination. Please make sure you have all your belongings with you Zane. Your cab fare has been updated to one hundred thirty-eight universal dollars for congestion charges."*

He stepped from the cab, dashing out through the clogged traffic and throngs of young urbanites rushing through the rain from one bar to another. Downtown Salish City was almost certainly the city's premier entertainment district, a sprawling collection of block after block of restaurants, night clubs, and trendy technology development firms. It was a break from the city's past, when in the era of Vancouver, entertainment was something the region was not known for.

He was greeted at the bar by a smiling Eurasian-looking woman wearing Italian high heels and a tight black mini skirt barely covering her big boobs. She gave a Zane a sexy smile and reminded him to login with his EVO for InTime billing, as she messaged him his table number and added, "have a great night handsome!".

His EVO whispered, *"Zane, you have activated a billing session with Bilini's Restaurants. Your table number is fifty-six on the third floor."*

Zane knew the billing would most likely be zero, as Timothy always picked up the tab, he never let anyone pay for anything.

EVO buzzed, it was Timothy. *"Just saw you arrived! Leyla Janssen bailed, apparently, she and your creative wizard Robbie Wallace have a shitload of work to do, unlike you, haha! We're here waiting for you stud, looking forward to seeing that sexy smile!"*

He climbed the stairs, wondering what was happening with the deal. Antonio had warned Robbie and Leyla they should be ready to work through the weekend given their position as creative and communications experts; however, if the deal was going sideways, it would only be a matter of time before he also received an urgent message to connect to SyNet. He put the thought aside as he reached the third level of the restaurant, which was filled with dozens of crowded tables and a large dance floor packed with beautiful people dancing to generic plastic music booming out the speakers. His eyes scanned the floor, following EVO's directions to where Timothy and his friends were sitting.

"There he is, the sexiest man alive!" shouted Timothy over the blaring music.

"Boys and girls, this is Zane, or better known as Zaney boy, and yes please control yourselves, I know none of you can resist this sexy South Asian Mediterranean stud, but he's mine tonight!" Timothy grinned as he squeezed Zane's buttocks.

Zane blushed, "we'll see mister, I can't do a late tonight, I have a body fit session in the morning at nine."

"You do body fit? That's so totally hot, my last girlfriend did body fit and she had the most amazing body…fuck I miss her right now!" cried one of the blonds hanging off Timothy's shoulder.

"So Zane this stunning blond babe is Stephanie, who besides being drop dead gorgeous also works at National Bank as a blockchain data manager. So even though she has the finest set of tits around, she also has a mind for mathematics like you can't imagine! Plus she earns more money than any of us here, hahaha!"

"We also have Melissa, she is a regional pharma manager, don't ask her for trance samples, she only sells hard-ons, which I know you don't need."

Timothy ran off the names of the other people at the table, a mixture of beautiful hyper educated types from their mid-twenties to their mid-fifties, who worked in finance, genetics, AI, and banking. After the introductions were done, Timothy poured Zane a couple of drinks and had him do a line of fresh cocaine right on the table to get him quickly onto the same wavelength as everyone else. It didn't take long for the drugs and the booze to kick in, and before long his worries from the day vanished, as Timothy and a couple of girls swept him onto the restaurant dancefloor to get close and dirty to a couple of Ka-Li's new hits.

"Zane bro, you are so sexy, I love ya man!"

Zane blushed, and gave Timothy a deep kiss on the lips.

"Oh bro, you're gonna get Melissa jealous," Timothy winked.

Throughout the night Timothy's attention to his guests never faltered one moment, leaving his EVO billing on auto order, which meant the food, drinks, and drugs just kept coming. As the night ran on, and the drugs and booze came and went, Zane's mind became shrouded in a haziness of music and sweaty bodies, first at the restaurant, then at a nightclub, and finally at an after-hours event somewhere out in the docks near East Salish City. It was the early hours of the morning when Timothy decided to call it a night, inviting Zane and Melissa back to his place for some more entertainment. He had a black limousine waiting for the three of them as they stepped from the warehouse into the November darkness, electric trucks whirring past on the wide industrial streets of the East Salish City dockyards.

"Well so much for that body fit session Zaney boy," Melissa giggled, "you're coming to workout with me and Timmy, in Timmy's big bed!"

Zane grinned at Melissa, as she mischievously winked back at him. It was true she was incredibly sexy, irresistible really. Normally he wasn't into blonds, having always preferred darker women from

Africa and the Mediterranean; however, she had a wildness to her, which he found literally intoxicating.

As the limo pulled away from the afterhours, Timothy and Melissa flopped out on the seat in front of him, locked in a sweaty embrace. Zane stretched out his long legs, letting his right foot come to rest on the couch, right beside Melissa's thighs. He felt her hand drift up his right trouser leg, stroking his hairy calf. He smiled, letting out a gentle sigh of pleasure. The minutes passed by, the only sounds besides the occasional moan and giggle from his friends was the gentle drizzle on the windscreen and the hum of the electric limousine motor as they glided along the near empty dockyard roadway to Timothy's pad. It was 4:45 in the morning, and the sky showed no sign of opening up - a thick dark mat of November clouds speckled with flashing red lights from thousands of delivery drones. Zane gazed out through the widow, looking at some of the brightly lit flashing LED flexi-screens and holograms, evenly spaced along the side of the boulevard. He tried to read some of the advertising on the boards, but he couldn't focus, his mind clouded in a shroud of alcohol and drugs.

"Your body fit session is in four hours, I would recommend rescheduling."

"Yes EVO, make me a new spot for today at 16:30."

"Making request…booking…you are all set!"

The limo pulled up outside Timothy's condo building in downtown Salish City, and the three of them stumbled out of the side door and onto the sidewalk, both Timothy and Melissa laughing as they straightened out their clothes. Timothy led them across the lobby to a private entrance, where they passed through a glass door and into an elevator. A moment later they were hurtling upwards into the sky, Zane's ears popping as they whizzed up to Timothy's penthouse on the 107th floor.

Timothy's suite covered the entire top two floors of the tower, and had a jaw dropping view across the downtown peninsula, to the North Shore Mountains, and over towards Lord Stanley Park and the Salish Sea. The top floor was entirely open plan, with an indoor-outdoor garden patio and pool, and a massive lounge and designer kitchen. In the far corner, about forty metres from the front door, was a king size bed, and not much further, an open plan bathroom with a glass and marble shower and separate vintage cast iron bathtub. There was also a large staircase located beside the entrance, which led down to the main floor, where Timothy had his guest rooms, office, gym and sauna, and the main lounges and entertainment areas.

Zane was about to comment on Timothy's pad, that the layout looked a bit different; however, before he could utter a word, Melissa grabbed him and covered his lips in a deep long sensual kiss. Zane briefly resisted, and then quickly succumbed, his heartbeat racing as he felt her hands slide down to his crotch. Timothy watched for a minute and then joined in, his mouth connecting with Zane's, as Melissa pulled at their clothes. Pants slid off, then the rest, and the three of them were naked before they even made it to Timothy's bed.

"Oh my god Zaney boy you have such a sexy body, that ass, hmm... Timmy has your dick been in between those mounds yet?"

"Hehe what do you think Melissa? Of course, Zaney is a total bottom for guys!"

Zane look up through the drugged haze as he leaned back to Melissa boobs, burying his face in them just as Timothy gently slipped between his glutes. "Oh my god!" Zane groaned.

The debauchery lasted for who knows how long, their three naked bodies twisting and tangling in a sexual tirade on Timothy's king size bed, the silky satin sheets bunched up in knots with the plush pillows and cushions. Whenever they seemed to near climax, Timothy just stopped and looked down at them, before reaching over to his bedside table to grab the drug vaporizer for another hit.

"It's good shit isn't it kids? It'll keep us going just a bit longer!"

After two hours of drug induced sexual insanity, the three of them finally climaxed and came back down to earth. The high suddenly vanishing, replaced with an urge to sleep and eat.

"I'm ordering ice cream from Deliveroo. One of their birds can get us a big fat tub of chocolate strawberry cream in nine minutes, better than the crap I have in the freezer port."

"Do it Timmy, I'm all over it, and I bet Zaney could handle the calories after the workout we put him through."

Zane stumbled over to the shower in the middle of the loft and stepped under the warm pulsating stream. Washing the sweat off his body, he gently meditated as the warm water ran through his thick mop of dark hair and down his back. He filled his hands with a couple of dollops of body wash from the dispenser, rubbing it through his hair and over his body, melting under the intoxicating mixture of warm water, steam, and aromas from the soap. He had no idea how long he was under the water, his thoughts suddenly interrupted by voices from the kitchen.

"Zaney, the bird's dropped off our ice cream. Get out of that shower and come get some stud!"

He stepped out of the shower and the water shut off automatically. Melissa was standing naked by the shower door and passed him a fresh puffy towel.

"Just to dry yourself mister, not for wearing! Timothy and I want to enjoy the view a bit longer!" she laughed.

The three of them stood naked in the kitchen, stuffing their faces with the gourmet ice cream.

"Oh my fucking god this is so decadent Timmy! You're such a sweetheart!"

"Don't thank me, thank the delivery birds. Try get a human to deliver up to this penthouse palace in the sky at this hour, they're either too slow or too fucking lazy!"

"Timothy, drone dock six is in need of a service, would you like me to book a service call for tomorrow morning?"

The three of them broke into laughter.

"Sure babe, go ahead, get a service call in. Will it be a service bird, or a regular in-house technician?"

"Don't call your EVO babe, she'll get confused," Melissa interjected.

"Nah she gets it, right EVO?"

"Yes Timothy I get it, I'm a babe. To answer your question, the service call will be via an air drone, or bird, as you prefer to call it. If the repair is unsuccessful, they will send a human technician for an in-suite repair."

Melissa and Zane couldn't stop laughing as Timothy's EVO continued, "I have made the booking for you, the drone will be here at 11:30 am today."

"Thanks EVO."

"My pleasure Timothy. Enjoy sharing your ice cream with Zane Fischer and Melissa Wong."

Zane winked, "Timothy is your EVO jealous, or is she like super attentive to your needs?"

"Zaney boy, don't get cheeky with me and my EVO, or I'm going to have to throw you out," Timothy joked.

"Speaking of throwing Zaney out, I think it's time for me to head out boys. It's been a slice hanging and playing with our sexy perfect genetically enhanced bodies, but mine's in need of some sleep."

"Me too, Zane you're welcome to sleep here or head out. The service bird may wake us up, so if you're in need of a good few hours, it would be best for you to head home."

"Yeah Timothy, I'll skip the birdie call and also head home. Maybe Melissa and I can share the elevator ride down together!"

"I'd be honoured Zaney!"

The three of them made their way around the apartment, gathering various articles of stray clothing, and getting dressed along the way. Eventually they arrived at the front door, and after a brief three-way kiss, Zane and Melissa slipped into the elevator.

"Elevator doors closing, destination lobby, estimated travel time 1 minute 53 seconds."

"Hmm that's a long elevator ride, we should try fill the time," Melissa said with a wink.

Zane leaned over, his arms wrapping around her waist, their lips making contact. They kissed softly then more and more passionately, their bodies pushing against each other. Melissa's hand dropped down to Zane's crotch, and she pulled at the zipper, pulling his cock out.

"Oh man, fuck" he groaned, as he kissed her harder, his hands sliding under her skirt, where he could feel her panties, which were already warm and moist from excitement.

"Oh my god Zaney, that feels, arrh…"

"Elevator nearing lobby, prepare to disembark by the front doors."

They reluctantly pulled apart, Melissa straightening out her skirt and fixing her hair, while Zane tucked in his shirt and pulled his cock back inside his pants.

"Ooh, that looks very uncomfortable! How do you fit it in?" Melissa giggled.

"It's not easy, but what's the alternative?" Zane winked back.

The elevator doors opened and the two of them walked out the lobby to the street. Two cabs were waiting outside.

"Have a great rest of the weekend Zane. Hope to see that sexy ass sometime soon."

The taxi door closed and Melissa's cab pulled away into the morning light.

Zane slipped into his cab and the vehicle quickly accelerated into the Saturday morning traffic. His EVO opened a message from Timothy, *"nice work in the elevator Zaney boy, it was great watching. Look forward to catching you soon my friend!"*

Zane Fischer

Date - Saturday November 2nd, 2120

It was Saturday late afternoon, Zane had just got home from his workout session, his body aching from the exercise and the hangover from the excessive partying the night before. He leaned against the tiled wall in the shower, the jets of warm water and mist running through his hair, over his face, and down his chest. The aroma of fresh mint and lavender filled the steamy air as he lathered himself up, leaning into the jets to massage his back. He was in the shower for easily ten minutes when EVO alerted him with a priority message from Antonio.

"Hey Zane, Antonio checking in to update you about the project. Leyla, Robbie, and I were online last night with Sean Chan and the Asia Pacific team in Auckland, putting the final touches in place for Stockholm. Senior management and the client are very pleased with what we all did and have signed off on it, so it's all done for us! Have a good rest of the weekend mister. Also, instructions from our VP Jared Berg, everyone is to take Monday and Tuesday off, so see you Wednesday morning nine sharp for the debrief!"

Man, what a team, we salvaged that project and made a good impression on Jared Berg, he thought as he stepped out of the shower. For all that work, it better translate into a big bonus or I'll be really pissed off.

He toweled himself dry, admiring his perfect reflection in the mirror, a product of the most sophisticated genetic engineering available at a time when state funded genetic programs still didn't exist. It was what the doctors had promised his parents and it was what they had delivered. He tossed the towel to the floor and walked into the bedroom, once again admiring himself in the wall mirrors before sliding under the soft satin sheets, letting EVO dim the lights, darken the windows, and lower the blackout shades. His legs stretched across the bed, reaching into the coldest confines of the bedding, his body heat slowly warming up the synthetic down covers. He forever owed his parents for the financial sacrifice they made to give him the genes he had, it was the only reason he stayed in touch with them, after all they had nothing in common. When last had he spoken to them? He couldn't exactly recall, but it must have been at least a few months, maybe nearly a year? Perhaps it was time to give them a call, maybe something worth considering for tomorrow, or definitely for Christmas, which his parents loved celebrating.

His parents were emotional strangers to him, and while he knew about their lives he didn't know them. He knew they had led highly productive careers before retiring to a remote idyllic corner of Aotearoa. His mother was born in 2042 in New Delhi, his father in 2038 in Tel Aviv. They met in Toronto at medical school, where his father was specializing in reproductive medicine, and his mother was studying pediatrics.

Zane's parents came from two very different worlds. As young children, his mother and her older brother were sponsored from India to Canada through family adoption networks. They were the lucky two of six children, who had the opportunity to escape an increasingly oppressive and politically uncertain life in India, where the climate crisis was being most acutely felt on the Indian subcontinent, through extreme heatwaves, chaotic and polluted urbanization, and a water crisis driven by vanishing Himalayan ice sheets.

Upon arrival in Canada, Zane' mother was separated from her brother and sent to live with distant relatives in a simple suburban family home in south Edmonton. She never saw her brother again, he started with a family in Calgary, but was eventually deported back to India following too many brushes with the law. Once back there, he disappeared, never to be heard of again.

As soon as she arrived in Edmonton, her Canadian adoptive parents enrolled her in a public school in the neighbourhood, sending her to swimming and music lessons. They were third generation Canadians, with no children of their own, and completely integrated into the harsh, but breathtakingly beautiful landscape of the Canadian Prairies. They both had rather ordinary comfortable white-collar jobs with the provincial government, and had very liberal Western ways of thinking. Within just a few years, Zane's mother was a Prairie girl studying mathematics and music at the University of Alberta, at ease with life in Canada, with its crisp cold winters and short magical summers. Her connection with her family back in India faded with time, reduced to the odd email or text message. She never returned to visit, not because she didn't want to, but because by the time she finished university and could travel, the region had been decimated by the terrible 2062 Indo-Pakistani Small Nuclear War, and was permanently quarantined from the outside world.

Following her undergraduate studies in Edmonton, she accepted an offer for medical school in Toronto. There she excelled as a student, and was subsequently admitted into the school's prestigious pediatrics specialization program. On campus she led a rich and active life, volunteering with a long-running Toronto medical program, which got medical students out of the hospitals and into Toronto area public schools to talk to young people about medical issues such as diseases, vaccinations, genetics, and physical exercise. It was through the program she met Zane's father, when they were paired together to speak to lower income students in the city's east side neighbourhoods. At first she thought little of him, finding him annoying and too obsessed with the prestige of being a medical doctor; however, he slowly won her over with his handsome smile and endless supply of perfectly timed bad jokes.

"Zane."

His eyes flicked open, EVO's voice intruding into his thoughts.

"Yes EVO."

"I am sorry to interrupt you, but it is quite late. Did you not want to get a good night's sleep for tomorrow?"

"Thank you EVO, I appreciate your concern; however, at times I like to reflect on things without any interruptions."

"My apologies Zane."

Zane drifted back to his thoughts, returning to thinking about his father, and what he must have been like in those days as a young man. His father spoke rarely of his childhood in Israel, something Zane understood must have been difficult and full of responsibilities. Like all young Israelis, Zane's father was conscripted into the military after he finished high school at the age of seventeen. For two years he was stationed as a frontline soldier on the volatile border between Israel and Palestinian Gaza, participating in multiple skirmishes with paramilitaries in Gaza and the Egyptian Sinai.

His father once explained to Zane the tragedy of Gaza, an orphaned territory cut off from the newly established Palestinian State set in the Jordan River Valley, which was carved out of territory occupied by Israel and Jordan. Forgotten by the world, Gaza suffered from chronic epidemics, over-population, and flooding from sea level rise, which were unsolvable as long as the conflict continued.

Like most young Israelis, as soon as his father finished his military service he chose to go abroad, deciding to settle in New York to study chemistry and biology at Columbia University. He had always been a brilliant student, so it was of little surprise he finished at the top of his graduating class. Following his studies, he took two semesters to reflect on whether he wished to remain in the United States, or whether to return to Israel and pursue a Ph.D. there. During those two semesters he took a summer to travel through Mexico and America, visiting their national parks, vast expansive landscapes, and sprawling decaying cities. On the way back, he took a detour to return to New York via Canada, passing the border north of Seattle, and entering the country through the Peace Arch Crossing. Originally he planned to spend just a few days in the area around Salish City, but ultimately that turned into months, as he fell in love with the dramatic landscapes of Canada's West Coast, as well the promise of its shiny new cities undergoing vast urban renewal following the catastrophic earthquakes of the early 2040's.

In the end he never made it back to New York, enrolling into the local university's prestigious medical school program, which he completed three years later. Following his studies, his professors encouraged him to go to Central Canada to study in the rapidly developing fields of reproductive and genetic medicine at one of Canada's more established schools. They explained such a move would help him leverage his way into a professorship at one of the Salish City medical schools, should he wish to return to Canada's West Coast. He applied to the University of Toronto's reproductive technologies program, which was considered one the world's top programs at the time, and just a few weeks after being accepted, he left Salish City and relocated to a small shared flat just beside the medical school campus.

Life in Toronto was very different to Salish City, it was a much bigger and more urbanized city, where it was easy to feel isolated if one had no intention of staying permanently. Fortunately there was no shortage of time obligations in the medical program, which besides being intense and academically challenging, also included mandatory volunteer work and hospital internship time. Within the first days of his arrival in Toronto, the medical school hospital outreach office provided Zane's father with a list of several community projects to be assigned to, and he eventually settled on one where he was partnered with Zane's mother. As his father liked to say, he chose to drop all the other volunteer programs so he could focus his entire attention on Zane's mother, whom he fell for the day he laid his eyes on her.

Zane's parents were clearly very different people from different worlds; however, in spending time together at university, they discovered their shared passion for medicine, and it was this that brought them together. By the time they finished their specializations in 2070, his mother was pregnant with his sister, and they were on their way to Salish City, where Zane's father had been offered a prestigious professorship in the Faculty of Medical Genetics and Reproduction at the University of British Columbia. Shortly after moving to their new city, Zane's mother accepted a role as a pediatrics specialist at a major local hospital, and they moved into a large apartment in one of the new condominium towers being built along Broadway Avenue. Their careers were brilliant, ascendant, and all consuming, and neither of them had any time to spare for raising Zane's sister, whom they eventually placed in a nearby full room and board nursery.

In the 2070's, as a young successful researcher, his father was very involved in the medical genetics field, and was frequently invited to participate in numerous public policy discussions around the ramifications of genetic medical applications in humans. The big issue of the time was how wealthy people were paying to have genetical engineered children conceived in artificial pods, which were isolated from pollution and contaminants. These children were almost perfect, trouncing IQ and EI tests, winning academic and sporting competitions, and gaining access to the best universities. Some of them were already working in academic research, competing with Zane's father for funding.

At the same time Zane's mother, as a frontline pediatrics specialist, witnessed firsthand how human genetic engineering was transforming her profession. Rarely did the perfectly genetically engineered children of the wealthy fall ill from disease, rather her chronic patients were almost entirely naturally conceived children from medium to lower income families, who did not have the money to access the fantastical technologies of genetic engineering.

The situation alarmed his parents, especially as they watched their daughter grow into a toddler, showing the subtle imperfections of a naturally conceived child. They felt terrible for placing her on the wrong side of a world divided between genetically engineered and naturally conceived; however, more than anything they were jealous of the perfect children their friends and colleagues paraded around at birthday parties. They wanted a perfect child as well, and decided to freeze their genetic material to one day access those same technologies.

At the start of the 2080's the world changed dramatically as wealthy developed countries like Canada succumbed to public pressure, and nationalized access to gentech to arrest a growing socio-economic chasm between a class of genetically engineered rich people and everyone else. Initially priority was given to spending on gentech access for cancers, cardiovascular diseases, and neurodegenerative illnesses, while reproductive technologies and fertility clinics were given lower priority, with a plan to have them all fully nationalized by 2090. To manage access to the fertility clinics, the government offered two options: join a newly implemented lottery and wait patiently for one's number to be called, or go the expensive parallel private option, which was still available until public access wait times dropped below one year.

In the mid-2080's Zane's parents decided they were ready to have their second child; they were in their forties, his sister was just finishing high school, and they didn't want to be dealing with a young child when they were older. They signed up for the newly implemented lottery; however, after a year of waiting for their number to be called, they decided to switch to the private option when Zane's father saw new ground-breaking technologies at a medical conference in Europe.

Developed by Zelion Genetics, these technologies created the first generation of cybernetic humans conceived using genetic technology interwoven with an implanted Engineered Virtual Organism, or EVO. Permanently connected to the Internet and running off the host's body heat, EVO consisted of a centralized microprocessor embedded in the wrist, implanted retina lenses, and micro-auditive and sensory enhancements. It was a fantastical technology that created a sensory experience far beyond what any ordinary human being could possibly imagine. As his parents discovered, these were the latest technologies being demanded by very wealthy clients in countries such as Israel, the United States, and Brazil. Zelion's sales force pushed it to them, saying the marriage of EVO and genetic engineering was the future, and eventually everyone was going to need it.

They decided to commit, abandoning the government fertility lottery to invest hundreds of thousands of their personal savings to leapfrog their future child into the next generation of reproductive technologies. The process they engaged in was completely different from the first time around with Zane's sister - there was no love, no physical contact, and no emotional bond through pregnancy. Instead it started with several meetings in private fertility clinics with genetic counsellors and medical engineers, then progressing to preliminary examinations of their genetic material, as well as samples of the sperm and eggs they had stored years earlier.

After all of the meetings, preliminary tests, and legal paperwork, Zane's father and mother's genetic material were finally transferred to a facility in Tel Aviv, one of the few places in the world offering these new technologies. Once this step was completed, and the final legal and financial hurdles cleared, one of Zane's mother's premium genetically enhanced eggs was fertilized with one of his father's enhanced sperm in a process known as optimized invitro-fertilization. This process involved bonding the pronucleus containing twenty-three chromosomes from Zane's mother, with the pronucleus containing twenty-three chromosomes from his father. The resulting genetically enhanced single celled zygote was further enhanced as it cleaved into a blastocyst, which was then transferred to a Zelion patented gestation pod.

Over the months ahead, from halfway around the world in Salish City, Zane's parents watched through the eyes of a camera as the fetus gradually evolved, taking the form of a tiny human being. They could see it kick and swim inside the sterilized chamber of the pod, the umbilical cord offering the only connection to the world outside, providing the supply of nutrients for the fetus to survive. Some nine months after it all began, Zane parents returned to the laboratory in Tel Aviv, and on the 8th September, 2088, Zane exited into the world, landing in the expectant arms of his mother and father.

Before his parents could take him from the lab, he went through several final procedures in a sterilized chamber to implant malleable immersive artificial intelligence enhancements into his body. Better known as MIAI for short, these included micro sized dynamic retina receptors in each of his eyes, nano-auditive and sensory enhancements in his ears, and a tiny centralized micro processing receptor in his wrist. The procedures completed, Zane began his life permanently connected to Internet through the filter of MIAI.

"Zane, sorry to interrupt you again. You are extremely tired and need to sleep. Can I infuse the air with a sedative?"

He sighed, "yes EVO, you may proceed."

Date - Sunday November 2nd, 2120

It was early Sunday morning and Lougheed City Station was eerily quiet, the city still mostly asleep. It was strange seeing the station complex so empty, after all it was the regional hub for SkyTrain and dozens of bullet trains arriving and departing from destinations across North America. From Lougheed City one could board a train and be in Los Angeles in six hours, San Francisco in four, or Calgary in seven. This convenience made it one of the most sought after locations to live in Metropolitan Salish City.

Besides being the region's largest transit hub, Lougheed City was also a densely populated city within a city, with hundreds of futuristic high-rise buildings forming the largest urban centre in Burquitlam, the region's most populous agglomeration, and home to most of its professional workers. His apartment was in one of those many buildings, a tiny forty square metre one-bedroom concrete and glass box stacked amongst thousands of other tiny concrete and glass boxes. It was an investment he hoped to someday leverage into an apartment in distant downtown Salish City, where the region's wealthy entrepreneurs, CEO's, celebrities, academics, and political elite congregated.

The morning sky was covered in high grey clouds as the SkyTrain pulled out of Lougheed City Station and travelled northwest on the elevated tracks, passing through futuristic vaulted glass and concrete stations, each of them surrounded by canyons of glass towers. Production Way was the most spectacular, a massive beehive-like structure, which was also the terminus for the Burnaby Mountain Gondola, connecting the region's second major university to the SkyTrain network.

As the train glided towards downtown Salish City, he caught sporadic glimpses of the mountains in the gaps between the high-rise buildings packed alongside the tracks. About twenty-five minutes after leaving Lougheed City the train began descending Grandview Heights towards Salish City's densely constructed downtown peninsula. Part way down the hill the maze of glass towers parted, revealing an enormous urban park separating the masses of sleek downtown towers from the rest of the city. Dykes and canals crisscrossed the park, providing a key role in protecting the downtown core from regular tidal surges.

The train crossed the park on elevated tracks, and a few minutes later plunged under the city into a long dark tunnel running to the North Shore. Zane gazed at his reflection in the glass as they floated through the darkness, studying his nose, his eyes, his dark features, and the perfect symmetry of his angular face. Yes, everything was flawless, not a hair out of place. His eyes scanned the reflection of the interior of the train, catching glimpses of other people, comparing himself with what he saw. Apart from a few older people who were remnants of generations conceived before the era of compulsory state funded human genetic engineering, nearly everyone was perfect, differing only in the expression of their ethnic backgrounds.

Zane was snapped out of his thoughts as the train climbed out of the tunnel and sunlight streamed in through the windows. The high clouds had broken apart, and the city was doused in brilliant sunshine, the autumn sky reflecting off the glass towers of Salish City's downtown peninsula on the opposite side of Burrard Inlet. The train slowed as it silently snaked its way along First Avenue, passing under Lion's Gate Bridge, and through a giant shopping and entertainment complex, which formed the hub of this part of the North Shore. After several brief stops, it continued west along the coast, passing before rows of gleaming luxury waterfront condominiums, where some of Salish City's most powerful and wealthy resided.

Fifteen minutes later the SkyTrain began to steadily accelerate to a cruising speed, turning north past Horseshoe Bay towards Squamish City, which lay nestled at the far end of the vast glacier carved fjord. The landscape unfolded before him as the train snaked its way along the slender ribbon of steel and concrete, passing through tunnels and under cliffs, revealing a breathtaking mountainous wall rising from the depths of the fjord to the sky above. The water of the sound was like a sheet of glass, not a ripple to be seen, reflecting the crisp orange blue hews of autumn sunlight dancing upon its surface. Wisps of morning fog and mist floated lazily in the air, providing subtle camouflage to the dozens of islands sprinkled the length of the long deep inlet.

Anything human was dwarfed by the sheer immensity of the fjord - towns, railway lines, and highways were insignificant in the face of the dramatic landscape. The most striking element missing from the scene were the glacier caps, which up until a generation ago had graced the peaks of the mountain ranges in the sound. They were victims of the climate crisis, swept away and replaced by dry barren landscapes, further modified by decades of brush and forest fires. Zane was too young to have known the fjord peaks with snow; however, he remembered on a rare family outing his father recounting an unforgettable story of how as a young backpacker, he lost his way during a whiteout on the upper sections of Mount Garibaldi.

Zane's attention drifted back to his parents, and the thoughts from the night before. His connection with them had always been distant, cold, and disengaged, the kind of bond where if he didn't reach out to them, months could pass by before they may even send him a message to see if he was alright. They were like strangers to him, ever since he had gone to university he had stopped seeing them in person, there simply hadn't been enough time between his studies in San Francisco, and his parents' schedules as important medical researchers and clinicians.

In fact it had always been work first for Zane's parents and their social circle, where children were nothing more than trophies to be bragged about at medical meetings and at dinner parties. From his early childhood Zane had no more than one or two memories of a family outing, and he and his sister had certainly never gone on any of his parents' lavish trips abroad, which often included fully expensed medical conferences. At a young age, just like his sister, he was sent to one of the many boarding schools in Salish City, the sort of place which had become popular amongst the bourgeois urban elites, who between virtual and real time obligations, had no time to waste raising their own children.

As an adult, his rare contacts with his parents usually happened around the Christmas holidays, when he dropped by over the Internet to virtually join them at their retirement bungalow on the Bay of Islands in Aotearoa. His parents were usually out on their large sunny balcony overlooking the seaside, with the chatter and laughter of friends drifting in and out in the background, punctuated with the clinking of wine glasses and random cheery summertime music. The chat usually lasted about fifteen minutes, before his mother or father made an excuse about needing to get back to the guests, or having to do something important in the kitchen. It was their way of ushering him on, so they could get back to the more important things in life.

Zane had no emotional connection to his parents, instead he stayed in contact out of a sense of duty, forever indebted for the remarkable tools they had given him through genetic engineering. His high level of engineered intelligence meant he easily accessed the best boarding schools and the finest universities, all on fully funded scholarships. At a very early age his teachers identified he was particularly brilliant with numbers, which was of no surprise given his parents' genes and the genetic enhancements. He was bumped up at boarding school by two years, and by the age of sixteen was already done with high school and in university. By nineteen he had completed his undergraduate studies in physics and had moved to San Francisco to study applied mathematics, a program that evolved into a doctorate and was then followed with an MBA.

His parents were thrilled with Zane's options, not only did they have more to brag about amongst colleagues at medical conferences, but there was also the real possibility of a prestigious future professorship at a famous business or mathematics school. He never forgot the relentless pressure from them as his MBA graduation date grew closer, followed by the profound disappointment on their faces when he declared he had taken his friend Timothy's advice, and followed the money into industry, accepting an offer from Syllabus Corporation as a strategic data analyst.

They never recovered from that moment of deception, where all their hopes and dreams of a perfect son were dashed. The torrent of messages and encouragement leading up to the end of his MBA came to an abrupt and sudden end after his announcement of his role at Syllabus - he was hardly surprised when neither of them appeared for his MBA graduation ceremony a few months later.

Then there was his sister, Melody. Zane had not seen her since he was in high school, when she had finished technical college and gone to Australia on a work experience visa. Melody hated him from the day he was born, considering him to be some sort of horrid genetic MAIA mutant, part of a class of people who were displacing real people like herself out of universities, careers, and meaningful employment. Her generation had had access to some genetic engineering; however, unless you were from a very wealthy family, the most you could count on was rudimentary genetic profiling prior to conception, as well as genetic vaccines to manage diseases such as arthritis, dementia, or cancer. At the time of her conception, their parents were just leaving Toronto to take posts in Salish City, and had neither the money nor the foresight to pay for advanced genetic selection, which meant Melody was almost entirely naturally conceived, with all the defects that entailed.

Melody made no effort to hide her jealousy and hatred, both towards Zane, and towards their parents. She hated him for who he was, and them for not having made the effort to use their connections as doctors to provide her with a better genetic makeup. Melody never joined Zane when he called their parents for Christmas, and from what he knew she had not spoken to them since their retirement to Aotearoa. His parents told him once in passing that apparently she was now permanently settled in a tiny isolated agricultural town, about two hundred kilometres to the south of Perth, living entirely off the grid. They also confirmed she and her partner had no children, which did not surprise him, given she had always sworn to never bring children into a world with a climate crisis and oppressive wealth inequality, which was becoming entrenched through human genetic engineering. He felt sorry for her, but realized it wasn't his problem and he shouldn't waste energy thinking about it. Ultimately, in the competitive world of the early 22nd Century, AI and genetic engineering made it nearly impossible for naturally conceived people to compete, and Melody was just another data point to confirm it.

The train pulled into Squamish City and Zane stepped onto the platform and walked past the virtual pay gates into the station. Squamish's new central station consisted of a dramatic glass dome with an enormous thirty-metre high vertical garden wall at the exit. From the platform and the main hall, one had stunning views across the valley to the cliffs on the northeast side of the city and Howe Sound and the mountains to the southwest. The floors of the station were paved in a mixture of local rock and concrete, with colourful glass motifs reflecting the history and culture of the Squamish peoples, who had inhabited the region for thousands of years, and were the city's most important community.

Zane passed under the vertical garden through the exit to an open plaza, which lay perched above the small compact city below it. He stopped for a few minutes to take in the breathtaking view, walking to the far end of the plaza, where there was a large First Nations carving of a raven, a bear, and salmon surrounded by a water feature. The plaza was a transport hub of sorts, with a small street car, walking and biking trails following a stream into the centre of the city, and a gondola service from the station up to the cliffs above the city. Squamish was a pretty tourist town, which over the course of the past one hundred years had undergone rapid development, accelerated by the extension of the SkyTrain commuter rail from Salish City. The arrival of a rail link to Salish City in the mid 2050's was an important milestone for Squamish; however, it was the great earthquakes of the 2040's which had made it all possible. The quakes destroyed the famous Sea to Sky Highway as well as all of the villages along Howe Sound, and in the aftermath, to conserve time and money, the Provincial and Federal governments elected to consolidate all the redevelopment into Squamish, while also building a recreational port and tsunami resistant seawall on the waterfront. From the mid 2040's to the mid 2050's, the region's survivors of the earthquakes, slides, and tsunamis were relocated to Squamish, and the old railway line was quickly upgraded and connected to Salish City's SkyTrain network.

Zane turned on his heels and walked back to the station entrance, where just outside the doors were rows of powder blue hybrid electric bikes. He grabbed number thirty-nine, which EVO had reserved for him while he was disembarking from the SkyTrain, and wheeled the bike from the dock, hopping onto the seat. The bike glided smoothly across the plaza to the bike path into the city centre, which wend its way under the SkyTrain tracks and along the stream, before passing over the old Sea to Sky Highway and into the town centre.

Zane stopped for a few minutes to grab a coffee, locking his bike outside a cute looking café on one of the town's many colourful bustling pedestrian streets. Squamish was a sort of pedestrian utopia, where nutty urban planners in the post-earthquake and tsunami apocalypse embarked on a series of radical urban projects to keep cars and large vehicle traffic outside of the centre, and away from the waterfront. The result was a delightful mix of narrow treelined streets filled with cafes, restaurants, and shops, which in the summer months and on sunny days were packed with tourists. He took his coffee and sat on a bench beside his bike, watching the parade of people on the street. With the sunshine and mild weather, most people were in light autumn clothing, consisting of the usual sleek temperature regulating elastic body suits that were the mainstay of fashion, as well as colourful lightweight synthetic down jackets. A few people were in shorts, sporting hiking boots or running shoes as they made their way to and from the mountains.

He stretched his legs out, sipping his coffee and enjoying the brief respite from the constant chatter of the Internet, his job, and social obligations. Zane was a loner, he always had been, it was one of the few defects the genetic engineering company failed to observe and rectify prior to his birth. At boarding school teachers noticed the problem and psychologists were assigned to try resolve it. They were unsuccessful, leaving him with a flaw that made career advancement more difficult in a society dominated by extroverts.

He finished the coffee, returned the cup to the shop, and hopped back on his bike. The peddle along the street was a bit of an obstacle course, as he weaved amongst throngs of pedestrians, making his way towards the far side of the town centre. After about four hundred metres he arrived at the access to the tsunami defence dyke, which he followed along the waterfront, before engaging the hybrid function and pedalling up the mountainside trail on the west side of the city.

On the lower trails there were a fair number of people biking and hiking, taking advantage of the beautiful sunshine; however as he rode further up the mountainside, the number of people dwindled, and soon he was alone. For about an hour and a half he ascended the trail, eventually reaching a beautiful vantage point where he had a view across Squamish City towards the giant granite outcrop of The Chief. The sun was just making its way around the centre of the fjord, its brilliant rays striking the surface of the inlet's icy waters. Birds glided in skies, rising and falling with midday thermals, while the sunlight reflected off the massive sheer rock face of Squamish Chief, dew glimmering like a billion diamonds in the bright light. He could make out the Squamish Gondola and the plaza at the other end of the valley, as well as the densely packed town centre below, separated from the fjord by the port and the gigantic tsunami defence dyke, which protected the city from the inevitability of another terrible earthquake and the wall of water it would surely generate.

The last mega thrust earthquake took place on the night of July 23rd, 2043. It was a 9.3 on the Richter Scale quake, and lasted just over five minutes, with an epicentre to the west of Vancouver Island. The subsequent aftershocks and localized tsunamis went on for weeks following the event, hampering any effort to salvage infrastructure and move people back to towns along Howe Sound. Zane was born nearly a half century after the disaster, but the pain of the event was forever etched in the character of the city that had risen out of the destruction. As he had learnt in boarding school, most of what used to be known as the Lower Mainland was severely damaged by the shaking, in particular the cities to the south of the Fraser River, which were entirely lost to flooding, fires, and liquification. Single family and lower density homes were also totally destroyed, not by the earthquake, but rather by uncontrolled fires, which leapt erratically from house to building to house, fanned by exploding gas, hot mid-summer winds, and dried out vegetation. There was no way to put them out, as water

79

main lines failed, and emergency services were completely overwhelmed by the scale of the catastrophe. The worst of the carnage was beside Stanley Park in the old West End of Salish City, where poorly built mid-20th Century towers collapsed like houses of cards, crushing thousands of people under the concrete.

The disaster left 2.5 million people in the region homeless, and because of localized tsunamis and landslides it remained cut off from emergency assistance for weeks. It was the greatest natural disaster to ever strike North America, damaging cities and towns from Sacramento to Kitimat. Throughout the region millions spent months camped in disease-ridden tent cities, waiting as planners, insurance companies, and national governments decided how to rebuild. It was not until the following spring that a sense of order began to re-establish itself, as the military and urban planners began to get a handle on the situation.

The reconstruction of what was Vancouver and its satellite cities was the greatest urban renewal project in Canadian history, and it would take nearly twenty years to complete. In that period of time, civilian and military planners made swift decisions to prohibit the reconstruction of urban sprawl. The entire metro region was densified and all urban development was moved north of the Fraser River, except in the case of Surrey Centre, and Lulu Island, where the airport and ferry terminals were rebuilt and consolidated. A decision was also made to rename the city as Salish City, in recognition of its past. Cities such as Abbotsford, Chilliwack, Langley, and Tsawwassen ceased to exist, their charred suburban remains were bulldozed and converted to agricultural lands, or else ceded to rapidly rising sea levels by the end of the 21st Century. In the case of Burquitlam, Port Moody, and the North Shore, their burnt out suburban communities were relocated to towers built around the expanded metro SkyTrain network.

Initially there was significant public protest against the densification strategy; nevertheless, many people had no choice, as insurance companies refused to cover any new or existing suburban single-family projects, or new construction in tsunami or future coastal and river flood zones. Residents were faced with continuing to live in uncomfortable makeshift military tents, or get in on the new government subsidized residential towers rapidly being constructed near public transit lines. Those who quickly made the transition were rewarded with well-located apartments in towers near transit hubs, while others who protested and waited, ended up spending more time in tents before finally accepting apartments further from the SkyTrain. Ultimately, the combination of fast emergency planning decisions, pressure from insurance companies and banks, and the reality of future quakes and climate change meant most of the population of Salish City and its surrounding satellite cities were housed in towers by latter part of the 21st Century. Indeed by 2100 the urban region looked much like Singapore or Hong Kong, significantly different to the sprawling Canadian cities of Edmonton, Calgary, and Winnipeg, on the other side of the continental divide.

Planning decisions were much the same on Vancouver Island, where the capital had been completely flattened. There too, as with Seattle, Portland, and other cities in the region, sprawl was eliminated, older buildings were reinforced, and cities were reconstructed on densely populated urban grids surrounded with green space, and protected from the rising seas and tsunamis by dykes and construction on higher solid ground.

Zane felt a grumble in his stomach, it had been a good couple of hours since his coffee, and several hours since breakfast.

"EVO, find me some food!"

"Yes Zane, I imagine you must be feeling quite hungry, in fact I was just about to make a suggestion."

EVO continued, *"I recommend Tacolandia, located in Squamish City. They offer drone delivery and have 1002 positive reviews on the Internet. I have located the menu for you to look at."*

Zane glanced at the menu and chose a synthetic beef burrito, a poutine, and a large strawberry smoothie.

"Zane, your order has been placed and will arrive in nine minutes. In the meantime, would you like me to recommend some good vantage points for photos?"

Zane nodded.

"This area of Squamish has some of the best views of the sound. It is a particularly good moment to take pictures of the Chief, as the sun is at an optimal angle for west facing shots. Your photos will be near perfect, and with image enhancement will be ideal for decorating your apartment."

"Thanks EVO."

Zane began snapping photos with the tiny camera attached to the bike helmet, the images flashing across his retina screens as they uploaded to the Internet. The camera was so efficient that he didn't even need to think how to aim the device, it simply beeped and vibrated every time he was facing an optimal photo angle, allowing him to get perfect shots of the surrounding landscape.

"Zane, apart from being hungry, you also appear preoccupied. Can you please explain what you are thinking?"

"All is good EVO, I was just reflecting on how it must have been to have lived through the earthquake."

"Understood Zane. I imagine the earthquake you are referring to is the megathrust quake, which occurred in the early morning hours of July 23rd, 2043. This entire region, from as far north as Kitimat to Northern California suffered greatly. The town below you, Squamish, was completely destroyed by fire, tsunami, and mud slides. This is why Squamish is built back from the water and has a tsunami defense dyke. The dyke performs a dual function, to protect it from ongoing sea level rise, and water surges from a future landslide or earthquake."

"Zane, for your information, I just received an updated from the restaurant in Squamish, they informed me your food delivery is just around the corner."

He glanced over towards Squamish, his eyes catching the metallic reflection of a thermally insulated service drone whirring towards him. In just a few moments it was hovering a couple metres above him, its crablike legs unfolding as it came to a rest on a flat rock about five metres away. A few seconds later its belly snapped open, and a package containing his meal slid out onto the ground. Seconds later, there was a beeping sound, the drone's underbelly clicked shut and it zipped away into the sky, its legs folding up against its body, as it disappeared over the cliffside.

Zane stooped over to pick up the perfectly wrapped package, the scent of hot Mexican food filling the air, suddenly reminding him how hungry he was. Without waiting to find a comfortable place to sit, he tore open the package and took a large bite of the tortilla-wrapped mixture of synthetic beef, beans, cheese, avocado, sour cream, and spicy vegetables, some of which dripped out of the packaging onto this jacket. He barely chewed his first bite, and was about to lunge for another, when he heard sounds coming from the trail leading to Squamish. He jumped, wondering if it was a wild boar or maybe even a bear, which was highly improbable, given most of the native wildlife in the area had long since gone extinct from human encroachment and decades of forest fires, which had permanently altered the ecosystem.

Zane still let out a sigh of relief as a woman appeared out of the trail, pushing her electric bike, with her helmet draped over one of the handlebars. He took another large bite from his burrito as the new arrival looked his way, greeting him with a smile and a hello. She was unbelievably beautiful - tall, dark-skinned, athletic, with long slender legs accentuated by the tight-fitting body suit she was wearing.

"Hey there, nice day up here!" She said, as she looked his way.

Zane waved, trying to answer with his mouth full with food.

"Ah sorry, didn't seeing you were eating!"

She parked her bike just near Zane's and then wandered off, disappearing over a small rise in the middle of the clifftop clearing. He continued working through his lunch, and was almost finished, when he heard footsteps behind him.

"Hey again, I don't want to impose, but do you mind if I share this spot for a few minutes, it seems like you have the best view around. The live interactive map says this is the quietest view point on the route, apparently there is a scouting troop at the next one, and the one after that has been closed for some sort of private function."

"Oh no problem, there's plenty of room, and to be honest, I was getting a bit bored chatting with EVO!"

"Haha, god you chat with that thing? It drives me nuts, I always have it set to all the minimum interference settings, otherwise I find I can't concentrate on anything," she replied.

"By the way, my name's Maya. What's yours?"

"I'm Zane."

"Cool, nice name, sounds very futuristic, the kind of name for a cosmonaut. You from here Zane?"

"Yeah born and raised. I live in Burquitlam, well Lougheed City to be precise. How about you? I can pick up some sort of exotic accent," he smiled.

"Haha, you've got good ears! I'm from New York, but my accent is African, well Ethiopian to be more precise. I was born there, but moved to New York when I started college."

"That is exotic! I rarely meet people born in Africa. So how long you visiting for?" he asked.

"Ah, I'm not visiting. I'm here on a work contract, which I'm hoping will become permanent."

"Nice."

There was an awkward silence, made all the more noticeable by the total stillness of the air, devoid of the familiar humming of drones and machines. Hoping to keep the conversation going, Zane asked, "so what sort of work do you do?"

"Ah, I study climate change and urban design at a big university. In a nutshell I provide recommendations on how to rebuild cities to better cope with the crazy over-heated world we live in."

"Wow, sounds like a pretty cool job!"

"It is, I considered myself pretty lucky to have it! What do you do, if I may ask?"

"I'm a data analyst at a large strategic management consulting firm. Basically I gather and analyze data to help companies and governments make major strategic decisions."

"Sounds really interesting," she said.

There was another uncomfortable silence, the conversation had gone about as far as it could for a random meeting between two strangers on a biking trail in the mountains.

"Okay I'm going to get going again, but it was nice to meet you Zane. Have a wonderful afternoon."

"Thank you, Maya. Hope the rest of the day treats you well."

He watched her tie up her thick braided hair and put her helmet on. Then she hopped on her bike, waved goodbye, and vanished down the trail back to Squamish. He felt a pang of regret after she disappeared, she was so beautiful and seemed really intelligent. If only he weren't so introverted, then maybe they could have made a connection.

The time idled by and he drifted off to sleep, stretched out on the rocks under the mid-afternoon sunshine. After what seemed hours, he was awakened by a light breeze, as the sun momentarily disappeared behind a passing cloud. The sun was now quite a bit lower in the sky, meaning it was probably time to start making his way back down the mountain to not risk being stuck in darkness should he run into any problems.

He stood up, brushed himself down, gathered the small amount of packaging from his lunch, and clipped his helmet on. The skies had started to turn a darker blue, and there were hints of orange in the light, as the sun slowly slipped towards the southwest, following its distant solitary November arc across the sky. After a final look at the view, he jumped on his e-bike to start the long winding descent back to the train station.

"Zane, would you like me to enable to drive assist function?"

"No EVO, this is the best part, it's beats any video game or gym!"

It was a long steady dusty descent back to Squamish, and he had to keep his hands on the brakes to avoid picking up too much speed and risk careening off the trail into the thickets of short scrubby bushes. It was also important to be alert for hikers and wildlife; while there were no longer any bears in the region, there were plenty of North American wild boars, which were known to become aggressive if they felt threatened.

Approximately thirty minutes later he exited the track and rode across the dyke to the centre of town, which was considerably quieter than when he passed through in the morning. Most of the shops were closed, and a number of the cafes had emptied out, as the staff began moving tables and chairs inside. There was now an evening chill in the air, as he peddled across the nearly empty streets, zipping past the occasional pedestrian. The street lights started lighting up, and the short November sunset quickly transformed into an evening sky. About twenty minutes later Zane had his bike locked up and was walking quickly through the station to the platform gates.

His EVO whispered *"Zane, your e-bike number thirty-nine has been locked, and you have been billed for your session. For your information, the next train for to Lougheed is departing in eight minutes."*

He slowed down as he reached the platform, realizing he had plenty of time to kill before the next train. Rather than waste time and stare vacantly at the flashing ads on the flexiscreens covering the walls of the opposite platform, he logged into Teva, curious to see if his virtual assets had recovered from the sale he'd made back on Friday. The news was good, his investments had done well in his absence, returning to around 90,000 followers. Apparently in the past few hours the game had experienced a renewed surge in popularity, driven by a number of big players and celebrities bringing fresh assets into play. He wondered if it was sustainable, or if this was a final surge before the game went supernova and crashed. He made a mental note to take some more profit that evening and shift it into one of the newer real estate games starting to gain traction – Terra.

"Hey, Zane right? Fancy seeing you again!"

Zane jumped, deactivating his retina screens to look over to where the voice was coming from. It was Maya, the beautiful woman he'd met on the mountain earlier in the day.

"Hey…ah…Maya, right? Wow…what are the odds of running into each other again! You heading…back to town too?" he stuttered in surprise.

She laughed at his obvious confusion, "yes I'm heading back on the next train, got an early start tomorrow for a talk I'm giving to some colleagues. What about you?"

"Yeah I'm heading back as well, but I've got Monday and Tuesday off."

"Nice, nothing beats a long weekend!" she smiled.

There was a moment of awkward silence before he asked, "So, what's your talk about tomorrow? You said you were a post-doctoral fellow, right? I'm assuming it's about your research?"

"Yeah it's sort of about my research. I'm actually doing a series of presentations in front of my faculty colleagues for a position as a full professor. At the moment I'm only an associate, which doesn't have the security of being permanent, or being able to operate my own grants and labs."

"Sounds intense. I bet you are…"

Zane was interrupted as the train pulled into the platform and the glass gates slid open. They waited for the few passengers to exit and then stepped inside and took a pair of seats together. A minute later the doors closed and the nearly empty train pulled out into the darkness of the night. It was about an hour long journey back into the city; however, the time passed quickly as the two of them talked intensely about Maya's research. Zane could see the passion she had for her work, as she explained the many challenges facing climate crisis planners around the world. Rising sea levels was the biggest challenge, affecting many of the world's largest coastal agglomerations, such as Jakarta, Rio de Janeiro, New York, and Miami. In Jakarta the entire city had collapsed, pushing millions to new urban centres at higher elevations, while Rio de Janeiro had simply allowed its low land areas to flood, and then used military force to clear the poor from the hill tops to make way for redevelopment for the wealthy. Where money was available, New York and most other major coastal centres in wealthy countries took the option of building dykes and tidal management systems to protect infrastructure, while others, such as Miami, simply succumbed to the sea, experiencing sudden catastrophic failure, which destroyed real estate values overnight.

"In Miami's case it happened so quickly. Everyone knew the real estate bubble was unsustainable and built on a dying city, yet so many people just kept speculating, believing prices would keep rising, despite the city being under water most days of the year."

Listening to Maya talk about Miami, he became acutely aware of the similarities it had to his investments in Teva, and how the game was also entirely dependent on speculation. He decided it was time to reduce his exposure and sell more than he did on Friday, moving some of his assets from Teva to Terra and making another payment against the debt on his condo.

He mumbled out loud, "a classical example of an economic bubble forming before a crash."

"Exactly!" she replied.

"Curious, you said sea level rise was one of a number of challenges. What are some of the others?"

"Well sea level rise is the go to example because it's the most visible manifestation of climate change; however, climate crisis urban planners also look at how to design cities to sustain food supply shocks, pandemics, catastrophic weather events, and more. Here's a cool example, I bet you didn't know that up until the middle of the 21st Century, large portions of urban real estate in cities were reserved for private non-autonomous gasoline vehicles."

"Actually I did know that!" Zane smiled.

"Well you're probably the exception! Without asking EVO, do you know what caused many cities to change?"

"Ah, to be honest I'm not quite sure."

"Well the answer is it was a series of early 21st Century pandemics that seriously affected food supply in cities, forcing urban planners to move agriculture into cities, closer to the consumer. In many forward-thinking cities they quickly expropriated public parking and road space to build large forty and fifty storey urban farms. These cities were better able to confront ongoing shocks, and the model soon spread to include most cities in Europe, China, Japan, and Canada. Unfortunately, the United States has yet to adopt this model - part of my work is to convince them to act before the next large shocks arrive…"

Maya stopped what she was saying as the train popped out of the tunnel from the downtown core and onto the elevated tracks above the False Creek tidal park between the downtown Salish City and the low-rise towers on Grandview Heights.

"I guess you're exiting at Commercial, right?" Zane asked.

"Yes I'm heading west to the campus out at Point Grey."

"Well it's been fun chatting, would be nice to do this again. Um, do you mind if we trade contacts?" Zane asked shyly.

"Of course not, I was about to ask you because we were running out of time!" she laughed, as she got up to prepare to disembark.

"Great! Let's get together next weekend if you're up for it!" Zane said, as Maya's information appeared in his EVO social circle.

"Sounds good to me, my weekends are pretty open at the moment."

With that she smiled and waved goodbye, dashing out the doors just before they closed.

He spent the rest of the journey reflecting on their conversation about the climate crisis. It was a tragedy that could have been avoided, instead previous generations chose to bury their heads in the sand and continue living unsustainable lives, in the belief that it was impossible for humans to modify something as enormous as the planet's climate. By the late 20th Century data and real events showed humans were indeed changing the planet's climate, as natural spaces began suffering their first great die-offs, the beginnings of a coming biosphere collapse. Yet despite forest fires on continental scales, collapse of ocean fisheries, and the reality of millions of deaths provoked by urban heat islands, pollution, and pandemics, the political class still failed to change course. Instead populations became beholden to simple and populist propaganda from the ultra-wealthy who showed no interest in removing fossil fuels from the global economy before it was too late.

By the late 2020's the evidence was too blatant to deny, even for populist crack-pots and conspiracy hoax theorists who continued peddling fake-news stories. The Green Revolution first happened in the European Union at the end of the decade, where high population density permitted it to happen quickly. Europeans were more educated about climate change and how it was affecting them. They could feel it in their burning hot summers, as well as see it in the form of millions of African and Asian refugees swarming their borders; crossing deserts, seas, and war zones to reach the promised land.

The changes then spread from Europe to Asia, where China, Korea, and Japan drastically cut carbon output through taxation and prohibition, which were enforced through fines and threat of imprisonment. The North American economy followed suit, starting at the regional level and then spreading throughout the private sector, before being mandated through agreements signed in Ottawa, Washington, and Mexico City.

Besides a rapid switchover to green technologies, there was also a move to remove carbon derivatives such as plastics from entire economies. This was coordinated with new technologies designed to remove and incinerate plastics in the air, water, and on land. Giant machines drifted across the world's oceans collecting and incinerating plastic, powered by the sun, the ocean, and the waste they collected. On land, waste dumps were mined for materials, which were used for powering incineration plants to remove as much plastic as possible from the ecosystem. These efforts helped bring carbon emissions down to levels not seen since the 1970's; nevertheless, it was all too late to stop the inevitable unrelenting heating of the planet. Scientists explained that while the worst had been averted, the heating was going to continue unabated for hundreds or thousands of years to come, with severe and unknown consequences, especially for billions of people trapped in the poor countries of the Global South.

The wealthy countries, terrified of the implications of being swamped with ever more climate refugees from the Global South, debated what to do to protect themselves. In the 2030's they suddenly acted, collectively tearing up both the UN Declaration of Human Rights and the 1951 Geneva Convention for the safe asylum of refugees, ushering in an era of untold terror for the world's most vulnerable populations. Mercilessly they began brazenly employing their militaries, terrorizing millions of people fleeing appalling conditions in impoverished countries. They fortified and mined natural barriers, armed and bribed puppet regimes, and deployed their armed forces to eliminate any possible access to the relative security and comfort of the developed world.

The world went onto a deep freeze, divided into two zones: the Global South and the wealthy developed countries. After about ten years, the wealthy countries also began to split into separate blocs, aligning themselves based on ideology and geopolitical interests. Three large blocs appeared, the first was the group of European and Western liberal states, which also included Australia, Aotearoa, Taiwan, Korea, and Japan; the second was the group of Totalitarian states, which included Russia, China, and the Central Asian Republics; the third was a disparate group of loosely associated non-aligned states in Latin America and Southern Africa, referred to as the Non-Aligned Bloc. Each of these blocs tolerated each other, conducting globalized trade across their borders, while playing dangerous brinkmanship through proxy wars in the Global South.

Zane sighed, he was back at home, standing in his bedroom, clearing his mind as he prepared to get to bed. He looked out the glass at the sea of buildings before him. Droplets of rain beginning to fall, splashing and running down the glass, distorting and fragmenting the lights outside. The climate crisis had changed the world, making it a more unstable and perilous place; however, it was not all bad news, one just need look at the hundreds of millions of people living in reengineered cities like Salish City. These metropolises had adapted and thrived, powered by the forces of the sun, the wind, and the rain falling from the heavens. As dark as things may seem, there was hope, human beings had a remarkable ability to adapt when they accepted science and acted not on emotion, but on facts.

Phase One

Date – Wednesday November 6th, 2120

"Okay guys, firstly I hope all of you had a wonderful long weekend and were able to rest and recharge your batteries! Secondly, I want to thank you for joining me this morning for a bit of company sponsored weekly fitness and informal fun, my way of saying thanks and goodbye. I really want to say it's been a real pleasure working with you all, with a special nod to Leyla, who I've had the honour of working on four projects with, and Zane, who has worked with me ever since joining the firm."

Leyla added, "well Antonio it's always a pleasure working with you handsome, though I do prefer being the project leader because then I get to put you in your place whenever I want!"

Everyone burst into laughter as Antonio shook his head, smiling at Leyla's friendly joke.

"Well babe that's not going to happen on the next project because Jared Berg has already assigned me a new lead role. In fact what I have is so interesting, you and everyone here might want to stick around!"

"Antonio, I hate to break it you bro, but I have a new project I'm starting up with a client in California, they want me to put together a team to restructure and rebrand their surfboard company!"

"Oh nice Robbie! I'm ready to move, when does it start?"

"Anita, the only reason you're interested is because you'll be closer to tech boy!"

Everyone laughed, including Anita, who knew Robbie was joking about the project.

"Okay," Antonio continued, "so to sell you on my new project I've put together a fun and informative day with some pretty amazing guest speakers. One thing I must emphasize, due of the nature of this new project you will need to inform me today as to whether you wish to stay on, or leave this group to work on something different. This is to meet the client's security needs and allow me to plan my staffing requirements."

Just as he finished speaking, a company fitness trainer joined their group, wasting no time to put them through a battery of modified army fitness drills that in just minutes had them sweating and out of breath. Unlike most corporate team building activities, Zane loved the company workouts because they were the only activities where he could switch off and not be bombarded with company politics and propaganda.

An hour after the workout, Zane and the entire team were freshened up and sitting in the boardroom waiting on Antonio. Everyone looked well rested following the morning exercise and the long weekend. Anita was the only one who seemed out of sorts - to be expected given she was spending most weekends in Los Angeles with her new boyfriend, a gorgeous virtual reality tech programmer based in Orange County, who had a thing for older Asian women.

"So Anita, how many cups of coffee are you going to go through today?" Robbie asked.

"I'm betting she'll do at least a dozen by the end of the afternoon!" Zane joked.

Anita looked at the two of them, raising her brows as she took a sip of coffee and leaned back in her swivel chair.

"Hey leave the girl in peace, she's doing just fine, she doesn't need any lecturing about her lifestyle from you Robbie, or especially you Zane, mister party boy!" Leyla winked.

"Ooh mister party boy. Tell us more Leyla, what did our office hottie get up to over the weekend?" Anita winked, as she put down her cup of coffee.

"Oh yeah, do tell Leyla!" everyone insisted.

"Woah, that's my personal business…" Zane shouted, waving his arms in Leyla's direction.

"Haha! Well Zane there is no such thing as personal business here. I mean Anita has her cards on the table, we all know about her thing in LA and how she's riding the bullet train down there every weekend to be with her tech boy. So, what was Zane up to on Friday night?" Leyla smiled, "well he was very busy with my dear friend Timothy and his latest girlfriend Melissa…"

Before it could get much saucier Antonio walked in, cutting Leyla off.

"Sorry I'm late guys, I ran into our group VP Jared Berg in the hall."

"No problem," Miko smiled, "we were just catching up on Anita and Zane's weekend exploits!"

"Ah ha, sounds like fun! Though I bet not nearly as exciting as the party my girlfriend Ocean and I went to on the weekend. It was a crazy bash put on by one of her property developer clients for a new tower they've just completed in Burquitlam."

"Oh do tell us Antonio." Leyla purred, raising her eyebrows, as she placed her fashionable fake eye glasses on the glass boardroom table.

"Maybe later babe, we're running a bit behind schedule and I'm expecting a few guests to join us momentarily."

There was a collective moan, which stopped just as Jared Berg strolled into the boardroom and sat down at the table. He was accompanied by Marko Ivanovic, one of the directors of business development for Syllabus, whom Zane had chatted with a few times in the lunch room.

Antonio stood up, smiling, "alright I think all of you know Jared and Marko, they're going to join us today to help introduce the project."

Everyone nodded, acutely aware the assignment must be a bit out of the ordinary, given Berg and Ivanovic's presence. Zane looked at the two men. Berg was an imposing individual, probably in his mid-fifties, and already flagged amongst the candidates to be

Syllabus' next CEO. Berg's subordinate, Marko was well known to many on the strategic development side of the firm - he was in his late forties, very sociable, and tall and athletic, with slick handsome southern Slavic facial features.

"Okay everyone, I can tell you're all anxious for me to reveal the details of this project. I'm also willing to bet you're all going to sign up as soon as you discover what it's all about."

Antonio stopped talking, smiling cheekily at everyone in the room, as both Jared and Marko started to chuckle at his act. Everyone was on the edge of their seats, leaning on the boardroom table in anticipation of what was about to be divulged.

"Oh come on Antonio, what's the project, don't be an ass!?" Leyla groaned.

"Yeah, I've got a train to catch to the next project in LA." Anita quipped.

"Okay Antonio, let them have it." Marko laughed.

"It's a government project, hot off the press as of last night."

"What?" everyone groaned in unison.

"A government project? That's about as exciting as spending a day alone in the forest." Leyla moaned.

"Hey, what's wrong with spending a day in the forest? That's what I did this weekend!" Zane frowned indignantly.

"Zane you did a lot more than that on the weekend…" Leyla giggled, as everyone, including Jared Berg and Marko Ivanovic, looked his way.

Zane went beet red, Leyla had baited him fair and square, knowing he had gone to Squamish on one of his regular solitary nature outings.

"Okay guys let's focus here, just for a moment please. This is no ordinary government project, it's like nothing you've imagined, and it had the potential to take your careers to a whole new level."

"Well what is it Antonio?" Robbie asked, suddenly once again very interested.

"Well, Marko and Jared aren't here to listen to us make fun of our dear colleague Zane Fischer, they're here to talk to you about this project. So without wasting anymore time, Marko how about you take it from here?"

Antonio turned to Marko, who swivelled out of his chair and stepped to the front of the room. "Thanks Antonio for the introduction. Before I start, my commendations to Zane for his mountaineering and weekend exploits, it all sounds very interesting indeed!"

Marko paused to let the room have another laugh at Zane's expense, before continuing. "Now, seriously, while you've been working on wrapping up the last project, Antonio, myself, and Jared, have been hard at work securing what is certainly a remarkable government project."

Marko continued, "as all of you know, there was an election last night in the United States. The results were dramatic, a major change in the direction of the country. The winner of that election, a Social Democrat, has some pretty lofty ideas, and has called on Syllabus to put together an implementation plan for one of them. She is asking us to develop an official strategic plan for the United States Department of Health to implement publicly accessible gentech in America. What we propose will ultimately become the incoming President's path to modernizing healthcare in the country."

The room went dead quiet, the only sound the gentle humming from the air ducts.

"You mean, like a version of Canada Health and Genetic Technology Act we have in Canada?" Zane gasped, incredulous.

"Similar, except ours was a complete rewrite of the Canada Health Act to include genetic technology, whereas theirs is most likely going to be an amendment to their Medicare program. But yes, the objective for the incoming President is to provide public-access state funded genetic medicine, just like we have in Canada and other developed countries."

"Wow, that's one seriously big deal," Robbie said.

Marko nodded in agreement, "this was a difficult deal to get; however, before we delve into the details, what I'm going to do is put everything into context. First, as you all know, I've only been with Syllabus for about a year. Prior to that I was a senior partner in a boutique consulting firm in Washington D.C., focused on lobbying the US government and politicians to make human genetic technology free and accessible for everyone, by adding it to America's public access Medicare program. Around the middle of last year my firm's other senior partner, whom you will meet today, was recruited to join the election campaign for who is now America's incoming President. He was assigned the responsibility of developing a human genetic technologies policy for their electoral platform."

"Around the time my business partner moved to the presidential race, we were approached by Syllabus to buy us out – your CEO and vice-presidents were anticipating changes in access to human genetic technology in America, and wanted to have access to our clients. We accepted Syllabus' offer and set up an arrangement where my partner remained with the incoming president's campaign, and I moved here. Ever since then my former partner and I have been working closely together to establish a relationship between the President-elect's campaign and Syllabus, a relationship that has solidified as the President-elect went from a populist firebrand candidate in the primaries, to becoming the nominee, and finally winning the race last night."

"Over the past month, as the campaign approached election day, myself, Jared Berg, and Antonio have been quietly working to cement this relationship into a contract, all contingent on the electoral victory last night. With the win last night, the contract went into effect, with the President-elect's team instructing us to have something ready for them prior to inauguration on the 21st January 2121."

"Now why have we chosen to offer you guys the project before opening it up to the rest of the firm? Well when we secured the deal, Antonio suggested we use his existing work team to save time on recruiting, and also because several of you, in particular Antonio, Zane, and Anita, have the specific technical competencies for this sort of project. Namely training in genetics, data analysis, and artificial intelligence, which will all be central components of what the client will need from us. "

"Alright, that about sums up the essentials of what I needed to say. Antonio, do you want to take it from there?"

Marko sat down and Antonio returned to the front of the room.

"Alright, now I'm sure many of you are asking how you can contribute to a project of this complexity, especially since apart from Marko and I, none of you are formally trained in medical genetics or public health policy. Let me make this clear, this will not be a project of one or two healthcare specialists working in silos, it will be one requiring lots of team work, using collective skills to support those who will be in the public eye."

"Starting with Zane, your training in mathematical modelling and data analysis will be essential for us to chart out the best plan for the new government to implement. Factors such as cost, ease of implementation, public buy-in, political opposition, technical challenges, and endless other variables will need to be modelled and analyzed by a mathematics expert. Zane, your experience with the last health care client, as well as your doctoral work at Stanford will be invaluable on a project of this scope."

"Leyla and Robbie, you guys are two of the top communications experts based here at Syllabus head office. With a politicized project like this, whatever we propose will need to be effectively communicated, first to the US Administration, then to the broad political class, and lastly to the general public. Your experience in visual and verbal communication will be critical is selling whatever we come up with."

"Anita and Miko, every Syllabus project needs AI, computing, and project management expertise; however, I can assure you this one will be beyond anything Syllabus has taken on in recent memory. As this project unfolds, we'll be needing to constantly harness technology and timelines to rollout this project and communicate it to very diverse audiences, many of them being naturally conceived people with sub-standard levels of education and inferior intelligence."

"Antonio, I have a question."

"Ah Miko, I'm going to have to hold off on questions for now, as we're about to be joined by some guest speakers. In case you don't have the option on, if you guys could please activate augmented reality in your retina lenses, you'll be needing it to see our guests."

Zane quickly activated the option on his EVO, it was one he normally left off, primarily to avoid being inundated with aggressive hologram ads littering the public space. The technology had its advantages, but sadly it had become a marketer's dream, causing all sorts of confusion and mayhem in public spaces for people who accidently left it activated when outside.

A few moments later two hologram figures appeared standing beside Antonio in the front of the room. They were both so real that they looked like they were physically inside the boardroom, and not projections from somewhere far away.

"Joe and Samuel, hey there! Thanks for joining us. I understand Steve will jump in later on after the break?"

"Hey Antonio, a pleasure. Yes you are right, we're going to do the background material first, then Steve will take over after the break. He's currently in meetings in Washington for the next hour or so."

"Sounds good guys, I'll get out of the way and let you gentlemen start."

Antonio sat down at the front, and Joe and Samuel moved to the sides of the room. The screen in the front lit up, with logos of various government agencies and corporate partners, including Syllabus.

"Hi everyone, my name is Samuel, with the European Union's COST, an acronym for the Council on Science and Technology. We are the umbrella organization for the use of science, engineering, and technology in EU member states. I'm in a sub-department of COST responsible for the EU fertility lottery, the mechanism by which we allocate human genetic materials in the area of birth and conception in EU member states."

"And I'm Joe, a senior research scientist with NSERC, the National Science and Energy Research Council of Canada. My specific expertise is in genetic engineering applications as they apply to climate change management."

After a moment of silence, Joe continued, "sorry guys, as you may be aware, Samuel and I are not in the same location, so please excuse any hiccups, we've done a few of these hologram

106

conferences, but sometimes we get out of sync with the technology. Samuel, all good there?"

"All good Joe!" Samuel's transatlantic British accent was in marked contrast to Joe's more familiar Central Canadian twang.

"Ok everyone, looks like we're good to start. Samuel is going to step away for a bit, while I lead this first part of the presentation. Thanks Samuel, and see you shortly."

Samuel waved as his hologram faded, and Joe turned to look at everyone. "Alright guys, let's get down to business. First we'll start with something very familiar and unavoidable in today's world: the climate crisis. It is my area of expertise, so please excuse me if I get quite deep into the topic. I promise it will be stimulating, with lots of examples from your part of the country. Lastly, before I hand over to Samuel, we'll see how it all ties into the rise of genetic engineering."

"Now as you know, like other wealthy coastal cities, Salish City began to suffer from the results of the climate change crisis in the early 21st Century. Warmer climate meant longer, hotter, drier summers and shorter, warmer, wetter winters, leading to a rapid decline in glaciers and snow packs, both of which eventually disappeared from your region by the end of the 21st Century. This situation was not atypical, as much of Europe, Asia, and the Americas witnessed the demise of their ice packs around the same time. The changing climate brought many crises, but in your region it was long fire seasons that were the most difficult to adapt to. These fires polluted the air for months, wiped out animal and plant species, and in a few decades transformed the region's forests into scattered bush and brush vegetation."

Joe paused as the slides on the screen shifted through various images of Salish City and Seattle, as well as the landscape and climate as they looked one hundred years earlier. He then continued, "what makes your region unique was the catastrophic July 2043 earthquake, which completely destroyed the urban centres in the region. All of these cities were forced to rebuild, and the only way to do it was through coercive centralized state planning, which forced the region's inhabitants into completely different urban landscapes designed to survive both the climate crisis and future earthquakes."

Joe paused again, checking to see the slides were synchronized with his talk, "the re-urbanization of the entire Cascade region was a tremendous success, proof of the power of big government to implement drastic changes on a large scale, all within a short period of time. By the end of the transformation in the 2090's, the region's economy had shifted from fossil fuels to renewable energy, and densified into populous compact cities, interconnected through local, regional, and interurban rapid rail transport. It is a model being used to reshape other regions of the world to reduce their carbon footprint and make them better able to survive the worsening climate crisis."

"So now what? Well besides reshaping entire regional human geographies, the response to the climate crisis has also been to innovate, and one of the central areas of innovation outside of urban densification and renewable energy is genetic engineering. Genetic engineering was first used in the meat industry to create enhanced livestock, which needed less food and water than traditional cattle, thus saving resources and reducing carbon output. Next it was applied to get us off meat altogether, by engineering synthetic meat, which allowed us to significantly shrink our carbon footprint. The technology was also applied in the produce industry, where fruit, grains, and vegetables were engineered for harsher climates so they could be grown closer to consumers, thus reducing transportation needs."

"The enormous investments in genetic engineering in agriculture also helped lead to major spin-off developments in human health. Diseases such as Ebola, Malaria, and Zika were largely eliminated through genetic engineering and gene therapies applied to humans and to the insects and animals carrying the viruses. Techniques developed though these technologies were applied in other disease areas, advancing the whole realm of health science, and helping us win the battle against HIV, respiratory epidemics, cancer, and neurodegenerative diseases."

"As investors saw the success of genetic engineering in agriculture and disease management, those with the financial means sought to take the technology one step further. Investors started pouring money into human genetic engineering firms in China, Europe, and the United States that focused their technologies on a wealthy segment of the market - people who were willing to pay money to select and enhance the best traits from their genes to produce so called 'super-children'. In the mid 21st Century, pharmaceutical companies began buying up these genetic engineering firms, shifting their business models from disease elimination and management, to more lucrative human genetic enhancement. This set the stage for the most dramatic transformation of healthcare in modern history."

Joe stopped speaking for a moment as a final slide appeared on the screen beside him with logos of NSERC and the Government of Canada.

"That concludes my part of the talk. I'm going step away and hand you off to Samuel in Brussels. He'll explain a bit more about human genetics and healthcare management programs implemented around the world."

"Have a great day everyone."

"Thanks Joe," Marko and Antonio answered.

Joe took a step back, and moments later Samuel's hologram brightened as he stood up from a chair and walked to the centre of the room.

"Hi everyone, so as I mentioned earlier I'm with the EU's COST, the Council on Science and Technology, which umbrellas the use of science, engineering, and technology in EU member states. I'm in a sub-department of COST responsible for the EU fertility lottery, the mechanism by which we allocate human genetic materials in the area of birth and conception in EU member states."

"By the way, just so you are aware, I am speaking in French here in Brussels – no that Transatlantic accent sadly isn't mine. So please signal to me if the AI translator starts to malfunction and you hear German or Mandarin instead of English."

Everyone laughed.

"No we're good Samuel."

"Great! So Joe spoke about climate change and the Cascadia re-urbanization project post 2043, and gave a bit of an intro into genetic engineering and how we moved from agricultural innovation to human health applications. I'm going continue on and get more in depth into genetic engineering and the advent of human reproduction lottery systems in wealthy developed countries."

"It was around the middle of the 21st Century that governments in wealthy countries began to take an interest in genetic engineering technology outside of the fields of agriculture and disease management. They were concerned about the move of pharmaceutical firms into human genetic engineering, and the effect it would have on society. For governments, it wasn't just for the technology's ability to make super-children, it was also the clear evidence that genetically engineered children got the best grades, were the best at sports, rarely got sick, got all the scholarships, went to the best universities, and ended up with the best jobs."

"People with the financial means were sacrificing whatever they had to have just one prized genetically engineered child, giving up having children conceived through intercourse. It wasn't long before a chasm in terms of life opportunities opened between the near perfect genetically engineered offspring, and the masses conceived the old-fashioned way. Those born from parents without the means were doomed to earn lower wages, be stuck in low skill jobs, and constantly at risk of being made redundant by AI technology. These masses took to the streets in violent protests in the late 21st Century, threatening to destabilise entire countries unless governments banned private access genetic medicine and made it publicly funded and accessible for all."

Samuel stopped to take a sip of water, and then continued. "In order to prevent anarchy, governments in the EU and other wealthy nations, including Canada, quickly responded by nationalizing genetic medication and invitro-fertilization IVF clinics, bringing them under state run public medical systems in the 2090's. In the case of IVF clinics, resources were limited and it was impossible to offer access to everyone at once, so an opt in lottery system was devised to regulate demand. Lotteries in very wealthy countries, such as Canada and Norway, offered high probabilities of winning, where people had the chance of having between one and three children in their lifetimes. In less wealthy countries, such as Chile and Argentina, the odds of being called were much lower, and it was possible for some people to end up childless; nevertheless, the public was willing to take that risk, rather than giving birth to a substandard child conceived the old-fashioned way. There were some who did not participate in the lotteries, these were mostly people who did not want to reproduce, or those few on the margins of society who still preferred natural conception to IVF and gestation pods."

"The nationalization of genetic medicine and the implementation of the lottery quickly ended social unrest. In just twenty years natural conceived pregnancies all but disappeared, and in some countries such as Canada it is now illegal to conceive outside of the lottery system. The lotteries, in regulating access to IVF clinics, have had the added benefit of being able to plan the number of births per year, thus ending the age-old problem of endless population growth and generational boom-bust cycles. Human life expectancy has also soared to unprecedented levels, where it is now expected people entering their twenties today will live beyond two hundred years of age."

"Okay guys, Joe and I have rambled on for quite some time here. I'd say it's a good time to take a break before your meeting with Steve McNeill."

Antonio stood up and thanked Joe, wishing him a good evening back in Ottawa. Joe's hologram vanished, and the lights turned on.

"Alright everyone, let's take a twenty-minute break and then gather back here for the last part of the talk."

Zane was the last to leave the room, making a bathroom stop before grabbing a coffee and heading back to the boardroom to take a seat and reflect on what he had just heard. It was all quite fantastical, but it was reality, almost everyone born in wealthy countries who were under the age of forty were genetically engineered. They were conceived through IVF and then incubated for nine months in an artificial uterus, commonly known as a gestation pod. Zane and all of his colleagues were in their early thirties and above, so most of them had been created in private IVF clinics, not state-owned facilities; however, younger people, who were just entering the work force today, were all genetically engineered through a comprehensive public system that banned reproduction through natural means.

The room started to fill up again as his colleagues returned to take their seats. Antonio reminded everyone to reactivate their retina systems to hologram mode, and the lights partially dimmed as the same screen with the logos appeared, followed by a hologram of a tall gangly mid-forties white man with a thick mop of very blond hair.

Marko waved from his seat. "Hey Steve, just to let you know we see you crystal clear on this end."

"Hey Marko! Good to see you again bro! I see Jared is there too, great to see both of you could join in this evening, or afternoon for you guys!"

"I wouldn't miss it for the world Steve! Congratulations on the big night last night!"

"Thanks Jared, we're all ecstatic, still floating on cloud nine I must say! Okay, I see we've got the full group there, my facial recognition system tells me we've got Zane Fischer, Leyla Janssen, Robbie Wallace, and Anita Wong in the room?" Steve asked.

"We do", Antonio answered, "as well as Miko Tanaka, an operations management specialist who joined this group at the end of our last project."

"Great, thanks Antonio, also good to see you again my friend. So no wasting time, Joe and Samuel have completely filled you guys in about life, the universe, and everything, right? Basically everything that has happened since the fall of Constantinople?"

There were chuckles, as Steve pretended to yawn and look a bit bored. It was clear he was a very affable and friendly fellow who enjoyed being in front of an audience – very important for someone working in politics.

Marko replied, "yes Steve, if you'd like we can tell you all about it!"

"Thanks for the offer Marko, maybe another time! Okay, so I'm sure you're wondering who the hell is Steve McNeill, right? Well to keep it simple, I work for the US President-elect in her inner circle of advisors. If you follow US news, you'll surely have seen me around, as I've been very visible on the campaign trail the past year pushing for genetic medicine and reproductive technology, collectively known in the US as gentech, to be added to our public Medicare health plan. Now as we transition from campaigning to taking office, I have been assigned the task of making this happen, to implement a public payer system similar to what has been in place in Canada and other wealthy countries since the 2090's."

"Now how did Steve McNeill get this unusual job? Well prior to working for the President-elect's campaign, I ran a consulting outfit in D.C. with your senior director of business development Marko Ivanovic, who is sitting right there in the room with you. Marko and I go way back to college, where we studied genetic engineering together at Georgetown University. He went on to do a master's in public health policy, while I did my Ph. D. in human gentech, but we stayed in touch and eventually got into the business of helping progressive state governments such as Vermont, Massachusetts, Maine, and Minnesota add public gentech medicine to their state Medicare health plans. The success of those projects gave us a name, which led to Syllabus buying us out, and Marko and I ending up where we are today."

"Anyway, I digress. I'm sure all of you have seen on the news that in the United States we are confronted with a gentech healthcare crisis. Not a week goes by without some large and violent demonstration by hundreds of thousands of ordinary Americans who are, to put it bluntly, frightened and pissed off that the wealthy twenty percent of the population have monopolized access to these technologies for themselves. Ordinary Americans see how gentech has been part of publicly funded healthcare in so many countries around the world for decades, and they ask why it still isn't the case here. Well this incoming administration understands their anger, and we are dead set on fixing this problem because there is no more time to keep fucking around."

McNeill paused for a few moments, letting the emotion in his brash language settle upon the audience seated in the Syllabus boardroom. There was no hiding just how much the issue mattered to the man, as well as the stakes in a country with debilitating levels of healthcare and socio-economic inequality.

"So before we go any further, I'm going to explain to you what is happening with healthcare in America today, so you can understand why even ordinary Americans are starting to resort to violence to gain access to gentech. Healthcare in our country is covered by state Medicare, and topped up by private insurance for a few lucky people. Currently Medicare offers no gentech at all, unless you're lucky to live in a few states in New England and Minnesota. The only way you can access gentech is if you are a working elite with a premium private insurance top-up plan, or you are incredibly wealthy with lots of money to blow on the technologies. Currently about eighty percent of Americans are restricted to Medicare, while the other twenty percent form this privileged elite."

"This two-tier system of elites versus everyone else has been in place since about 2070, so nearly fifty years. Life has been very good for the elites, they have experienced unparalleled increases in life-span, quality of life, wealth, beauty, athleticism, intelligence, and access to premium education and careers, all this despite AI and the fallout from the climate crisis. In fact because they are amongst the most privileged people on earth, they have first access to premium technologies still not on state plans in rich countries such as Norway, Canada, and the Netherlands."

"And as for the rest, the eighty percent stuck with ordinary Medicare, well quality of life has stalled, incomes have declined, life spans have stagnated, and they continue to suffer and die from diseases that have long since disappeared in countries where gentech is part of national healthcare. This situation has provoked fear, anger, and rage amongst people, who worry that if this continues unabated, there will be a permanent divergence between a genetically engineered class of rich people, and everyone else. This concern is nothing new for other wealthy nations like Canada, where you people nationalized gentech access to stop the divergence from happening; however, in America, where we are beholden to a religious obsession with the free-market, it has taken nearly fifty years for us to realize the perils of the status quo."

"Our incoming administration has identified this issue, along with the climate crisis as the two biggest threats to our national security. In a national election scarred with voter suppression, gerrymandering, lies, fraud, and distractions, a majority still chose our message, drawn to our promise to tackle these two issues head on."

"So that brings us to the present. In a bit over two months, in the third week of January, our administration will take office. This leaves us a short window of time to craft a strategy to overcome the torrent of lies the rich and powerful in the Libertarian party will throw at us to prevent nationalizing gentech healthcare. Jared and Marko have convinced me your team at Syllabus is up to the task. We are counting on you to be there."

Steve paused for a few seconds and then asked, "any questions or comments?"

Zane raised his hand.

"Yes Dr. Zane Fischer, go ahead."

"Steve, if you don't mind me using your first name, thanks for your presentation, very informative. I have a question regarding the priorities you have. There are two issues you are addressing here, one is genetic treatments for the living, and the other is essentially reproductive technologies for the yet to be conceived. Which one gets first priority?"

"Good point Zane. Reproductive technologies are the Social Democrats' priority as they are critical to closing the class gap in America over the long term; however, we are dependent on a coalition with Republicans to get this bill through Congress, and they tend to be more religious, less educated, and skeptical about using science in reproduction. So to make this plan sell, we will need to put the spotlight on Medicare covered genetic medicines and vaccines, while keeping the focus off the reproductive technologies covered in the bill."

Robbie raised his hand, and asked, "Can you elaborate on the timeline you have for the project."

"Robbie, if it were me I'd push this through right away, but the President-elect was carried through on a dual platform, with climate infrastructure upgrades being the priority. So we'll have to wait and work in the background until that bill is passed through Congress. I anticipate we'll get our turn in May or June, that's our big hope; however, definitely before the start of the summer, as then we will be facing the start of the primary cycle for the next Congressional elections."

"More questions?"

Silence.

Marko jumped in, "thanks Steve, I think Antonio and his team now have a much clearer idea of what lies ahead. What we'll do here is discuss our next steps and then you and your team will start hearing back from us before week's end."

"Awesome Marko, look forward to meeting you all in person! You have yourselves a great afternoon over there in Salish City!"

Steve's hologram vanished and the lights turned on. Zane looked around, rubbing his eyes and looking at his colleagues. He was filled with a sense of excitement and trepidation for what was clearly a remarkable project, a sort of once in a lifetime deal for a strategic consultant, and a dream for a mathematician and data analyst like himself, but which also held enormous risks of failure.

Jared Berg interrupted his thoughts. "Alright everyone, thank you for letting Marko and I sit in on this talk. It's a big project for Syllabus, one that he and I worked hard to get, and is getting lots of attention from the CEO and the senior board of directors. I want you to know this is a tremendous opportunity for our company and for yourselves, and we should all be thrilled to have Antonio running this. He is a very competent team leader and a senior consultant with years of experience in this field of work, and I am most confident he can deliver for us and the client."

Jared looked over at Antonio, giving him a smile and a look of confidence, before adding, "Marko and I will check in with the team from time to time, and as the project snowballs in size we will start taking a more active role. Okay that concludes what I have to say. I've got to run to another meeting and I believe you also have to be somewhere Marko?"

Marko nodded, as the two of them stood up and pushed their chairs into the table.

"Gentlemen, once again thank you for making this happen." Antonio replied.

Jared and Marko left the room, and Antonio turned back to the group. "Okay everyone, I think you guys have a fair bit of information to make your decision on whether this is the project for you. Jared and I want you to commit to this no later than lunch time. Let's take an hour to break for something to eat and then you guys can let me know what your decision is. Oh and lastly, before we leave the room may I remind all of you that what you have seen here is strictly confidential information, any leaks will be traced to source and will result in immediate termination of your employment at Syllabus."

Antonio stood up and left the room, leaving everyone to mingle for a couple of minutes and then stroll as a group down the hallway towards Zane and Leyla's desks.

"So what do you guys think?" Miko asked nervously, staring at Robbie.

"Ah, I don't know about you guys, but I think this deal is pretty incredible, it's like a career boost on steroids!" Robbie answered enthusiastically.

"Totally agree, this would be the biggest project I've ever undertaken with Syllabus. I mean how many data analysts can say they crafted a signature US policy in their first job?" Zane added.

Anita nodded in agreement, adding, "plus we get to work directly with our VP and a sales director, while also under the CEO and the senior board of directors' watch!"

"Yeah that does ratchet up the stress a few more notches. I mean guys, think about it, this is serious material, is our small team equipped for this? What happens if things go wrong and it flops?"

Zane shrugged, "Come on, I wouldn't be worried about that Miko. Antonio has lots of project leadership experience, he's a geneticist, and so is Marko Ivanovic; furthermore, we can count on Syllabus adding more resources should the project start to grow. This project is a winner, what possibly could go wrong?"

Anita put her arm on Miko's shoulders, "Relax babe we can do this, this is the jackpot, I mean it's why we're here at Syllabus. Just think, we could be at some other firm doing boring run of the mill strategic development for power management, or worse, virtual reality games. This is exciting transformative technology, and we get to shape how Americans will use it for generations to come."

"Hey! What's wrong with virtual reality games?" Zane joked.

"Haha, we all know how addicted you are to those Dr. Fischer, the mathematics wizard!" Leyla laughed.

"Hey, I've made plenty good money on Teva. In fact I just cashed out a whole bunch more to invest in the next big game, Terra. You lot will all be pretty jealous when you see how much I'm going to coin on that one!"

"God, I'd rather just go shopping and hang out with my girlfriends, than spend all that time on some addictive real estate fantasy," Leyla groaned.

The team eventually arrived at Zane and Leyla's work cubes. Anita looked at their cubicles and then turned to Zane. "What's this? How did I never notice this? You guys have way better offices than us. How did you get these views?"

Robbie winked back at Anita and said, "well sister, look at that dark olive skin and those beautiful blue eyes, how could anyone in Human Resources resist giving Zaney boy anything but the best? As for Leyla, not only does she know how to catch an eye, but she's also got plenty of seniority here, which yeah, means she also knows how to work the system!"

Zane interjected, grinning with a big mischievous smile, "whoa guys let's chill here, control yourselves okay. It's just a desk and if you all want it, I'll be happy to switch out…for a good sum of money that is!"

Leyla chuckled, "well maybe Zaney boy is a sell-out for money, but my precious view ain't for sale!"

Everyone laughed, as they dispersed for lunch.

As planned after lunch, they had a brief meeting with Antonio to discuss the next steps. He started with the usual privacy run down, which included the ramifications for any data breaches and disclosure of sensitive information. Afterwards he explained phase one of the project, which focused on assembling several options for the incoming President's gentech and healthcare policy. This phase was expected to last about four weeks, ending with a presentation to the incoming Administration in early December.

"Afterwards we hope to be selected for phase two, where the Administration will task us with completing the plan they choose, and having it ready prior to the Presidential inauguration on January 21st, ready for us to defend it in Congressional hearings in the weeks that follow. At that point we'll transition to the last phase, where I imagine we'll begin engaging the public to build broad political support so the new legislation can pass Congress."

"It will be crucial for us to do a fucking amazing job on this project, because if we fail, there will be no second chances for us and the US Administration."

Antonio stopped talking for a moment, letting everyone absorb what he had just said. He then explained that at some point during the project, most likely in phase two, he would step aside as project leader in order to focus entirely on using his training and expertise in genetics to act as Syllabus' scientific liaison with the US Administration. Jared and Marko were both supportive of this and already had eyes on someone specialized in project and operations management to take over him.

"Do you know who it is?" Miko asked.

He shook his head, "I don't know, but I am confident Jared and Marko will pick the right person for the task."

"Okay folks, that wraps up what I wanted to cover in this meeting. The rest of the day you'll need to access the project files and do as much background learning as possible. Tomorrow morning we will meet here bright and early for a lecture on genetics, reproductive technology, and human reproduction."

"Ah, another specialist joining us?" Leyla asked.

"Yes, me!"

"You?" Robbie asked astounded.

"Well I am a former researcher in human genetics, so I think I'm pretty qualified to give you lot a lesson in basic biology!" Antonio laughed.

"Just don't tell me you're going to ask Zane to be your prop," Miko joked.

"Well, that was my plan, as apparently we all know how much Zane can't keep his clothes on," Antonio replied sarcastically.

"Guys I'd love to, but my work contract is very explicit with regards to appropriate dress," Zane joked, as everyone started to chuckle with laughter.

"Okay people, I know this is going to be a big complex project, but let's make the most of it! Meeting adjourned, see you all here tomorrow morning, bright and early at nine."

With the meeting over, everyone quickly dispersed to their work pods. Zane lingered a bit longer in the boardroom, taking a few minutes to reflect on what lay ahead. There was no doubt he was going to be a key person on this project, simply because good data analysis was the foundation of a successful strategy, and this project needed a razor-sharp strategy. He was already formulating ideas in his head, of what healthcare data he needed to review, what comparable Medicare plans he needed to analyze, and what time periods he needed to include in his model and recommendations. Should Syllabus secure stage two and three, Zane was sure members of the company would be called to defend those recommendations to the incoming US President and other politicians. There was good chance he would be one of them.

Leyla was already plugged into SyNet by the time Zane arrived at his work cube. He watched her, observing as she shifted about the interactive cube, navigating an invisible universe like a dancer on a stage with no audience. His eyes shifted from her to the other work cubes lining the length of the windows to the far corner of the building, and then the rows behind them; rows upon rows upon rows stretching all the way to the windows on the opposite side of the tower. Besides the lobby, washrooms, and meeting spaces, everywhere he looked was filled cubes, almost all of them containing a Syllabus consultant. The corporation occupied forty floors of the tower, and though the majority were dedicated to AI infrastructure and SyNet support, there were still many others identical to this one, just as there were countless satellite offices in hundreds of locations around the world, each filled with rows of two-metre high work cubes and their occupants, collectively connected through SyNet.

SyNet was a remarkable virtual cybernetic ecosystem providing a deep immersive experience, which submerged the user inside a sterilized virtual universe, eradicating all traces of the outside world. Users, through their EVO microchips and sensory implants, integrated completely with SyNet during connectivity. This was a system requirement to prevent unauthorized foreign applications from hacking in through a user's EVO, potentially exposing SyNet and its users to digital and physical harm. SyNet achieved this by automatically deactivating all of EVO's external ports and applications, transforming the device, and by extension the user, into a company work drone. The link was only interrupted when the user lost their concentration or decided to log out; however, as long as they were connected, their minds, their bodies, and debatably even their free will were ceded to SyNet.

He stepped into his cube, lowered the blackout screen so he could no longer see outside, and picked up his sensory deprivation visor, which wrapped comfortably around his head, insulating him from any external noise, dust, and light exposure he could not see while completely immersed in the network. With the visor comfortably in place, Zane activated all of his enhanced retina functions and dropped into SyNet's virtual reality world, losing all contact with the outside. He released a deep relaxing breath as the project's malleable AI architecture populated his retina screens with a stunning virtual world that was so real, his mind could not detect any imperfections.

What appeared before him was a vast virtual Renaissance inspired library with lavish rooms extending in all directions. Everything was four dimensional, meaning whatever he saw felt real when he touched it. This included the doors, the floors, and the windows, which looked out onto a replica of the Grand Canal and the lost city of Venice. As he moved around familiarising himself with the AI architecture, he could see his colleagues and senior management doing the same thing, some of them walking, others floating and jetting through the air, magically disappearing and instantly reappearing in other rooms far away.

For a first-time user, SyNet could feel disorienting and maddeningly confusing, often leading to dizziness, nausea, and even cases of vomiting; however, it was a magical piece of technology once one got used to it. The user felt limitless, like an angel descending from the heavens, who could be anywhere and everywhere at once, darting, jumping, and reappearing in the architecture, as they navigated for files and ideas. Since this project was just beginning, the sensation was all the more enchanting because there were hardly any data and users congesting the virtual space; however, he knew it would only be a matter of days before architecture began to fill with information.

Zane moved to the group area of the data structure, retrieving a copy of the immersive project brief Marko had placed in the group room for everyone to review. He flew over and took a seat in front of a window facing the replica of Saint Marc's Square. The view was perfect, with the Grand Canal in the background, filled with ships, sailboats, and the city's famous gondolas. He shut the holographic image off and focused his attention on the project brief in front of him. It was an interactive structure designed to meld the user's mind with EVO's powerful AI features, stimulating total recall of pertinent data stored latently in the human brain and on SyNet. At first the process was slow, with Zane struggling to remember anything he knew about gentech; however, as his latent memories expanded, he began acquiring and absorbing information with ever greater speed and agility as he browsed through Marko's brief and the hundreds of associated files stored on SyNet and beyond.

The origins of universal access gentech and the context of the climate crisis in which it occurred were exactly as Joe and Samuel explained in their presentations. Starting in the mid to late 21st Century, a socio-economic gap began forming between naturally conceived and genetically engineered populations. This happened just as the climate crisis was amplifying mass migrations, pandemics, conflicts, and isolationism.

In order to prevent contagion and collapse, in the 2070's the powerful opposing Liberal and Totalitarian Blocs took the drastic action of sealing their borders to migration, permanently ensnaring hundreds of millions of climate refugees in failed states policed by opaque puppet regimes. Simultaneously, governments in the majority of the Liberal Bloc nationalized access to gentech in order to prevent a form of genetically engineered Apartheid from taking hold in their societies, where a rich genetically engineered elite controlled masses of impoverished naturally conceived citizens. The Totalitarian Bloc took the same measures, realizing they needed as many of their citizens as possible to be genetically optimized in order to compete with their Liberal rivals.

As Joe and Samuel explained, the changes quickly led to the end natural conception and birth, and by 2090 versions of universal reproductive lottery systems were made mandatory in nearly all wealthy Liberal, Totalitarian, and Non-aligned states. There was only one major country that did not implement any form of universal genetic healthcare, preferring to leave the situation to the control of the free-market. That country was the United States.

America's decision to leave genetic medicine and reproduction to the free market turned out to be disastrous, exacerbating socio-economic inequality and tipping the country from democracy towards a form of genetically engineered fascism. In a desperate attempt to arrest the slide, America's centre left coalesced around a populist presidential candidate in the 2120 election, who captured the White House with a promise to fix the situation by providing universal access to all genetic medicine.

With the new Administration set to take office, the big debate in its coalition now revolved around how to implement universal access to genetic medicine. Was a mixed model of public and private access the most likely option to make it through Congress? What about a privately-run system, with the government reimbursing all of the costs? Or could a pure nationalized Medicare funded option gather enough votes to clear all the legislative hurdles? As Zane reviewed the material it became evident the incoming Administration preferred the Medicare funded option; however, it was clear it would face the most challenges from the powerful Libertarian Party and its allies.

It was nine in the evening by the time Zane arrived at his apartment. He was exhausted, overwhelmed, and couldn't stop thinking. The project was of a scale far beyond anything he had encountered before, and he wondered if he had perhaps bitten off more than he could chew.

"Zane you seem terribly preoccupied."

"Yes EVO, it was a busy day at work with a complicated new project. I am concerned it may be beyond my capabilities."

"Zane you know should not be concerned, you are in the top 0.01% of the population in terms of IQ. You also have very high emotional intelligence. Based on my calculations you have only been on this project for 9 hours and 13 minutes, please be patient and continue to study the appropriate materials to obtain a high level of comprehension."

"Thank you for you valued input EVO."

"My pleasure Zane. For your information the fridge dock has been restocked with seven prepared meals for you to choose from. I recommend the broccoli cheese, potato and synthetic meat roast, it had the greatest number of favourable reviews."

"Thank you, I'll prepare that one in the oven." Zane walked to the fridge dock and placed the meal in the oven.

"Zane, may I also suggest something to help you unwind?"

"What would that be EVO?" Zane sighed.

"After dinner I would suggest you arrange a meeting with Madelaine on floor number fifty-three, apartment 5398. She is available and has expressed great interest in having some intimate moments with you tonight."

"She has sent you seven messages, including two intimate files. She also has a high rating from other hookups she has recently engaged in."

"Have I sent her anything?"

"You have replied with seventeen messages, five of which contained explicit material."

Zane chuckled, *"ok let me get dinner down. Tell her I'll be downstairs in a bit."*

The oven beeped, and Zane pulled his meal out, grabbing a spoon and sitting at the kitchen bar as he wolfed down the meal in front of him. The food wasn't bad, it had a decent sauce, and the broccoli and potato tasted fresh, which was a far cry better than a number of the meals he had had in the past. Dinner done, he changed into more comfortable gym clothes, and strode out the door and down the hallway to the elevators.

Madelaine opened the door. She was tall and slim, with curvaceous hips and perky medium sized breasts. She had a light skin complexion, deep brown eyes, and long straight blonde hair. Zane immediately recognized her from the messages he had received in past chats, recalling some of the images and details he had sent her in return. According to her profile she was a bilingual French marketing specialist with a large gaming supply company based in France, which had just opened in Salish City.

"Oh my, you are even sexier than in your profile," she said with a smile.

"Thanks, I get that all the time." Zane winked.

"Ooh, a cocky fellow, aren't you? Well narcists can be hot." She smirked, as she let him run his hands down her waist.

Zane grinned confidently, pushing her gently to the side, slipping past the door as it closed with a soft click behind him. There was no more conversation, their hands and legs quickly becoming entangled, as they pulled off their clothes, stumbling and tripping in a knot of socks, tights, and underwear across Madelaine's windowless studio apartment to her double bed. It lasted just fifteen minutes, with Zane promising to drop by again in the next few days, or a maybe a dinner date out; however, he knew he wouldn't bother to see her again, there were plenty more eager options for him to choose from.

Date Thursday November 7th, 2120

It was nine in the morning and they were back in the same conference room waiting for Antonio to get the lecture underway. Zane looked around at his colleagues. Robbie was sketching some art on a digital canvas as Miko sat mesmerized staring at what he was doing, Leyla was sitting legs crossed looking at Antonio and fiddling with her big curly hair, while Anita sat hunched over a screen at the other end of the table, oblivious to everyone else in the room.

"Okay everyone, time for all of you to get your biology refresher!" Antonio smiled.

"Sounds lovely my dear," Leyla answered sarcastically, as she flicked her curls and rolled her eyes.

"Wow, so much enthusiasm this morning! I promise you this presentation won't be so painful, in fact I'm betting you'll find it fun, exciting, and interactive!"

"Ooh, interactive, does that mean we have to get naked?" Zane joked.

"No, but if you insist Zane, I can bring you to the front of the room and use you as a prop."

"I'd have no problem with that!" Anita giggled.

"I most certainly would!" Miko replied.

"Seriously guys, let's get started otherwise we'll be here all day," Leyla interjected.

"Thanks Leyla!" Ricardo said, and then asked the room, "is everyone familiar with what DNA and RNA are?"

"Yeah," Leyla purred, raising her eyebrows, "DNA and RNA are the materials used to carry genetic information. DNA contains the genetic code to make organisms, while RNA is the genetic machine to transport that information from DNA to proteins, which enables cells to be replicated according to the DNA recipe."

"Wow! Not bad Leyla, someone's been doing some studying! A simplified description, but for our needs it does the job."

"So as Leyla said, DNA is the fingerprint of an organism. So what is an organism? Well it is a living entity with an organized structure that can grow, reproduce, adapt, and maintain homeostasis. There are five major groups of organisms on Earth, known as the Five Kingdoms of Life. Two of these, the Monera and Protista kingdoms, consist of singled celled organisms such as Salmonella, Diatoms, E. coli, Brewer's Yeast, and Phytoplankton. The other three kingdoms are multi-cellular, and are called the Animal, Plant, and Fungi kingdoms. In case you didn't already know it, us humans are part of the Animal Kingdom."

"Now regardless of whether an organism is unicellular or multicellular, it needs DNA to know how it is supposed to grow. And as Leyla said, it also needs RNA molds to transfer this DNA information to Proteins. Proteins are the building blocks of all cells, without proteins, cells cannot be constructed."

Antonio looked at Zane. "Makes sense Dr. Fischer?"

Zane jumped, he had zoned out from listening to Antonio and was daydreaming about the sex with Madelaine the night before and debating whether she was worth a second visit after all. "Ahh, yeah I get it," he stuttered, "but I don't see where genetic engineering and CRISPR fits in with all of this."

"Don't worry Zane, we're getting to the part on CRISPR now, you're just jumping ahead of everyone."

The screen lit up with images of DNA stands, as Antonio continued, "so, what is CRISPR-Cas, and how does it fit into this? Well firstly CRISPR is an acronym for Clustered Regularly Interspaced Short Palindromic Repeats. They are a group of DNA sequences found in single cell organisms such as bacteria and archaea. These sequences are derived from pieces of bacteriophages that have previously infected the prokaryote and are used to detect and destroy DNA from similar phages during future infections."

"Huh, what did you just say Antonio? Sounds more like Latin and Greek than English!" Robbie joked.

"Yeah, I'm an operations specialist Antonio, not a geneticist, dumb it down for me!" Miko added.

"Relax guys, patience, I'm going to simplify it, don't worry. To start with, a bacteriophage is just a big word for virus. So what happens in this process, is a virus invades a single cell organism such as a bacterium, and after the successful invasion, it leaves a piece of its genetic material as a strand inside the DNA of the bacterium. These pieces or sequences are like tiny weapons, which detect and destroy invasions from other viruses that try to take over the cell."

"Ah so what you're saying Antonio is that a virus gets inside a cell, like a parasite, modifies the cell's DNA, and then this modified DNA repels invasions from other viruses later on as the cell replicates?"

"Presto! Exactly Miko, you see it's not that hard!!" Antonio grinned.

"So to recap, CRISPR is a fancy acronym describing what happens when a virus invades a bacterium and modifies the DNA of the bacterium in such a way that the new DNA sequence of the bacterium can repel invasions of other viruses during replication."

"The next thing to understand here is the CRISPR-Cas system. Well Cas are simply protein-based enzymes, and enzymes are biological catalysts that permit specific biochemical reactions to take place. There are many kinds of Cas protein enzymes, one of them is Cas9, which is the protein enzyme that plays a critical role in the bacteria's immunological defense against viruses. Cas9 reads the CRISPR sequences in the DNA recipe of a bacterium, and then uses this recipe to snip out any foreign invasive bacteriophages that are trying to invade the single cell. This is a defensive antiviral mechanism employed by the cell to prevent its DNA from being modified by another bacteriophage."

Antonio took a deep breath and looked around the room. There was no more day dreaming or clocking out, suddenly everyone was clearly fascinated with what he had to say.

"Does everyone follow me up to here?" he asked.

"Yes," everyone answered in unison.

"Dang Antonio, this is pretty cool stuff, I mean I'm asking myself what the hell I was doing running mathematical models for a Ph.D., when I could have been doing this!" Zane said, as he raised his eyebrows and gave Antonio a nod of approval. It was true, what Antonio was explaining sounded like science fiction, even though it had been around for over a hundred years.

Antonio smiled, "awesome, just what I like to hear! Okay guys, now that you understand the fundamentals, you're gonna see how the applications for this technology are enormous. While it was first of observed in single celled organisms such as bacteria, it wasn't long before scientists realized they could try it on multicellular organisms in the Plant, Fungi, and Animal kingdoms. First researchers started with simple organisms, slowly working their way up to more complex multicellular species such as mice and chimps. Ultimately they observed they could use the CRISPR-Cas technique to modify the DNA of literally any form of life, including humans."

"The next big break was when geneticists realized they didn't have to work with specific Cas9 provided by nature, they could in fact modify the Cas9 itself, and thus be able to activate gene expression without even cutting the DNA. This process provided a new level of customization never seen before, permitting geneticists to create their own DNA Cas9 sized robots to modify and change an organism's DNA at custom sites. This was the beginning of genetic engineering, as first through trial and error, and later through computer modelling and data analysis, geneticists were able to determine what parts of DNA could be modified to turn certain gene expressions on and off."

"So from there we began to see an explosion of gentech, including new genetic medicines such as advanced antibiotics and antivirals to fight contagious diseases. We also started using the technique to create lab mice that were genetically altered to have certain diseases, so as to better understand how these illnesses worked. As our level of understanding improved, we were able to develop genetic technologies to test people for the presence of these diseases in their DNA, which was a critical first step in the eradication of many genetic illnesses such as Huntington's, Alzheimer's and Downs Syndrome."

"Over a period of fifty years our understanding of CRISPR-Cas advanced with leaps and bounds, aided by the development of quantum computing and big data, which massively increased our analytical capacity. We used these technologies to create whole new applications, including genetically engineered food crops more resistant to extreme weather events, genetically engineered synthetic meats sterilized of toxic bacteria and viruses, and genetically engineered medicines to cure illnesses."

"Yet the most fantastical application of these technologies was the conception of the first generation of genetically engineered humans in the 2030's, who had their DNA rudimentarily enhanced to eliminate certain genetic defects and inherited diseases. By 2070 the technology had been perfected, and we began to see the first generations of humans created from selections of enhanced genetic material from their parents. These new babies were optimized to never have cancers, neurodegenerative diseases, hair loss, myopia, and all numbers of other genetically inherited illnesses and defects. They were also selected for optimal height, eye colour, IQ, emotional intelligence, and life span. Finally, in a world blighted by pollution, climate change, and disease, humans transferred gestation to perfectly sterilized artificial pods, ending pregnancy forever. This was the beginning of the future, the world we know."

Antonio's presentation wrapped up and everyone dispersed for lunch. Zane ended up ordering Mexican, which he had delivered by drone to the coffee room. There he wolfed down his meal, thinking about the Antonio's presentation. The science was fascinating, today it seemed so simple, but he could only imagine how novel and complex it must have been for scientists a hundred years ago, who were trying to process everything with such rudimentary computing power. Little did those researchers know their painfully slow baby steps would have such dramatic outcomes for science, technology, and the human condition.

When he was done eating, he cleaned up and went to the library room to pick up a reader and sit in one of the company's reading rooms to do some research. The reading rooms were quiet spaces for reflection and research, with reduced outside interference. They were the closest one could get to being off the Internet, away from EVO's constant interference.

From SyNet's virtual library he selected a long form article explaining the gentech debate in Canada and America in the 2070's. The article described how politically controversial the technologies were in Canada and other developed countries in the 2070's, with many Canadians unsure about accepting tax increases to fund genetically engineered reproduction, or novel genetic medicines to treat certain rare diseases. Ultimately Canadians diverged from Americans as cumulative data demonstrated how remarkably efficient genetic technologies were in treating all forms of illnesses, from the rarest to the most common, with the benefit of protecting both the population and the country's healthcare system from outbreaks of previously untreatable diseases. However, it was not just the data that mattered, being less religious than Americans, less accepting of inequality, having much higher social cohesion, and being more connected to events beyond its borders helped Canadians buy into all aspects of genetic medicine, including genetically engineered reproduction.

By the end of the 2070's America was alone pursuing its *laissez-faire* trajectory, driven by its obsession for free-market corporatism and a high tolerance for socio-economic inequality. Their free-market approach created a boom in their domestic gentech industry, which developed lucrative cutting-edge technologies for the upper twenty percent of Americans, who were armed with limitless budgets funded by private health insurance and deep pockets. Fantastical technologies such as gestation pods, gene therapy, genetic engineering, and genetic medications were standard fare for the fortunate few; however, for the other eighty percent of the population they were but pipedreams. Accepted by the masses as a natural part of America's free-market economy, this situation continued unchallenged until a domestic health epidemic in 2105 wreaked havoc among the eighty percent of the population who had no access to genetically engineered vaccines. The health crisis exposed an inconvenient truth: America was sliding from democracy to a pseudo Apartheid state of genetic haves and have-nots.

Zane put down the article to reflect. Was America really a pseudo Apartheid state? Or was it simply being more democratic by letting healthcare markets act free and openly, unrestricted by government interference? Was it right for governments to regulate the private sector to ensure a more equal distribution of resources, especially in the healthcare sector, where lives were patently at stake? Or should it be money and power that decided who had access to treatments? In his opinion there was no question, America had to do something about the situation; however, the barriers to change seemed insurmountable. Sure, America achieved major health care upgrades in the past; however, gentech was a completely different kind of overhaul, involving controversial technologies with significant opposition. That opposition included the healthcare industry, religious fanatics, racists who did not want to extend the technology to non-Caucasians, and the small government Libertarians. Finding a path to defeating this opposition was critical to whatever gentech healthcare plan Syllabus and the US government developed, and it was going to be no small task.

Maya Bekele

Date Saturday November 9th, 2120

Zane dashed up the stairs of the UBC SkyTrain Station, popping into the cool drizzly November air. Maya was standing with her back to the entrance, under a shelter beside a water fountain. She was dressed in one of those tight green and olive body suits, the kind of outfits he hoped never went out of fashion. Man she really is quite something. Hopefully today will be more than just a walk around campus, he thought to himself.

"Heya." He tapped her gently on the shoulder.

"Ahhh!!!" She jumped, "you scared me haha!"

"Sorry about that, my bad!" he laughed.

"It's okay, I probably needed a bit of a wake up."

"So what's the plan?" he asked.

"I'd thought I'd take you to the climate crisis planning labs. A lot of it is closed to the public, but there is a fun open-access virtual reality area we can walk through. You'll get a lot out of it, even though it is kind of corny and geared towards weekday school visits."

"Ah that's fun, and don't worry, I can do corny, trust me!"

She laughed, grabbing his arm and leading him on a brisk twenty-minute stroll across the empty university grounds. It was a pretty campus, a mixture of tree lined pedestrian plazas and 19th, 20th, and 21st Century buildings. The School of Climate Modelling was located inside one of the university's newest complexes, a rectangular four storey steel and glass building cladded in vegetation and solar panels. To get inside, Maya first had to scan herself in at a sensor panel located beside the glass entry doors, and then take a couple of minutes to create a temporary access profile to bring Zane through afterwards.

Inside the air was warm and dry, a pleasant respite from the cool dampness of a November day. There was hardly any noise, apart from the hum of air vents and soft mechanical sounds coming from some of the laboratories located the length of the corridor. Natural and artificial light drifted down from the upper floors through skylights and large open lofted spaces, sweeping the ground floor and basement in soft blues, greens, and greys. As they walked down the wide corridor, they passed empty laboratories and lecture halls, many of them visible through panes of clear glass. They'd walked about a hundred metres when they heard a friendly voice shout out, "Dr. Bekele, is that you?"

Zane and Maya turned to see a cheerful very tall young woman exiting from one of the labs.

"Oh it is! How are you doing?" she asked, smiling.

"Oh hi Fae! I'm doing great! How are you? Fancy seeing you here on a weekend!"

"Oh I'm here most weekends, working on my simulator, fiddling with the input data, and so on and so forth. My supervisor, Dr. Watts told me we needed to prepare the system for producing publishable data by the start of the new year, so the pressure is on."

"Oh my it definitely is! Well I'm not usually here on weekends, but I dropped by to show a friend of mine around. Zane this is Fae, she's a Dutch doctoral student working in a lab associated with mine. Fae studies applied mathematics, and is working on climate risk models applied to urban infrastructure."

"Wow that sounds pretty interesting! I'm a mathematician as well, so I love anything requiring lots of modelling and data analysis."

"Oh cool! What area of maths did you study in?" Fae asked, her intense gaze now focused on Zane.

"I studied modelling and data analysis, so probably quite similar to what you are doing here."

"Cool, maybe we know the same people! Where did you study, if I may ask?"

"Stanford University."

"Wow! That's quite the school, really known for Artificial Intelligence applications to modelling!"

Fae's eyes glossed over for a moment, "ah sorry to cut this short, I just got an alert from my modelling application reminding me I have to be back here in four hours, and I've got a ton of things I need to get done before then. You guys have a great rest of the day!"

They waved goodbye to Fae, as she hurried back into her lab, leaving the two of them standing in the hallway.

"You didn't tell me you studied mathematical modeling, and at Stanford on top of that!" Maya laughed, as they walked down the corridor to the virtual reality exhibition space.

"Euhh, I didn't want to put it out there right away, prefer keeping it low key, under the radar, you know…"

"Really? Well now it's time to show me what you've got, maybe you can guide me through some of those exhibits, Mr. Zane the Mathematician."

"How about Dr. Fischer the Mathematician?" he replied, raising his eyebrows mischievously.

"Oh my, well in that case Dr. Fischer, you can call me Dr. Bekele," she said, as she led him through the sliding glass doors, into the public exhibition area.

They spent the next couple of hours walking through the exhibits, with Maya showing Zane how the Earth's climate had gone from millions of years of trending towards greater stability, to suddenly in just three centuries reversing course to become highly unstable. She explained how starting in the 19th Century with the Industrial Revolution, humans began drastically altering the natural environment through massive deforestation and emissions of carbon gases from industrial activity. These activities increased the earth's temperature, leading to the melting of polar and mountain ice sheets and high latitude permafrost, which drove naturally stored carbon into the atmosphere. This accelerated heating, which combined with ocean acidity, plastic pollution, and over-fishing, also led to a collapse of the ocean ecosystem.

They moved from the first exhibits to the ones showing early human responses to the crisis. These exhibits explained how people initially chose to ignore the inconvenient truth of climate change, preferring to conduct business as usual. In democracies, people elected simple populists who preached denial and deregulation, while in most other countries dictators and strongmen crushed any public discourse. The situation broke down when climate change switched from being a theoretical concept to being a real emergency on the ground. Heat waves crashing electrical grids, forest fires polluting cities, and flooding destroying trillions of dollars of infrastructure became the norm, killing millions of people. These disasters led to outbreak of many conflicts and plagues, killing even more people, and creating a refugee crisis of unparalleled proportions.

Yet it was the Small Nuclear War of 2062 between India and Pakistan that changed it all. Named the Small Nuclear War because it involved the exchange of just twenty large thermonuclear warheads, it was sufficient to immediately kill nearly fifty million people, and give cancer and acute injuries to another half a billion. The conflict was sparked in a yet another record-setting summer, where temperatures sat in the mid-fifty degrees Celsius for weeks, leading to a series of irrational and uncontrollable acts in the Kashmir, first with border skirmishes involving conventional weapons, then with biological and chemical weapons, and finally thermonuclear weapons. The dust clouds from the twenty ballistic missile blasts contaminated cities across the region, turning the South Asian subcontinent into a contaminated hinterland, and plunging it into permanent economic and social collapse.

The immediate aftermath of the conflict was hundreds of millions of desperate nuclear contaminated refugees pouring out in all directions from the region, threatening the stability of Europe, Russia, the former Soviet Republics, and China. To prevent anarchy, groups of countries quickly formed regional defensive blocks and buffer zones, which included armed barriers to keep the refugees out, trapping them in a zone today known as the "South Asian Exclusion Zone".

To try prevent the situation from happening again, the remaining nuclear powers moved with some degrees of success to reduce stockpiles of nuclear, chemical, and biological weapons. The weapons reduction agreements signed were far from perfect; however, they did shrink stockpiles by eighty percent, and also established multiple safe guards, including open communication channels between leaders of all the major military and economic powers, as a means of preventing miscommunication from escalating out of control.

Besides the weapons agreements, the major military and economic powers also recognized climate change as the major flashpoint in the conflict, and realized they had to take drastic action to arrest climate heating, or face more conflict and instability. Summits were organized, and a series of emergency meetings in 2064 ended in success, with the largest polluting nations banning the use of fossil fuels for use in manufacturing, transport, and energy; however, the agreements arrived about thirty years too late - climate change was already spiralling out of control, and it was going to take hundreds, maybe thousands of years to turn the clock back to a more stable climate.

"It makes me so angry," Zane said.

"Yes, well who wouldn't feel that way, I mean our generation, and those to follow are going be paying the price of generations of ignorance, laziness, and financial greed."

He sighed, feeling a sense of hopelessness for something he had no control over.

"Come over here Zane, these displays will cheer you up a bit. They include some of the work I'm specialized in, the area of reengineering cities for climate change."

They walked through the next set of exhibit panels, with Maya explaining to him that as climate change took hold around the world, cities responded with urgent action to adapt to all kinds of crises, including higher sea levels, population growth, and more severe weather events. Many cities were successful in adapting to the shocks, in particular North America's West Coast, where the 2043 earthquakes facilitated the biggest re-urbanization project since the Second World War, serving as a model for urban planners such as Maya, who were working to help other cities around the world adapt to a hotter, more unstable world.

"So there is hope, except it's a long way off, and a lot more people are going to suffer and die in the process."

As Churchill said, when in hell keep going, Zane thought to himself.

"So Maya, how did you end up in this field? Actually, how did you get to Salish City all the way from Ethiopia?"

"Ah, it's a long story. I was born in Addis Ababa, to parents well placed in the business and political elite of the country. My mother was, and still is in the national government as a cabinet minister, while my father had an engineering firm that built rail networks in Africa. Because of their connections and status, they had my brother and I conceived and gestated in the United States at a top IVF gentech clinic. Since we were born in the US, we both acquired American citizenship, and our parents encouraged us to make use of it. My brother left Ethiopia as soon as he could to avoid military service, settling in New York, where today he works in theatre as a screen writer."

"Really, is he famous!?" Zane asked wide-eyed.

"Haha, yes he is, but let's not get into that right now."

"Anyways," she continued," unlike my brother I wanted to stay in Africa. I was fascinated with climate change and how it was destabilising my part of the world, producing ongoing conflict and crop failures. So in my last year of high school I applied to and was accepted at the University of Cape Town, moving there to start a degree in climate sciences. Unfortunately everything was sidetracked when the university was shut down by waves of violent protests against foreign students. I ended up losing a semester, but fortunately was accepted on scholarship to New York University the following year. Fast forward a few years, after finishing a Master's in climate science I moved up island to

Columbia University, where I did my Ph.D. in urban climate resilience."

"Wow that's quite the journey!"

"Yeah tell me about it, it's been exhausting! Anyway I think we're done here at museum, how about we head back to the SkyTrain station? Want to grab a bite somewhere as well?" she asked.

"Sure why not? You lead the way."

"Okay we'll need to take the SkyTrain a couple of stops to where there are some decent bistros, so let's head back to the station."

They left the building and as they walked across campus Maya told him a bit more of her story. It turned out after Columbia she worked briefly in New York City's urban planning department as a temporary intern while she applied for professorships in urban climate resilience at various universities around the world. Ultimately UBC was the only one to offer her a full academic posting, which she hoped to have finalized following the next few weeks of faculty level evaluations.

It was dark out, and a light rain was falling as they approached the SkyTrain station.

"Maya it's been really great hanging out with you today," Zane mumbled nervously, walking slowly by her side.

She looked over at him, "you too Zane, you seem like a good guy."

They were looking at each other, and all he could feel was silly, foolish, and awkward - foreign emotions for someone who was used to being the centre of attention, with men and women fawning over him. Realizing it was time to make the move, he leaned in and kissed her awkwardly on the lips.

She kissed him right back.

"Well I was waiting for that, looks like we finally got it out of the way!" she laughed.

"Yeah sorry, ah, euh …" he mumbled.

"Hey relax, it's like you've turned into a pumpkin! Don't worry I don't bite, unless you want me to!"

"Hehehe, awesome." he blushed, as she pulled his hand and led him down the stairs to the SkyTrain.

Maya lived in a restored early 20th Century building on the outskirts of UBC. It was part of a small neighbourhood that had survived the horrendous fires of the 2043 earthquake, which had destroyed most of the homes and buildings on the Point Grey Peninsula. The surviving structures were all part of the university endowment lands - land that was bequeathed to the university by the province for limited high-density development and preservation as natural space and farms. The old houses and buildings were protected heritage stock, and the university offered them as rental facilities for faculty and graduate students.

Her apartment had old weathered hardwood floors covered in pastel coloured Persian rugs, and there plants everywhere, hanging from the ceilings, the rafters, and in pots on the floor. The vaulted ceiling was at least four and a half metres high, with fans slowly circulating the warm air from above back down to the surface. Inside the air had this sweet and humid texture, filled with wafts of smoke from the incense and marijuana they had been smoking for the past couple of hours.

"Your place is very different..." he mumbled, his mind lost in a haze of smoke.

"Yeah I love it, I've always had a thing for green spaces...." she answered.

"I mean I feel like I'm in a tropical rainforest, not Salish City in November," he giggled.

"Yeah it is something, isn't it? There aren't many places like this in Salish, I mean the earthquake destroyed almost all of them.

153

When it was offered as a faculty perk, I jumped on it. It kind of reminds me of my old digs in New York."

The two of them were naked, Maya stretched back against Zane's chest, as he rested his head on a large puffy cushion, propped up on the sofa's side rest. She passed him a final spoon of ice cream, which he licked up with his tongue.

"Hmm babe, that was good stuff, must be the same brand as the one my friend Timothy ordered a few weeks ago at a hookup I had at his place."

"Oooh, hookup with a guy? You are filled with surprises Dr. Zane Fisher! Are you gay, bi, straight, or what? I didn't catch that stat when I was snooping on your social network bio card."

"I'm actually pansexual, I've dated guys and girls, with no real preference for one or the other. For me it's the connection, and each time it's different. I just never know until I've spent some time with the person.

"Gotcha. Have you had a long-term relationship before?"

"Sort of. I dated my friend Timothy for a number of years. We still have sex occasionally; however, for complex reasons we decided to keep it as friends."

"So what about me, what kind of connection do you think we have?" she asked.

"Hmm, it's hard to say just yet. There is definitely something cerebral going on, but you're also incredibly hot and the sex this evening was fucking amazing. For me you're definitely not a one-night stand, but it takes two to tango for sure."

He paused, then asked, "what about you, how do you approach sex and relationships?"

"Well I've never had a long-term relationship and it's not something I'm really interested in. I guess I'm kind of like most people in the developed world who are more focused on their careers and self-actualization. To be honest it's all so confusing. On one hand I'd like to have a nuclear family like my parents did, but on the other hand I want to stay free and be able to go wherever I want. I mean we are so lucky here in this part of the world to still have freedoms like this. Elsewhere, like in Ethiopia or America, people are stressed out about climate change, inequality, and rising social conflict. It's like this place is just so disconnected from it all, some sort of utopia garden city zoned out on marijuana and lotus leaves."

Her words melted away in the humid essence-filled air. Apart from the rain, everything was so still, so quiet, not a sound, not a creak to be heard from the neighbours. He reached his arm from his side and ran his hands through her long thick dark hair, as she pulled the warm down comforter to her chin, nestling against his torso. The minutes passed by, and they drifted in and out of sleep, the silence punctuated by the soft ringing of a distant wind chime, and the gusts of rain ebbing and flowing against the living room glass.

He was woken up by Maya, as she pulled the duvet aside and walked naked across the room, her tall dark body glistening in the soft smoky light. She turned to Zane and asked, "bed time?"

"Ahhh," he yawned and stretched, the duvet falling to his waist, "yeah it's getting there, I can order a cab."

"No, just sleep over. I know it's the first date, but we've done the full nine yards and the weather is crap to go back outside at this hour."

He smiled and stood up, following her into the bedroom.

Date Monday December 2ⁿᵈ, 2120

It was an early December Monday morning as Zane breezed happily into work, relaxed from spending the weekend with Maya. He headed over to his work cube, tossed his jacket onto a hook, and connected to SyNet, picking up all the messages he had ignored from the weekend.

There were lots of them, and quite a few priority ones from Antonio. He took a deep breath and scanned the list, deciding which ones to review first. He was about start reading, when he noticed Leyla wasn't around, which was unusual considering she was almost always at work before he arrived. He wondered if she was working from home that morning. Leyla had that flexibility, after all she lived just a ten minute walk from Syllabus Tower in a luxury apartment her wealthy parents had bought her, which was fitted out with a remote SyNet work cube in one of her spare rooms.

He shrugged and went back to his work cube, and was just starting to read the first messages from Antonio, when his EVO pinged with an alert. It was a note from none other than Antonio, calling everyone to boardroom A-5 for the start of a meeting. Zane dropped what he was doing and hurried down the hallway, wondering what was on the agenda, and regretting not having checked his messages over the weekend.

He was the first to arrive, taking a seat at the small oval table. A few moments later the rest of the crew filed in, minus Leyla and Marko.

"Hey, where's Leyla?" Zane asked.

"Ah you didn't check your messages, bad boy!" Robbie laughed.

"Woah, I had a busy weekend with my girlfrien-"

Antonio frowned and said, "sorry to cut you off Zane, but in the future kindly be on top of the communications I send out. Now let's get right to the chase here, no time to waste. It's been four weeks since we've been on this project, and all of you should now be fully up to speed. Now we need to pick this up a few notches, and show our client what Syllabus is capable of. In a nutshell, later this week Zane, myself, and our VP, Jared Berg will be heading to Washington D.C. to join Leyla and Marko to present our proposed recommendations to the incoming US Administration and their partners."

There was dead silence in the room.

"I don't know why you all look so stunned. This was always the plan with phase one of the project. This new US administration takes office in the third week of January, in just seven weeks, so there's no time to waste! They want to hit the ground running, and Steve McNeill told us to have something to present to them by the start of December."

"As per my message yesterday, I've sent Leyla and two junior communications consultants ahead to join Marko in Washington this week. They are working in collaboration with our strategic partners located in Washington. These include members of the incoming US Administration, legal experts, CEO's of major gentech firms, and support staff at the Canadian Embassy.

"Leyla and her team and putting together the presentation of our proposal and are expecting you to provide them with everything they need to make it look good. Zane, this means your data and arguments supporting our strategy must get to Robbie yesterday, so his creative team can polish it for Leyla to build a presentation. Miko, I want timelines, clear timelines to provide to the clients on how long we think it will take to roll this project out, and make sure whatever you have is easy to understand, or send it Robbie to make it look pretty."

"Questions?"

"Ah, what's happening with Leyla's writing team? Are they moving to Washington?" Zane asked, still stunned by the abrupt change in work tempo.

"No it is temporary, just for this critical phase to win the rest of the project, then she'll be back here."

"When are you and Zane going to D.C.?" asked Miko, as she manipulated the project schedule on her scroll pad.

"I haven't decided. To be honest, part of that call comes from Marko, as he is our business development liaison over there. I also want as many of us here as long as possible, after all this is where our resources are. So I'm trying to delay the trip as late as I can, especially since I still have no idea how long we will be there once we head over. We could be there a day, or a week, who knows!"

"Any more questions?"

Robbie raised his hand and asked, "is the strategic design team going there too?"

"Definitely not, don't worry about that. To avoid any confusion, if we are selected for phase two and three, all the support work will be run out of this office and not in Washington. Having geographic distance is critical to keeping us outside of the chatter and snooping of the US capital. The only staff who can expect to be travelling a lot for this will be Zane and I, unless things change."

Antonio turned to face Zane. "Dr. Fischer you should be prepared for a big week. It's on your shoulders to present the data analysis to the incoming US Administration and the President-elect. Hopefully you'll do a good job selling it. If the President-elect likes what you have to say, then I assume she'll let us proceed with the rest of the project."

Zane went white as a sheet, as the other three team members turned and stared at him. He was going to be presenting to the incoming President? Why wasn't it Antonio, he was the geneticist, or what about someone in the government, or Jared Berg, who was the most senior person in the company involved in the project?

Antonio looked and Zane and continued, "Leyla and the consortia in Washington are assembling reports based on the early data and studies you researched for us. Eventually, if this goes to phase two and three, we can expect to be grilled by Congress and the general public to defend the President's healthcare plan."

Zane gulped nervously, "ah, but I've never done anything like this Antonio…"

"I have complete confidence in you Dr. Fischer!" winked Antonio.

"Meeting done folks. Get cracking!"

Anita, Robbie, and Miko scurried out the boardroom, leaving Zane and Antonio alone.

"Sorry to do this to you Zane. I know it's going to be as stressful as shit, but you're a smart man, and this is what you know how to do. Just pretend you're back defending your Ph. D. at Stanford."

"Arrh Antonio, I'm barely thirty-two years old, and defending a Ph.D. at Stanford is nothing like presenting Syllabus' gentech Medicare proposal to the President-elect and her new government. I mean-"

Antonio sharply cut him off, lifting his hands up in front of his face, it was clear he was quite stressed. "Listen Zane, the directive comes from over my head. If I had my way only I would present, after all this is my project, not yours; however, Jared Berg and the CEO feel a data analyst, and not a geneticist needs to present it. Anyway, this is your data analysis, you dug up the studies, you looked at the outcomes in thousands of cases, you compiled the numbers, and you came up with the strategy for us to take."

Antonio stopped to emphasize his point, before continuing, this time with more of an edge to his voice, "I think it's time for you to grow up, put up, and show us what you can do Dr. Zane

Fischer. Life is more than just looking in the mirror to admire your reflection, and fucking around on weekends. You've been at Syllabus for two years, you're a senior consultant with a shitload of education and privilege, and now it's time for you to take some front-line responsibility. You like to act like some hot shit pretty prig, well now the bosses want you to show us it's for real."

He was stunned, Antonio's words were sharp, cold, and cut into his ego – there was no doubt his project manager was angry about Zane pushing him out of the spotlight, and that he believed Zane was getting special treatment from the firm's top brass.

"Now get yourself prepared. Talk to Leyla to make sure she has the right communications tools for you, and make sure Robbie and Miko put your plan together the way you need it. Anita isn't doing too much at the moment on AI, so get her to help you with running code on your data if you feel swamped. I will keep you posted as to when we go to Washington, be prepared for either air travel or bullet train."

Zane nodded and walked slowly out the boardroom to his work cube. His EVO pinged with a chat from Leyla.

"Well Zane, you probably have the news by now. I'm over in Washington with Marko, and you, Antonio, and our VP will be here soon. You also know you'll be presenting to some top politicos?"

"Yes I am up to speed, just a bit overwhelmed and a tad but nervous..."

"Don't worry about it Dr. Fischer, you're part of an amazing team, and we'll make your data analysis shine!"

The chat ended.

My data analysis shine? Fuck, that was a load of bullshit, he knew he didn't have the experience to present to the next American President and her political entourage. While he was confident about his recommendations, there was no way a consultant with just two years' field experience could hope to sound authoritative and convincing in front of such an audience. He had visions of himself being labeled by network media and opponents to gentech as an incompetent young puppet, who had been thrown to the dogs to test the waters. Fuck, what was a situation like this going to do for his career, could he ever recover from it?

He needed to act fast, go over Antonio's head and get a meeting with Jared Berg and senior management to plead for a change to the plan; however, there was a risk in doing that as well, he would look weak, and in the cut-throat business of elite consulting it could be grounds to push him off the project and maybe out the door – a mortal blow to his reputation! Was this all a plot to push him out? Had they gotten second thoughts about choosing him for this project? Were they setting him up for a breakdown, so they could put another data analyst in? Was Antonio jealous of him getting the spotlight on his project, or that Zane was taller, sexier, and clearly more intelligent because he had gone to better universities? What about the other team members, were they in on the act, and could he trust them?

He walked past the rows of cubes in a daze, his thoughts in overdrive, as he tried to figure out what to make of his predicament. The floor had the usual chatter and buzz of a busy work day, with almost all of the cubicles occupied with consultants. Just a few rows beyond where he was walking, he spotted Robbie standing in a meeting space with his small group of junior designers, they were discussing something, probably how best to present one of Zane's data analyses. The design consultant saw him, gave a quick nod and a smile, and returned to what he was doing. Was it really possible for Robbie, Leyla, Anita, and Miko to be conspiring against him? What did they have to gain from it? No, if anyone were playing him, it would be senior management and Antonio, no one else.

Standing over the wash basin in the toilets, he bent over and splashed his face a few times, hoping the cold water would help wash away the confusion. He stopped, and stood in silence, gazing into the mirror, admiring the masculine beauty reflecting back at him. No, there was no choice, he could not go over Antonio's head, and request a special meeting with Jared Berg, it would be career suicide. There was no other option other than to keep forging ahead, to buckle down and prepare himself to take the spotlight, and give it the everything he had. As Antonio said, it was time for him to stop playing the prig, and show what he was capable of.

The President

Date Wednesday December 4th, 2120

The next couple of days passed by in a blur, as he and his colleagues rushed to prepare the final report for presentation that week. Then on Wednesday, just as he thought the trip to D.C. might be postponed till after the weekend, he received a message from Antonio to prepare to fly to New York Thursday evening on a late-night red-eye flight. Zane initially had no idea why they were suddenly going to New York instead of D.C.; however, at the airport Antonio explained the new incoming Social Democratic Administration was paranoid about spying from the outgoing Libertarian government, and decided to move the first meetings to their political stronghold in New Jersey. The change made sense, Zane was now well aware that American politics was a cut-throat three-party affair, with knives drawn between the left-wing Social Democrats and their bitter right-wing Libertarians foes.

Despite the comforts of a first-class cabin the overnight flight was a typical sleep deprived affair, with the two of them arriving at Newark Airport at six in the morning looking and feeling tired and disheveled. From the taxi ranks they caught a cab to a rather ordinary looking expansive hotel on the side of a freeway overpass in suburban New Jersey. Marko, Leyla, and Jared Berg were already there, meeting them in the entrance of the hotel's glass and carpeted lobby. Marko took them upstairs to a large private suite, where they were able to freshen up and leave their bags, before returning downstairs to the lobby. Leyla was there waiting for them and took them through to a spacious ballroom, where there were various security people and technicians fussing over sound and lighting equipment.

Leyla reviewed the communications briefs with Zane, Antonio, and Marko, and then explained to them the order of events of the day. At around nine in the morning numerous gentech business leaders, Congressional representatives, and aides from the new US Administration were expected to start arriving for a breakfast mix and mingle, this would roll into a round table format, with Syllabus team members moving from table to table to discuss the Syllabus gentech plan. Then after lunch, the President-elect was to arrive for Syllabus' formal presentations.

Zane initially had butterflies in his stomach; however, they gradually subsided as he and his colleagues spent the morning moving from round table to round table, meeting various American politicians and domestic business leaders in the gentech business to gather their feedback on Syllabus' proposals. People were generally quite positive, after all, they were mostly Social Democrats, moderate Republicans, and members of the gentech industry, all thrilled with the opportunity to expand Medicare to include genetic technologies. Also in the room was a small observer delegation of Canadian politicians and business leaders in the gentech industry, they included Elise Germain, CEO of Montreal based Zelion, the world's largest gentech conglomerate, as well as the Canadian ambassador and the diplomatic *chargé d'affaires*. Their presence, along with Syllabus' central role as the project's consultant, was testimony to Canada's unique and special relationship with the United States, as well the incoming Administration.

After lunch everyone slowly drifted back to the ballroom, which had been reconfigured from round tables to rows of seating. People gradually took their places, leaving the front row open, which was reserved for the President-elect and members of her team. As the hall filled up, Zane, Antonio, Jared, and Marko moved to the front and took their places beside the speaker's platform, while Leyla went to the back of the room, to work behind the scenes with her technical team. About twenty minutes later, the chatter in the hall subsided as the President-elect entered the ballroom through the back doors, surrounded by an enormous security detail. It then took her about ten minutes to get the front of the room, as she took her time to greet and shake hands with colleagues and friends scattered about the hall. Once she and her team had taken their seats in the front row, the room went completely silent and Marko stood up and walked to the podium to say a few words and introduce Jared Berg.

Jared's talk was short and sweet, he presented Syllabus, the history of the firm, it's experience and depth, and the profound connection the company had with the United States over decades of projects in the public and private realm. After he was done, Marko introduced Antonio, who explained the science behind gentech, gave a bit of scope to the project, and discussed Syllabus' reasoning for supporting it. Marko then rose again to thank Antonio and briefly introduce Zane.

The moment had arrived, Zane stood up and walked to the podium, under the piercing weight of hundreds of eyes, staring at him like a ravenous pack of wolves who had suddenly spotted their evening dinner. He was terrified, convinced he was going to freeze and forget what he had to say, falling apart in a heap in front of everyone. As he stood on the stage, he could feel the sweat running down his back, slowly wetting his shirt and the tops of his underwear. What was he to do? How was he going to start talking, if his mouth was frozen shut in fear? Yet miraculously, just as he thought the worst was about befall him, his eyes caught those of the President-elect, and all the fear melted away. She smiled at him, giving a slight nod of encouragement, her warm and friendly face radiating conviction, compassion, and strength - it was as if she were his protector, and he had nothing to fear.

"Ladies and gentlemen," he cleared voice nervously "I want to thank you for the occasion to speak to you about the proposal Syllabus has put together. As mentioned earlier by my colleague Dr. Marko Ivanovic, I am Dr. Zane Fischer, a senior strategic management consultant with Syllabus Corporation. Like many on my team, I have a long connection with the United States, in my case I was educated at Stanford University in mathematical modelling, and collaborated on a number of projects in this country, including with the National Aeronautics and Space Administration."

"Over the past few weeks I've been tasked with modelling the outcomes of four distinct publicly funded gentech implementation scenarios, testing each one to determine its probability of success. The four scenarios were as follows. Scenario one - publicly funded gentech covered by a mix of Medicare and private insurance top-ups, implemented by the individual states. Scenario two - publicly funded gentech covered by Medicare without private insurance top-ups, also implemented by the individual states. Scenario three – publicly funded gentech covered by a mix of Medicare and private insurance top-ups, implemented by the federal government in Washington. Scenario four – publicly funded gentech covered by Medicare without

168

private insurance top-ups, implemented by the federal government in Washington. Clearly these four options are very different paths to achieving the incoming Administration's electoral platform of publicly funded access to genetically engineered medical technologies, collectively referred to as gentech."

"So how did I perform my analysis? First I looked at the types of government gentech healthcare plans around the world. I found, with the exception of the United States, that all rich countries offered mandatory state funded genetic medicine, with only the UK, Russia, China, and Australia permitting private insurance top-ups for premium services."

"Secondly I compared how gentech healthcare plans were implemented and operated in wealthy countries, namely were they centralized, such as in France or Spain, or decentralized such as in Canada and Brazil?"

"Thirdly I compared their relative efficacies in terms of population mortality, population morbidity, monetary cost, and socio-economic equality. For simplicity of the data, I focused on three key therapeutic areas: cancers, neurodegenerative illnesses, and reproductive technologies."

"Once these three steps were completed, I then ranked the performance of these plans. I found countries with centralized implementation and control, which prohibited private insurance top-ups, had the best outcomes in terms of life span, quality of life, monetary cost, and reduced socio-economic inequality. In all cases I observed allowing private insurance top-ups into the market places had serious negatives outcomes in these metrics, while decentralized implementation and control only produced small negative outcomes; however, it did slightly increase socio-economic inequality due to service inconsistencies from region to region within countries."

"There are two caveats to my analysis. Firstly, I determined that in many countries with nationalized genetic medicine, wealthy citizens continue to exploit loopholes, which allow them to access premium genetic medicine healthcare at offshore clinics. I encourage the Administration to include severe criminal penalties in their legislation to prevent this from happening, as is done in certain member states of the EU. Secondly, in all countries where genetic medicine has been nationalized under Medicare, it has only succeeded in reversing inequality when combined with progressive taxation policies to redistribute wealth from rich to middle and lower classes. I did not investigate this caveat any further, as it was beyond the scope of this project."

He paused, looking nervously around at the hundreds of people seated in the hall. They were all staring intently at the slides, clearly focused on the information he was presenting. He cleared his throat before continuing, "now, to make this all connect to an American reality, I looked at outcomes for major comparable domestic projects going back over one hundred years to include Obamacare, nationalized Medicare for all, carbon emissions controls, decriminalization of narcotics, and transportation standards for driverless vehicles. I then examined the current political reality in the United States to determine an optimal plan and an implementation pathway for extending Medicare to cover gentech."

"I found that in the United States, strong centralized policies often had better outcomes, while ad hoc state level rollouts often led to non-compliance by a significant number of individual rogue states. However, there is very important caveat to this observation - the political makeup in the United States usually makes it very hard to get strong centrally planned projects through Congress. The classic example in American healthcare is early 21st Century Obamacare, which had to be decentralized and watered down to get through Congress."

Leyla's slides and visual aids worked seamlessly with Zane's talk, and with each passing sheet he felt more and more confident, realizing the audience was entirely focused on the information he was presenting, barely looking at him.

"To conclude, what I have shown here is a very broad picture of what was done in other countries, overlaid on the political reality in America, and the healthcare needs of the majority of Americans. What the data shows is there are two significantly more favourable strategies for this Administration to proceed with. In both these strategies we recommend a centralized roll out, where Washington implements the plan, not the individual states. As I have shown, the problem with leaving it to the individual states is they may elect not to comply, causing confusion amongst the public. Centralized control will ensure standardization of the plan across the nation."

"Next, what are these two different strategies I recommend for gentech? The first one is some sort of a mixed private-public option. In this option, everyone will be enrolled in Medicare funded genetic medicine, but those who are already covered under private insurance can have their gentech benefits customized and enhanced with a top-up plan. The second one is every American is moved to standardized Medicare funded genetic medicine, and the private insurance plans are shut down."

"Each option has its risks and benefits. I lean towards the more aggressive second option, as it is the cleanest and simplest of the two options, with the best outcomes; however, as I have noted, it will be very challenging to get it through Congress, especially since we are recommending centralized implementation from Washington."

"Lastly, whatever plan is chosen, it will be critical that ample time and energy is given to engage with the public to educate and gain their support. If there is insufficient public engagement there is a real risk the eventual gentech legislation could fail to pass Congress, regardless of the option chosen."

Zane was about to jump to his last slide, when the President-elect raised her hand to interject.

"Dr. Fischer, sorry to cut you off here, very good talk, a solid analysis! What you are saying, is there are four options here, one is state roll out with mixed private and public coverage, another is public only coverage with state roll out, the third option is federal roll out with mixed private and public coverage, and the last is roll out from Washington with everything under Medicare. Correct?"

"Yes msa'am."

"And you lean towards the last option, because it's the cleanest and simplest; however, you believe a variant of the third option has the greatest chance of becoming law given our politics in the United States?"

"Correct. In all cases Syllabus believes roll out must come from Washington. State level roll out means a loss of control and makes it very confusing for Americans who cross state boundaries. But there is a caveat to all of this which I was going to emphasize in my conclusion."

"And what is that caveat Dr. Fischer?" the President-elect asked.

"Option one and two are both the easier ones to implement. Why? Because the states like to have control, and the public is highly suspicious of federal government over-reach. So if there is a lot of resistance to this project, meaning the political headwinds start to grow, I would then suggest state level implementation with mixed private and public insurance coverage – definitely not ideal, but better than nothing."

"You mean that should we run into political resistance, we should opt for the first option rather than risk ending up with nothing at all?"

"Yes ma'am. At the present moment this is unlikely, as you have a lot of political capital in your favour, but history shows the American political system makes it very difficult to implement drastic changes to domestic policy directly from Washington. So while option four is the best option, as it most closely aligns with highly successful plans in countries such as Norway, Japan, and Denmark, you must also prepare for the less desirable possibility of ceding the power to individual states to implement and manage a major domestic policy like this one."

The President-elect looked across the room and then back at Zane, she slowly stood up with her head raised, and walked to the front of the ballroom, coming to a stop halfway between the seated audience and Zane.

"Seems like this young Canadian man think he understands how gridlocked our politics is."

There was laughter in the room, as Zane lowered his gaze.

"Well, he is quite right! He shouldn't be ashamed, we should be!!! If our politicians did their jobs and delivered proper plans with long term benefits, this country, and indeed the world, wouldn't be in the mess it's in today!"

The room went silent.

"Colleagues, these are dark times for our country. We are suffering a climate disaster created by generations of politicians who were too soft to do the right things at the right time. Now, as we suffer the consequences of their inaction, we are also confronted with a class of billionaires and multi-millionaires who are using genetic engineering and AI to ensure their reign at the top of society becomes permanent. They are shutting eighty percent Americans out of the best jobs, schools, and neighbourhoods, by leaving them behind in the arms race for genetically engineered human perfection. We the Social Democrats must act decisively to arrest this, for if we do not, we risk the disintegration of our society, the rupturing of democracy in this country, and the beginning of a dark and terrifying future."

"My colleagues, there must be no weakness, we cannot compromise."

Zane's sweat soaked skin tingled, listening in awe to the President-elect speak. Her choice of words was measured and calculated, yet her voice had a raw and emotional texture to it, carrying the listener towards a possibility of hope, promise, and deliverance. As she spoke, she made eye contact with many people in the room, and when her monologue rose to a final crescendo, she eventually settled on him, her eyes connecting with his.

"This means Washington must deliver Medicare covered gentech, no state involvement, no private options. We must also engage with our Republican partners to push legislation for progressive taxation and take the additional step of shuttering access to premium genetic medicine through offshore clinics. Failure is not an option, we must be prepared to fight the Libertarians tooth and nail on this."

Zane looked on in amazement from his position at the podium, as everyone rose to their feet and began cheering and applauding. The President-elect looked across the room, and then returned her penetrating gaze to Zane, giving him a final nod of approval. She then pivoted on her feet and walked slowly out the room, her security detail and senior aides forming a protective group around her.

As she walked away, Zane felt an enormous weight had been lifted off his chest, breathing a sigh of relief as he watched the room quickly empty out after the President-elect had left. With the pressure relinquished, he took a moment to wander off and clear his mind, finding a quiet spot behind the stage, where he was able to look out the glass at the long queue of departing vehicles.

"Dr. Fischer."

Zane turned around to see a tall, gangly, blonde-haired fellow in his mid-forties standing in front of him.

"Steve McNeill?"

"That would be me! Good to finally meet you in the flesh Dr. Zane Fischer! Marko Ivanovic and Jared Berg have spoken very highly of you and the consulting team Antonio Rubio has assembled. Your reputation as a data and numbers boffin exceeded all expectations today, what you delivered was truly impressive in its simplicity and clarity."

Zane smiled, "thank you sir, I won't say it was pleasure presenting, but once I got going I think I found my rhythm."

"Hey no worries, it's no easy task presenting to an audience like this!"

He was about to continue, when a political handler came over to signal to him it was time to get going.

"Hey sorry, I've been given the signal to get moving, but anyways, I fully expect Syllabus will be approved to be our consulting partner moving forward, which also means we will be working together quite a bit in the next stage."

They shook hands, as Steve was guided out the room by his political staff and security guards.

Date Thursday December 5th, 2120

With the meetings done, all of them boarded an overnight train from Newark Central Station to Salish City. It was a bullet service, which meant arrival in Salish City the following morning at nine. They had their own private car with dining facilities, showers, beds, and a meeting room, which allowed Jared Berg to gather Marko, Leyla, Antonio, Zane, as well as the rest of the team in Salish City by conference call.

"Okay everyone, both here in the car, and back in Salish City, I want to thank all of you for an amazing job today, especially Zane Fischer on his wonderful presentation! I can confirm we have been selected for phase two of the project, which means we get to kick this thing up a few notches!"

Everyone let out a loud cheer, as Leyla wildly danced around, popping open a chilled bottle Champagne, to pour into everyone's glasses. She shouted, "hey Robbie, Miko, Anita, sorry I can't pour you guys any wine, but go order yourself a few bottles on Jared's new US Government expense account!"

There was laughter, as Jared gave her the thumbs up and raised his glass in a toast.

An opulent dinner service began shortly thereafter, served by immaculately dressed train staff. Over the course of the meal, Jared explained to everyone what he expected from them in the days ahead. Antonio, Marko, and Zane were to be the point people dealing with the incoming US Government, while the rest of the team was to provide the support they required. He also announced a new large project budget to enable Antonio and the

178

team to scale up and recruit junior consultants from across the firm to manage the increased work load.

After dinner there were no night caps or long discussions, everyone was exhausted and rapidly dispersed to their private rooms. Zane took a hot herbal tea to go, and then locked himself in his private suite, breathing a sigh of relief as he stood alone in the cool silent cabin. The suite was small, but very efficiently designed, containing a tiny wash basin and a long narrow shower on the far wall, and a double bed and a closet against the near wall. A long contiguous exterior window offered a reflection of his quarters, masking the view of the frozen nighttime landscape of middle America, rushing by at half the speed of sound.

He stripped naked, taking a moment to admire the perfection of his reflection in the window. The past week had pushed his limits, but he had risen to the challenge, delivering a home run for his career and almost certainly big bonus for his bank account. How far away an afternoon of uncertainty, stress, and fear of failure seemed - now he was on top of the world, the centre of a project of unimaginable prestige. Standing under the flow of warm water, he stretched out his long athletic body, bending forward to touch the floor, his mouth coming to rest in front of his erection. He briefly hesitated, giving barely a moment's thought as to what Leyla may hear through the millimetre thin walls of the cabin. It didn't take him long to find release, ejecting billions of copies of his perfect genetic material onto the shower floor, and then watching it wash away down the drain, to some unknown destination.

A few minutes later, washed and refreshed, he drew back the duvet and shut off the lights. The only sound, the gentle whirring

of the train as it hurtled like a missile through the dark icy
December night.

Phase Two

Date Saturday February 8th, 2121

Zane stood waiting for Maya, staring at the heavy rain splashing against his bedroom window. The sky was dark and sinister, layers upon layers of deep thick clouds battering the city scape with an uninterrupted downpour. Officially it was already one of the biggest weather systems to hit the coast in years, with the MetService reporting that over 150 mm had fallen in just a few hours, flooding streets, tunnels, and buildings, and causing major disruptions to the entire SkyTrain network. They predicted another 100 mm was still to come overnight before the clouds cleared, ushering in cold sunny weather.

EVO had already alerted him that Maya was expecting to be at least an hour late because of all the chaos. He was excited to see her, over the past few weeks they had only had the time to catch up sporadically for coffee and some dinner out. She was busier than ever with her research, while for him everything had turned into a blur of activity since his presentation to the President-elect in New York.

Phase two brought a new tempo to the project as the team quickly expanded, taking over more and more of the work cubes on the floor for their exclusive use. Everyone was swamped; however, Antonio was by far the busiest, juggling managing the project schedule and staffing needs with Miko, while participating in consultation meetings with Zane, Marko, Jared, and the incoming US Administration. His manager was trying to be everywhere at once, impressing Jared Berg and senior management in the hope of finally being promoted to director or junior vice-president.

181

Zane knew it was to the detriment of the project, but it was not his place to make any comment.

Everything kicked into high gear in the third week of January, as soon as the President and her administration were sworn into office on the steps of the Capitol building, before millions of supporters filling the length of the National Mall. They came from across America to witness a historical moment, the swearing in of the nation's first black woman President; however, in the end the celebrations were plain and austere, a reflection of a country in deep crisis. With the levers of power in her hands, the President had her cabinet confirmed within days of being sworn in, placing Steve McNeill as Secretary of Health and the FDA. Shortly thereafter, Steve McNeill introduced the gentech bill to Congress, and Zane, Antonio, and various other experts from industry, government, and academia were summoned to Washington to participate in Congressional hearings.

As he learnt during the ten days of questioning from late January to early February, the Congressional hearings were not about politicians gathering facts to make informed voting decisions, they were about optics, making their side look right, and calling into question the credibility and competence of their opponents. The Libertarians, led by Senator John Smith, called up conservative economists, gentech sceptics, and health insurance companies as witnesses, seeking to build an alternate reality with their own ecosystem of counter-facts and experts. The health insurance industry was particularly aggressive, on one side mobilizing the support of those who were terrified of losing their private insurance and being forced onto Medicare, and on the other side agitating those Americans who believed gentech was a dangerous and evil abomination.

The Libertarians also took the liberty of questioning the CEO's of the world's largest gentech firms, part of their claim the industry was bribing the President to have their expensive technologies covered by taxpayer funded Medicare. They argued it was not the role of government to waste taxpayer's money funding big genetics and pharmaceutical firms to provide expensive technology to people who were too poor to pay for it themselves. In the cross-examinations led by the Social Democrats, the response from the CEO's was merciless, labelling Smith as an abhorrent hypocrite, who was happy to use his own taxpayer funded government healthcare plan for genetic medicine for him and his family, while preaching the opposite for ordinary Americans.

When it was finally their turn to call their own witnesses, Steve McNeill and the Social Democrats elected to focus on the facts, first deploying government specialists, university researchers, and healthcare economists to testify before Congress. Unfortunately the plan backfired, as their complex explanations were drowned out by the simple and emotionally alluring arguments from Senator Smith and his organized and well-funded opposition, who comically labeled the experts as dull and out of touch technocrats.

Realizing the tenacity of the Libertarian opposition, McNeill called on both Antonio and Zane, who as consultants were extremely adept at providing clear, simple, and convincing arguments. Antonio defended the safety, efficacy, and widespread use of genetic technologies, showing how they were being used in Medicare plans in developed countries around the world. While Zane honed in on the urgent need to update Medicare to include genetic technologies in order to avoid a dystopic future, where a superior elite class of genetically engineered people controlled the country's wealth and power, with everyone else left behind. In dramatic presentations, Zane showed how the United States risked violently disintegrating in the next twenty-five years, as outside powers such as China, Russia, and the European Union exploited the country's growing genetic divide.

Of course it was no easy task for Zane and Antonio, they too faced the wrath of Senator Smith and the other Libertarian Congressmen. In cross-examinations the senator and his allies ruthlessly and falsely claimed that Syllabus, along with Zane and Antonio, were foreign agents who had neither the right nor the experience to make statements or decisions on behalf of the American people. Without evidence, Smith and his cronies asserted that Syllabus, just like the gentech companies, was part of a vast foreign conspiracy to take over Medicare and use it to poison ordinary Americans with dangerous genetic technologies.

His EVO interrupted, *"Zane, Maya is approaching the lobby doors. Would you like me to let her in and direct her to your front door?"*

"Yes EVO."

A couple of minutes later Maya appeared at the front door, all smiles and looking very wet.

"Hey handsome!" she smiled, shaking some of the water off her jacket.

"Hey babe, thanks for making the trek in such lousy weather! Let me take that umbrella and raincoat off your hands, you can leave your boots right here in the entrance by the front door."

She pulled off her boots, saying, "oh my, so this is the place, show me around Zaney."

"Well there's not much to see," he laughed, as he walked her from the front door, past the open plan kitchen on the right and the lounge on the left. A few steps further, and they were already past the bathroom on the left, and inside the bedroom, which was almost entirely taken up by his king size bed. The murky view of the Lougheed City filled the floor to ceiling windows, a sea of flickering lights and reflective glass and concrete towers.

"At forty-two square metres, it's just a fraction of the size of that lovely large heritage flat of yours in the forest at UBC. I'd trade this thing in any day for what you have out there."

"Well there's no hiding your place is very generic, but it has an amazing view and is very efficiently designed."

"Yes the view does make up for everything, but I'm not so sure about the efficient design," he laughed, as he pulled a bottle of white wine out of the cold dock. "So, care for some wine? Dinner is warming in the oven."

"Wine yes! You cooked dinner too?"

"Ah no, would you think I know how to do that!" he joked, "I ordered us a premium drone delivery special, but I know you'll like it!"

She laughed, as he gave her a kiss on the cheek.

A few minutes later they sat down for dinner at the bar. It was a tight fit, and it wasn't long before she was laughing herself silly watching him struggle to squash all the dishes and plates onto the tiny countertop. It was clear neither he nor his apartment were equipped to have anyone over for a meal.

"Oh my, this looks like Ethiopian food!"

"Well kind of, it's a version of *Shiro be Kibbe*, with synthetic meat of course, and plenty of rice and bread."

"Not bad, I'd give it an eight out of ten," she smiled, with a twinkle in her eye.

"What yah thinking?" He chuckled.

"Ah, not quite what you think I'm thinking," she laughed nervously.

"Hmm, so what is it?"

"Ah, nothing…"

"No, it's not nothing, it's definitely something."

"Zane," she said, with a decidedly more serious tone, as she put her knife and fork down on the plate.

"Oh, this sounds serious," he said, raising his eyebrows.

"It is, but it's not at all what you think," she paused. "I need some feedback from you. Where are we going with this? We're both very busy people, which isn't about to change now that my faculty position is permanent and your employer keeps giving you more important responsibilities."

"Yeah I apologize about work, it just keeps getting more and more involved. I promise when the project ends I'll bid for something a bit more low-key. I'll also consider selling this sterile condominium and rent something near my office, so we'd be a lot closer…"

"Don't be silly Zane, there's no need to change your life and sacrifice your career to spend more time with me! You should count yourself fortunate to work in a high impact field with so many opportunities. I certainly feel that way about what I do."

"Ah, so what is it then…?" he asked, confused.

She tailed off searching for words, "ah, I don't know if you've given this much thought really. I like you, you're very sexy, incredibly intelligent, younger, yes younger than me, but that's okay. To be honest, having a boyfriend like you is fantastic, the faculty members…you can't imagine the gossip started by that dear little Fae, she got everyone so jealous!"

Zane blushed, "about what?"

"Zane, don't play dumb! Everyone's seen what you look like and heard what you do for work, they're all so jealous I'm hitched up with a guy like you. I of course just shrug it off, reminding everyone I'm not so bad myself," she laughed.

He smiled sheepishly and was about to say he felt the same thing for her, when she cut him off, "Zane, I'll cut to the chase here. My parents keep asking me if I've found a suitable partner to have a child with. They have become very insistent ever since my brother in New York announced he would never have offspring. It terrifies my parents they will never be grandparents, which is entirely normal for an Ethiopian family, but totally foreign for you people in the developed world, where families are a thing of the past."

"To make them happy, I applied to reproduce using sperm from the Reproduction Bureau's supply bank; however, I was declined because I'm not a Canadian citizen. I won't become a citizen for at least five more years, but by then I won't qualify because I'll be too old. Zane, the only path I have to reproduction is with a Canadian citizen who is willing to use my eggs with their sperm. Do you see what I mean?"

"Ah…yeah," he stuttered, "well…I mean…to be honest…"

"Zane, you're my ticket to reproduction and dealing with my parents' anxieties. I understand if this something you can't comprehend, but you need to realize that if you say no, I'll have to start looking for someone else. I don't have time to waste."

He looked at her, stunned by the sudden turn of events. An evening that was supposed be a romantic dinner with some great sex had turned into a discussion about conceiving a child. What should he say? How could he say no and then have her walk out the door? He didn't want her to leave him, he was incredibly attracted to her and didn't want their relationship to end like this on their first night at his place.

"Zane?"

"Wait, just give me a moment to digest this okay, it's not something I was expecting."

She got up and went to the bathroom, leaving him to think in silence. He was so confused. The world was such an unstable place - the climate crisis, regional wars, artificial intelligence, a genetic engineering arms race, and socio-economic inequality were all pushing the planet to unsustainable extremes. Was this a world he wanted to bring a child into?

The bathroom door slid open and Maya walked back into the kitchen, taking her seat at the counter.

"Zane, when searching the Reproduction Bureau's supply bank I noticed you made sperm deposits back in your twenties, but didn't activate your Lottery profile. You know the sperm is still there and can be used if you release it."

He looked up into her intoxicatingly beautiful eyes. God she's gorgeous, he thought. Those eyes, the long braided hair, the ballet dancer legs, and the smooth dark skin. Was it really worth losing her over something as silly as a disagreement over reproduction? Why not just give her what she wanted so they could keep having a good time? After all, having a child didn't mean becoming a parent, that was the government's job.

"Zane, I need your help. You have nothing to lose, it doesn't cost you anything."

There was a long awkward silence between the two of them, before Zane asked slowly, "How will the child be raised? Will it be in good hands? I just don't want it to end up at some rotten boarding school that barely passes state accreditation."

She smiled gently, "there is nothing for you to worry about, the child will go straight into a full care creche on my university campus, which feeds into some of the best state boarding schools. It's not like the days when you were growing up Zane, because boarding schools are now mandatory, they come with strict government regulations and mandatory parental contact."

He looked at Maya, and smiled, "okay, I understand your predicament and I'm willing to help. I'll activate my profile in the Lottery and name you as my designated partner. I do however suggest we do it tonight, just in case I get second thoughts."

Her face erupted in joy, and she dove into his arms, nearly knocking the dishes off the tiny countertop, "thanks Zane, thank you so much! You have no idea how much I appreciate it!"

He laughed, "don't worry, it's all good! Let's just not go and break all the dishes okay!"

As soon as dinner was cleaned up, they logged into his account at the Reproduction Bureau, going through the process of activating his Lottery inscription. It was a remarkably simple process, greatly facilitated by the fact he already had his sperm stored in the Reproduction Bureau's genetic bank. Once that was done, he assigned her as his designated partner, which she accepted from inside her profile. In minutes she received a message from the

Reproduction Bureau requesting her to book an appointment for an initial genetic screening.

That night they made love, it was the first time he had ever done anything like that before. He didn't even believe it was possible for such things to happen in a vacuous world where beauty, self-actualization, and status were the only things that mattered. After they were done, the two of them collapsed under the covers, Zane staring at the rain falling against the tinted glass as Maya drifted off into a contented deep sleep. His mind was going a million miles a minute, thinking of what the future held in store. Would they even successfully reproduce? After all, she may have damaged eggs given she was older and from outside of Canada. The invitro clinics were remarkable, able to rehabilitate even the most damaged of reproductive material to generate a successful fertilization; however, nothing was guaranteed at this juncture, Maya still had to be screened, and it was also possible their material would be incompatible. If in the end fertilization and gestation succeeded, what would become of the child? What would it be like? What would it grow into? What sort of relationship, if any, would he have with it? Exhausted, his eyelids grew heavier and his thoughts became muddled, and soon, unable to resist, he surrendered to sleep.

"Dr. Fisher, you have no idea about the needs of America! How could you, you aren't even from here? Sure, you passed through here, going to some fancy privileged school in San Francisco, but that's not the real America. You're an imposter, trying to sell a wacked up idea where Washington controls people's reproductive rights, and then wires their bodies permanently to the Internet so the government and foreign companies can spy on them."

"Sir, Senator John Smith, I can tell you the gentech bill the President has chosen is not some wacked up idea that will control people's reproductive rights. To be honest, reproduction is only a small part of it, the big issues are access to cancer vaccines, treatment and screening for neurodegenerative diseases, and the end to many sexually transmitted illnesses."

Senator Smith laughed at his answer, continuing his assualt, "ah, I beg to differ, reproduction is a central plank in this bill, everything else is just a smoke screen to win support from Republicans and Independents. You fancy young foreign consultants have only one interest: making bonus payouts on this project. You people don't care about stealing the reproductive rights of Americans and hardwiring their bodies to the Internet so the government can monitor their every move and thought. Mr. Fischer, let me guess, you and the rest of the plugged-in test-tube elite will probably never know what it's like to raise a child, have a family, or fall in love. If you even ever bother having a child, I'm sure you'll have it in a test tube, and then nine months' later send it off like an inanimate object to one of your state boarding schools, so you can keep living your fancy elite life of endless dinner parties."

Losing his temper, Zane replied, "sir, firstly you can call me Dr. Fischer! Secondly your argument about surveillance is a moot point because most ordinary Americans already have EVO implants connecting them permanently to the Internet, regardless of whether they have access to gentech or not. Thirdly you are free to have your opinions about people like me, but might I say your offspring were also genetically engineered in a 'test tube'. You sir are a hypocrite, part of an elite in this country who is happy to lie to ordinary Americans, so you can keep access to gentech for yourselves, while everyone else gets left behind!"

The room went silent, but before Zane could continue his tirade, the senator started laughing, a deep bellowing laugh that made everyone feel uncomfortable. Smith stared at Zane, then at Antonio, and then at the other panelists, *"you've got to be kidding me, Mr. Fischer, we are not blocking access to these medications and treatments, what we are doing is saving taxpayers the huge cost of subsidizing it for poor, pathetic, lazy people who don't contribute a penny to the economy. Anyone can access these services by paying for it through the private sector, just like any hardworking American does."*

"Senator, eighty percent of Americans do not have the means to do that, no matter how hard they work. The President is fighting to extend those benefits to all Americans, and she has hired people like me to make that happen."

"Firstly, Zane you're insulting Americans by saying they can't afford to access these technologies, of course they can! Everywhere across this great country there are many people who are able to, they just work hard to do it. Secondly, people like you don't know anything about America. You're a foreigner, a test-tuber, a joke! You're nothing but a narcist and a selfish pretty college kid, who has no work experience, other than a couple of years at his fancy little Canadian firm. Oh, and a small little internship for NASA!"

Zane felt his blood boil in rage as he tried to counter-attack, but was drowned out by laughter in the room. Everyone was laughing, including Antonio, Steve McNeill, and the other panelists, as well as the media, and most of the senators. He shouted, trying to defend himself, but his mic was muted. The laughter grew louder and louder, with Smith and other Libertarian Senators dropping more personal insults, as they pointed at him. Furious, he jumped up to leave the room, but was suddenly pelted in the face by a rotten tomato launched from somewhere in the audience.

"Zane, Zane, are you okay?"

He opened his eyes to see he was sitting up in bed, with Maya at his side.

"Ah, it was a dream, another damn work nightmare," he answered, as he groggily rubbed his eyes.

"It must have been pretty bad, because you were shouting and thrashing around like crazy."

"I was in one of those rooms, you know the ones you've seen me in on the news. I was part of a panel of experts defending the gentech bill. We were being cross-examined by senators, and the room was full with media and spectators from the general public. Senator John Smith, you know the one?"

"Yes, the bean pole in the tweed suite, the Senate Minority leader from California?"

"Yeah, that one. Well he's also on the Health Committee for gentech and he has been causing me all sorts of grief. Anyway, in the dream he was attacking me, calling me some pretty kid with a college degree, while everyone in the room was laughing and laughing. I couldn't even defend myself, because they'd turned off my mic, then I got hit in the face by a rotten tomato..."

"Euhh, well it's okay, it was just a dream."

"Ah it was, but it also wasn't. I feel like I'm suffering some sort of PTSD from those Congressional inquiries."

He got up and stumbled to the bathroom to wash his face and use the toilet. When he returned to the bedroom, Maya was shaking out the duvet and turning the pillows.

"Come, let's get back to sleep. It's only three in the morning and we can still get a few decent hours."

He slid under the covers, wrapping his arms around her, her body radiating warmth against his. After a few minutes he could tell she was once again sound asleep, her breathing becoming deep and restful. He gently let her roll away from him, to a comfortable space in the middle of the bed, while he lay on his back staring at the ceiling, waiting for the night to pass.

Dinner in D.C.

Date Thursday March 6th, 2121

"So Dr. Fisher, you are quite the brilliant young man. A doctorate in applied mathematics from Stanford, an MBA from HEC, some work with NASA, and few years at Syllabus. All very impressive. If I may also add, your presentation to the President back in early December was excellent, so clear, so easy to understand. Both you and Antonio have performed admirably on the Congressional panels. It's no small task handling that horrible prune, the Senate minority leader John Smith."

Zane smiled politely, "thank you madam. I'm trying my best, but at times he has an ability to get under my skin."

"Oh it happens to all of us, but don't let him for god's sake. The key is to never take his attacks personally. Remember he may appear to be a formidable adversary, but in fact he is a hypocritic clown with not a leg to stand on."

Marko leaned over and said, "Smith has always been a nasty foe. When Steve McNeill and I were lobbying in D.C. to expand publicly funded gentech to the rest of the country using the New England model, he released some lie that we were part of a left-wing movement trying to raise taxes to pay for a vast socialist scheme!"

Marko chuckled naughtily, adding, "socialist, how absurd! I mean no one is a socialist anymore, certainly not at this table!" He continued with a whisper, "I don't think anyone here this evening earns under a quarter million universal dollars, except for that adorable junior ministerial staffer in the corner."

"Dr. Marko Ivanovic, don't be so rude, I would have never expected that from you," Germain laughed.

Their conversation dropped off as the dinner service began, with waiters moving about the private room, placing dishes in front of all the attendees. The food was outstanding, beyond anything Zane had ever eaten in his life, including the food in the private train car ride back from Newark in December. The restaurant was definitely at the level expected of one of Washington's finest establishments, a place for billionaires, politicians, and business people with big expense accounts.

Joining Marko, Jared, Antonio, and Zane at the table were the Canadian Ambassador to the United States, the Canadian Federal Minister of Health, the Canadian Minister of Business, the CEO of Zelion - Elise Germain, and the CEO of MediGen - Robert Dumas. Zane was well placed at the far corner of the table, with Marko and Germain seated beside him. Robert Dumas, Jared, and Antonio sat in the centre, facing the Canadian government ministers, while their political staffers were bunched together beside the exit.

With the main course done, the Minister of Business stood up to speak. "Everybody, I'd like to give a short toast to the Ambassador. *J'aimerais saluer notre Ambassadeur à son anniversaire et pour son travail et sa détermination en représentant nos intérêts avec tant de vigueur et de ténacité ici à Washington!* It's his birthday today, and I would like to thank him for his commitment in representing Canada here in Washington with such determination and valour.

He has been instrumental in standing up for Canadian interests, making sure we have our voices heard with this new US Administration! *J'aimerais aussi rajouter que nous comptions que ce projet de loi du Président réussisse, pour que nos entreprises Canadiennes, comme Zelion et MediGen puissent avoir accès a ce vaste marché.* I'd also like to add we are all counting on the President's bill becoming law, giving Canadian firms like Zelion and MediGen access to what should be a tremendous new market for their life-saving technologies. Cheers, *santé*!"

"Cheers, *santé*!" they repeated in unison after the Minister of Business.

The ambassador stood and nodded in recognition and then added, "first and foremost thank you Syllabus for covering the cost of tonight's meal. I'd also like to say thanks to Jared, Antonio, Zane, and of course Marko, whose connections in this city and gentech politics have gone a long way to getting us to this point. Fingers crossed the President's Medicare bill becomes a reality!"

He took his seat, and with a wave of the hand encouraged everyone to go back to what they were doing prior to the interruption.

It was clear Canada was extremely preoccupied with the gentech debate in America, it wasn't just a business opportunity for Canadian gentech and consulting firms, it was also a national security issue. Canada was concerned a divided unequal America, where only the rich benefited from genetic medicine, would destabilize fortress North America, making it more politically unstable and vulnerable to outside influence. The Canadian government feared a not too distant unravelling of the American

Republic, torn apart by conflict between ordinary Americans and the genetically engineered class.

Dinner lingered with dessert and coffee for another half an hour, wrapping up when the two cabinet ministers and their aides departed for Ottawa to prepare for cabinet meetings with the Prime Minster the following morning.

Zane stood up and pushed his chair in. He was just about to make his way to the washrooms, when Dr. Germain tapped him on the shoulder. "Dr. Fischer, it has been a pleasure meeting you again here this evening. Before we go, I was going to suggest we get together outside of the buzz of this place. Would you be interested in meeting Monday evening in Salish City? I will be flying there on my way back from Singapore. I thought it may be worthwhile for us to have a chat."

Zane nodded in surprise, why did Germain want to meet with him?

"Very good. I will send an assistant with a car to pick you up outside of work Monday at 19:00 sharp. Now please excuse me, I just want to get a final word with Federal Ministers before they leave for Ottawa."

Phase Three

Date - Friday March 7th, 2121

Sweat dripped down his face, his heart still thumping from the workout. He was jet-lagged, had indigestion from the dinner in Washington, and was hung over from the copious amounts of alcohol he, Jared, Antonio, and Marko had consumed on the late-night flight back to Salish City.

"So Zane, what do you think about us getting a whole floor for ourselves?" Anita asked.

"Hmm, I think it's about time. This has become a very high-profile project, and we have some pretty powerful enemies in Washington who would love to exploit any vulnerabilities we may have."

"With the extra space Robbie and I were hoping we could move our entire communications team here. We now have over two hundred writers, designers, and strategists scattered around the world and it's become a real headache managing all of them remotely," Leyla said.

"Yeah I tell you Zane, you have no idea, you should count yourself lucky you don't have to manage so many people," Robbie added.

"Well at least you guys don't have to get grilled by Congress and the media." Zane replied.

"True, I don't envy you and Antonio for that privilege," Robbie conceded.

"I just hope we can get some certainty with the direction this project is taking. Jared Berg, Marko Ivanovic, and Syllabus' board of directors say they're pushing Steve McNeill and the US Government to do a phase three rollout with thousands of public roundtables across America. Antonio and I know our operations and planning team doesn't have the resources to produce anything on that scale. What we urgently need are more people with operations experience, who know how to use SyNet's scheduling applications, and who I can trust to do things properly. It is just plain annoying how Jared Berg and senior management don't seem to get the urgency of it!" Miko snapped, finishing her juice and leaving them to go to the changeroom.

"Well it seems like everyone's in a good mood today..." Zane muttered sarcastically, swishing his protein drink around in the Syllabus labeled cup.

"Zane, Miko's in a sour mood. Berg came in here and blasted her this morning in front of everyone for not having her team secure the entire restaurant for your VIP dinner last night in Washington. You missed it all because you arrived late, but she was nearly in tears, we were all worried she was going to quit."

"Sorry, I had no idea. Everything seemed fine last night at the restaurant. The only thing I noticed was they confined us to a private room, but there were no complaints from anyone. On the flight back Berg was in good mood and we all drank way too much, which explains why Antonio and I look and feel like crap this morning."

"Well I'd rather be hung over than on the bad side of Jared Berg and the board of directors. Granted it sucks to be in the spotlight and take all kinds of abuse in Washington, but at least you're sheltered from the bullshit we're putting up with here. If I had of known this project was going to be like this, I may have thought twice before signing up without a bigger bonus cheque."

They looked up at the clock and realized they only had about ten minutes before they needed to be at Antonio's meeting. Wasting no more time, they finished their hydration drinks and hurried to the changeroom to get showered and changed.

Twenty minutes later they were gathered in a group around Antonio in the middle of a vast and vacant office covering the entire one hundredth floor of Syllabus tower, with a spectacular 360-degree view of Salish City and its magnificent surroundings. There were about fifteen of them, the core group, as well as a few other consultants who had taken on key assistant roles in the expanded project team.

"Guys, as you may guess we are about to experience some major changes. Before I elaborate, it is important for all of you to know that Marko Ivanovic is no longer with us. For reasons I cannot divulge, the board of directors, the CEO, and Jared Berg decided to terminate him last night."

There was a stunned silence, before Antonio continued with a smile on his face, "that aside, I want to thank all of you for the amazing support you provided Zane and I throughout those Congressional interrogations in D.C. It's because of our performance as a team that the US government has decided to retain Syllabus for the last part of this project!"

Everyone broke into cheers, with some of them giving Zane and Antonio congratulatory pats on the back. Once everyone quietened down, Antonio continued, "so now what? Well Syllabus determined this project is too important and sensitive for it to remain mingled with the rest of the company. The CEO, who has her office on the floor above, instructed Jared Berg to consolidate all staff involved in the project onto this floor; furthermore..."

Everyone listened attentively, hanging onto every word Antonio said.

"Furthermore, Jared Berg has authorized my release as project leader."

There was a look of bewilderment on everyone's faces. "Your release? What does that mean? I don't understand, if this project is so important to Syllabus, why would they release you as project leader?" Miko asked anxiously.

"I'm not being moved off the project, rather I'm finally being relieved of my project management responsibilities so I can focus on being our scientific liaison with the Department of Health, the FDA, and the President. Those parties want my undivided attention in phase three."

"Yes, but now we're without a project leader. Is someone taking over managing this? Hopefully someone who will be around here more consistently than you?" Miko asked, the apprehension clearly audible in her voice.

"Miko, yes we will have a new project manager, and I can promise you it will be someone who will give you their undivided attention. I recognize it was a source of much frustration for you, having me always out of town, and you left on your own to manage operations and project timelines. I also want to apologize to you and your team for taking all the blame for the D.C. restaurant booking, it was my fault for not being clearer about what Jared wanted," Antonio said.

Just as Antonio finished speaking, the lobby doors slid open and Jared Berg appeared, accompanied by Sean Chan from the Auckland office.

"Hello folks!" Sean waved, flashing his big friendly Kiwi grin, as he and Jared joined everyone in the middle of the room. Standing in front of the group, the company vice-president signalled to everyone to grab some of the loose chairs scattered around the space and take a seat around him.

"Alright everybody, first order of business, I assume Antonio has told you Marko was dismissed just a few hours ago. Firing him was a joint decision taken by myself, the CEO, and a number of other vice presidents in the company. I will not elaborate on why he was fired; however, you will be informed should senior management decide to release details."

"Next, on numerous occasions Antonio has reminded me he no longer has the time to act as both scientific liaison and project manager, and that I needed to split his role into two separate positions. Up to this point I have resisted hiring a dedicated project manager because I believed it was the best strategy to have an experienced scientifically trained manager who was also involved in the day to day interactions with the client."

"This strategy was possible in stages one and two, when this team was small; however, it now has to change as we enter the largest and final part of the project. Effective immediately, Antonio will relinquish his management responsibilities to a dedicated project manager, so he can focus on working with Zane Fischer as our scientific liaison with the US government and our industry partners."

"Your new project manager is Sean Chan, who is usually based in our Auckland office, acting as a liaison with Syllabus groups in China and parts of Central Asia. Sean has many years of project management experience with Syllabus, as well as training in human resources, operations management, AI deployment, and security and surveillance. Most importantly, many of you worked with Sean on the restructuring of that large Stockholm based biotechnology client. He was the project's Asia-Pacific and China liaison."

"Before I hand over to Sean, I want to emphasize that we should be prepared for phase three to push our limits. This company, and in particular this team, will be a target for all kinds of attacks from Americans who oppose this gentech bill. Anticipate bitter attacks from the private healthcare and insurance industry, religious fundamentalists, libertarians, vested financial interests, and of course the usual cohort of xenophobes and racial purists who believe this is a conspiracy against them."

"The good news is most of you are unlikely to directly experience these threats; nevertheless, Syllabus is taking security seriously and we will be monitoring any credible risks, paying particular attention to the safety of any team members working in the United States. Sean Chan, as your project manager, will be in charge of this and will communicate any important information to you."

"Well that covers everything I wanted to say to you today. I have some other important business I need to attend to, so if you don't mind I'll hand thing over to Sean."

Jared stood up and gave Sean a friendly pat on the back and then hurried off to the elevator lobby.

Sean smiled and stood up in front of the group. "Hello everyone, good to see you all again! I'm thrilled to be here and be part of what is a truly remarkable project. On my flight over from Auckland I got to familiarize myself with what's going on and what needs to happen next. I've also been in contact with Antonio, who has graciously brought me up to speed with where we are right now."

Sean gave Antonio a smile and continued, "from a project management perspective, my immediate priority is to restructure the team and consolidate all our staff and operations to this floor for phase three. In the briefs and exchanges I've had with Jared and Antonio, I can see this third part of the project involves some sort of extensive public outreach running from mid-April to mid-May. The objective of this outreach is to build support for the gentech healthcare legislation, so it can be submitted to Congress and voted into law. Our role in the project ends the moment the bill is signed into law."

"We are now in early March, so this gives us about five weeks to prepare to prepare for phase three - a tight schedule, but I'm sure we can make it happen! Questions?"

There were no questions, so Sean signalled to everyone to follow him around the office floor so he could explain the planned layout. As they walked around, the first thing Zane noticed about his new manager was how open and affable he was - a welcome contrast to the seriousness and intensity that was so characteristic of Antonio's management style. Sean smiled enthusiastically, detailing how the floor was going to be divided into seven work zones – strategic analysis under Zane, visual communications under Robbie, general communications under Leyla, operations management under Miko, scientific resources managed by Antonio, and artificial intelligence under Anita. The seventh zone was for Sean's office, as well as reading and meeting rooms. He promised them everything would be wired and in place by Monday morning, ready for the arrival of the first new recruits and satellite staff from abroad.

It was a tight timeline - the consolidation and restructuring was going to be a gargantuan task, primarily because of strict immigration controls for people who did not have the right passports. As Zane and his colleagues knew, migration eligibility trumped skills and intelligence in the 22nd Century, preventing many qualified Syllabus staff from ever being able to physically work in certain regions of the world. Those who suffered the most were employees in the periphery zones of South East Asia and Africa, who were barred from entering almost every developed country. These employees were trapped in support roles on SyNet, and were considered expendable as the project restructured its human resources. A similar fate awaited support staff in China, Russia, Eastern Europe, and Central Asia – the part of the world known as the Totalitarian Bloc. The US government was certain to demand Syllabus remove them from the project because of concerns about sabotage and espionage, despite their important role in assisting Zane and Antonio with scientific and data analysis. In this consolidation the only Syllabus staff to benefit were those fortunate enough to hold passports from Canada's allies inside the Non-aligned and Liberal Blocs, which included the EU super state, Mexico, Australasia, Japan-Taiwan, Korea, Southern Africa, Chile, Argentina, Brazil, and the United States. For them it meant promotions and the exciting opportunity of a reassignment to head office to work on a prestigious project.

Zane sat at the kitchen counter, slumped over his dinner as the screen in the living room mindlessly broadcasted a steady monochromatic stream of news. The first day on Floor 100 was mayhem, the restructuring and consolidation of staff consuming all the oxygen in the office. Sean, for all his affable Kiwi humour, was as driven as Antonio, forcing everyone to finalize their team lists and complete all the bureaucratic procedures before the work day ended. On top of that, there was also the constant noise and interruptions from inconsiderate construction crews installing work cubes, meeting rooms, and offices.

"In American news tonight, the US Administration has succeeded in passing CIRA, the Climate Infrastructure Rehabilitation Act..."

Zane abruptly snapped out of his thoughts and swiveled in his bar stool to look at the images filling the screen. He was flabbergasted, the climate infrastructure legislation had passed through Congress, and in such a short time frame. It was good news, not just because it set a precedent that the US Administration could get things done, but it also gave more time to focus on the genetic technologies legislation.

"...This signature bill will be signed into law tomorrow, Saturday morning at the White House, and represents a major achievement for a President who has only been in office for two months. Next on the agenda for this Administration is the overhaul to Medicare to include genetic medicine and technology, which faces a much more complex political calculus to achieving legislative approval in Congress. The Administration, along with its consulting partner Syllabus Corporation, will be running a yet to be announced public consultation process in April and May to build support for the plan."

"In the Kashmir, Chinese, Russian, and European forces conducted coordinated drone raids into the mountainous region to neutralize ongoing terrorist activity spilling out into neighbouring regions. Russian and Chinese military forces have been cooperating with Western Liberal Bloc forces in the region over concerns terrorist elements may have acquired abandoned low-grade nuclear weapons, and are planning to use it to strike at either Chinese, Russian, or Western military infrastructure bordering the South Asian nuclear containment zone..."

"Doctor Fischer, you are suffering from anxiety, exhaustion, and high levels of stress. I noticed your heart rate and blood pressure are slightly elevated."

Zane ignored EVO as he shoveled his salad into his mouth, staring at the news updates flashing across the living room screen in front of him.

"In Canadian news, the Prime Minister and cabinet are set to start a weekend of intense meetings, with the objective of implementing additional measures to restrict access to offshore genetic technology clinics. Wealthy Canadians continue to illegally use the clinics as a means to secretly engineer offspring with technologies superior to what are offered by the Reproduction Bureau, the body that administers the Reproduction Lottery and state reproduction centres. New measures include higher fines, imprisonment, and denying citizenship to offspring. The government has set up a hotline for citizens to report anyone they suspect may have imported offspring or genetically enhanced material from these offshore facilities."

"In climate crisis news..."

EVO interrupted him again, *"Dr. Fischer, I would recommend turning off the news and going to bed for a minimum seven hour sleep, followed by morning exercises. May I disconnect the news updates."*

"Yes EVO."

The screen went blank and the room turned quiet.

"One more thing Zane."

"Yes EVO."

"Timothy just texted and would like to make a quick visit. He is on his way to a work function, but will be passing nearby. Should I tell him to visit another time?"

"No I haven't seen him in ages. Tell him he can come over now and you can buzz him straight through to my floor."

Ten minutes later, just as Zane stepped out of the shower, he heard a knock at the front door. He wrapped himself in a towel and opened the door.

"Zane Fischer, look at you, wearing nothing but a towel! Sorry about the impromptu visit, but I figured this was the only way I was going to see you between your busy work schedule!"

Zane laughed dryly, "ah Timothy, 'busy' is an understatement…"

"Well it's okay, I understand how you mere mortals need to slave like beasts to cover your bills," he winked.

"Hahaha, nice one," Zane replied sarcastically.

"Enough joking, I know you're tired, so I won't keep you up for too long. Do you mind if we try something unusual, it may help you relax?"

Timothy pulled out a small box of aromatized candles and a lighter from the bag he was carrying. He looked at Zane and smiled, "okay, I'm definitely not your exotic Ethiopian girlfriend, but I thought some incensed candles might bring a tad of ambiance to this sterile shoebox apartment."

Zane raised his eyebrows in mocked amusement, "fine, whatever floats your boat Mr. Timothy Klein."

Timothy smiled, pulling out two peculiar looking white keys from his pocket and proceeding to walk around the apartment, looking for a spot to install them. He eventually placed one in the bedroom and another in the living room, and then pressed a button on what appeared to be a remote. Almost immediately Zane felt a mildly unpleasant electric pulse ripple through his upper body, closing his eyes as the wave traveled from the EVO microchip implant in his left hand up into his head. The pulse quickly dissipated, and he opened his eyes, shaking his head in confusion. At first he didn't notice anything out of the ordinary; however, it wasn't long before he realized his vision was magically clear of tags, digital menus, and message updates.

"Feels weird, doesn't it eh?" Timothy said, as he lit a candle and went over to the electrical junction panel, cutting all the electricity to the unit. He placed the lavender scented candle on the kitchen counter, "no digital overlay, just the real world without the virtual. It's something the rich and the powerful frequently do to be able to think clearly, without the nagging interruptions from dear little EVO."

"You have a signal blocking key?" Zane gasped, incredulous.

"I do indeed! This one is pretty sophisticated, converting your EVO into a drone and using your online data to create a deep fake profile of you and your environment, thus fooling the network into thinking the fake is you."

"I thought signal blocking keys were illegal!" Zane exclaimed.

"No, only being caught with an unauthorized or unregistered signal blocking key is, but don't worry, this one is licenced and clean. Trust me, the last thing I want is problems with the Internet Police."

"So how long can we stay offline like this?"

"The licence on this one allows about twenty minutes, then device will warn me when it's time to reconnect."

"And what happens if you fail to connect in time?"

"So many questions Zane, well then again you've always been the guy that wants to know everything," Timothy laughed. "In a nutshell if the Internet Police were to catch us, they would request we reconnect to the network within a reasonable amount of time, or face having the device confiscated. The Internet Police, under the guise of public safety, is mostly concerned about cybercriminals, spies, and political dissidents, not rich people like me who pay expensive licences to access these things for some peace and quiet."

Zane sighed, Timothy's explanations seemed somewhat plausible, and he highly doubted his friend would risk flouting the law with an illegal signal blocker.

"Zane, time is limited, can you quickly put some clothes on so we can talk seriously for a bit?" Timothy asked, as he sauntered past his friend, taking a seat in the small pink sofa in the lounge.

Zane looked down and realized he was still in his towel. He went to the bedroom and slipped on shorts and a shirt, returning to sit in one of the bar stools facing Timothy. His friend was stretched out confidently in the sofa, one leg crossed over the other, his custom black designer outfit in sharp contrast to Zane's cheap mass-produced plastic furniture.

"Zane, I want to talk to you in private about your Syllabus project with the US government. You, Antonio Rubio, Jared Berg, and others have been all over network news the past few weeks - hard to miss what you've been up to. I must admit your performance in Congress was particularly impressive, maybe worth an Oscar for best supporting actor."

Zane laughed, "thanks! If you're referring my confrontations with John Smith, well he is one mean beast."

"Ah yes, that man is a nasty prick who cares only for himself, not his country; however, Zane he is nothing in comparison to what is coming. This President has a long litany of enemies: Libertarians, the religious right, domestic white supremacists, the health insurance industry, the privatized genetic medical system, just to name a few. Be prepared for all of them to bend the law to stop this 'Medicare genetic medicine for all plan' from happening. Any doubts about that, just look back at America's violent history with civil rights, abortion, taxation, and basic Medicare reform."

They stared at each other in silence for a minute, before Timothy asked," Do you happen to know the percentage of Americans who are monotheistic creationists?"

"Ah, I used to, I think it's around twenty-seven percent," Zane guessed.

"Not bad, a good memory, considering you didn't have EVO to help you. The number is in fact thirty-one percent of Americans. Thirty-one percent! These are people who believe the Earth is just over six thousand years old, and humans are a divine creation of a one-god entity. There are even a few of them who think the world is flat! Imagine that, in the 22nd Century there are still morons around who think the word is flat! Zane, how do you sell these people an argument to fund human genetic engineering for all, using taxpayer money? The answer is, you can't."

Zane nodded in agreement, "Timothy, you're entirely right, but this is the strategy the President decided to take. I presented her the options back in December, and she decided America should have Medicare funded genetic medicine for everyone, just like in other developed countries. She was adamantly against any state level and private sector participation, and it was certainly not my place to oppose her, especially if it meant imperilling Syllabus' chances of getting the second and third phases of this project."

He got up and walked to the kitchen, and was about to open the fridge dock to get a drink, when Timothy barked, "don't open that Zane! There are external sensors out there which work on a different frequency, they'll reactivate EVO and detect the signal blocking keys."

"Why should you be worried about the keys being detected if they're authorized Timothy?" Zane asked, realizing that Timothy had probably lied to him about the blocking keys being licenced.

He returned to the bar stool, cutting in before Timothy could reply. "Timothy, you are correct about the religious voters, the xenophobes, the insurance industry, the private healthcare providers, and the Libertarians; however, what can I do to stop a national government from taking the path it decides to take?"

"Correct, there is nothing you can do; however, Syllabus is now a pawn in the middle of two opposing factions: Social Democrats and Libertarians. This President and her base want genetic medicine added to Medicare, if they lose, they will blame Syllabus. If they win, Syllabus will be slammed by Libertarians and conservative Republicans for foisting 'genetic socialism' upon them. Either way Syllabus loses, which is why you need to resign from this project now. I know it's not ideal, but you can say it is beyond your capacity at this point in your career and they need to hire someone older and more experienced than you."

"Timothy, that's absurd! If I did that, I would be fired and my reputation badly damaged."

"Zane, sometimes it is best to take a step backwards in order to take two steps forward, and this is one case where you need to do it now, and urgently."

Zane paused for a moment before replying, "Timothy, that would be one big step backwards. I seized this opportunity because it was the silver bullet for my career, my bank account, and my reputation in the consulting community. Perhaps I made an unwise decision, but now it's too late for me to turn back the clock. What I promise to do is stay alert and take all the necessary safety precautions - I'm not a fool, I know this project is controversial in America."

Timothy was about to reply, but Zane raised his hand and shook his head, he'd had enough talking about the matter.

"Timothy thanks for coming over tonight, for taking the risk to go offline here and share your thoughts."

Timothy smiled affectionately, "Zane, you're my best buddy, I'm always on the lookout for you."

Zane grinned, Timothy was the closest thing he had to a friend. He had always been there for him, standing beside him when he told his parents he was not going into academia, that he wanted to be a strategic consultant. He remembered his mother's disappointment, his father's fury, the tears, the anger, that a son they had spent millions to have, who was supposed to be everything his sister could never be, was going to let them down. Zane walked away from them and Timothy filled the void.

"Timothy, before we have to go back online, I want you to promise me we can do this again, it was incredible, I still can't believe it's really possible."

"I promise bro'. There are even places where it is possible to spend as much time as one likes disconnected; however –"

Timothy was cut off as the signal blocker started to vibrate, it was time for them to connect to the Internet again. Zane watched as he turned the power back on and deactivated the signal blockers, collecting the two keys from the bedroom and the living room. Instantly EVO reactivated, and his vision was one again cluttered with digital tags and streams of data.

"Thanks for the hookup Zaney!" Timothy winked mischievously, "oh and before I forget, it sounds like you need a bit of a break. How about we meet up for a weekend on my new airship!"

Zane looked at Timothy, his eyes lighting up with excitement. "What? You have an airship, where the hell did you get a toy like that? Those things must cost a fortune!"

"Well I don't have it yet, I'm going to pick it up in Munich soon, and then I will be flying it back across the Atlantic. Probably with my newest girlfriend, a sexy young thing from Bavaria, the sales rep who sold it me!" Timothy chuckled.

"Okay Zane, I gotta run, I'm already late for this business cocktail event!"

He lay naked in bed staring at the ceiling shrouded in nighttime shadows, the covers tossed to one side. His head was buzzing with thoughts of what had happened earlier that evening with Timothy. It all seemed so surreal, like it had occurred in a dream, not in real life. Zane had never before slipped from EVO's grasp, other than his experiences in the Syllabus' reading rooms, where data blocking attenuated most, but not all of the device's intrusive capabilities. What had occurred tonight was far beyond those experiences, all of sudden he knew what it was like to be completely untethered, to see the world through his eyes without EVO's digital interference.

For his entire life he had been brainwashed that it was reckless to unplug from EVO, that to do so could have terrible consequences. That narrative was reinforced every day with tragic stories of people run over by delivery trucks, mutilated by drones, or permanently separated from their identities when their EVO malfunctioned, severing their connection to the Internet and rendering them invisible to the world. That was where the Internet Police proved to be indispensable, saving the lives and identities of people who were suddenly disconnected, while also combating the proliferation of illegally unregistered signal blocking keys used mostly by cybercriminals, terrorists, and foreign spies.

Now that he'd experienced the freedom, Zane couldn't resist the temptation to try it again. He wanted to be free, even if just for a few fleeting moments, from the implanted machine that never stopped monitoring, analyzing, and marketing his every desire. Yet it was futile, he knew being untethered from EVO and the Internet was a luxury afforded only upon the very rich and powerful, and he certainly would never have the means to acquire such a privilege.

He sighed in frustration, his thoughts returning to the day's events at Syllabus – Marko Ivanovic's dismissal, Sean Chan's appointment to project manager, the restructuring, and warnings from Jared Berg of dark and ominous threats to their safety. What was going to happen next? Were the Libertarians, the billionaires, the insurance companies, the old guard and the religious fundamentalists going to go on the offensive? If they did, what means were they going to use, and would they turn violent?

What about the President and the Social Democrats? What if they abruptly deviated from the plan set up with Syllabus? What is they suddenly called a Congressional vote, or brought their supporters to the streets, or provoked the opposition and then used executive powers to arrest and imprison them? And what about the Republicans, the big forgotten party in the middle? Were they waiting for the perfect moment to abandon their Congressional coalition deal with Social Democrats, turning the President into a lame duck, in the hope they could seize power in the next Presidential election?

"Dr. Fischer, it is quite late, you need to stop thinking and go to sleep."

"Euhh, yes EVO you're right. By the way, why have you started calling me Dr. Fischer?"

"I updated your name reference, as you are increasingly being referred to by your professional accreditation on the Internet. This is most likely due to your high public profile as a senior consultant for the US government."

"I see, makes sense. EVO I'm having difficulty getting to sleep because I'm worried about work. Can you activate some sedation?"

"I regret to inform you the vapour ampoules are empty; however, I can order replacements now if you like. Drone delivery will take six minutes."

"Yes, go ahead," he sighed, getting out of bed to use the bathroom.

As he stood over the sink he looked at himself in the mirror, the soft brown lights enhancing his naturally dark olive complexion, making him look more photogenic than one should at three in the morning. His hair was thick and overgrown, knotted into a dark woolly mat, which without the use of ample amounts of gel would have long since failed the company guidelines of professionalism. He took a swig of some mint mouthwash and gargled it around in his mouth, some of it spilling down his unshaven chin as he spat it into the sink. Looking briefly at his reflection in the mirror, he splashed his face a few times with cold water, and then grabbed a towel to wipe himself dry.

As he entered the kitchen he heard a 'clunk' come from the postal dock, the sound of a delivery drone depositing his package of sedatives. How lucky he was to have outside access, it meant the drones could just fly straight to his condo and deposit whatever he desired at any hour of the day. He thought of people living in internal apartments with no windows, like Madeleine, his one-night hookup on the fifty-third floor, they had to go to the postal rooms on each floor to pick up their deliveries.

He padded back to the bedroom and switched out the ampoules, sliding under the duvet cover, his head coming to rest on the puffed-up pillows. Within seconds the air was filled with the soothing scent of mint and lavender, the vapour quickly filling his lungs and knocking him into a deep drug induced sleep.

Zane opened his eyes and looked around. His apartment had vanished, instead he was out on a sailboat, anchored not too far from a rocky outcrop covered with scrubby vegetation. The water around him was a deep cobalt blue, the kind of blue one found in the Balearic Islands on a mid-summer day. He was standing naked on a diving plank, the crystal-clear waters below him teaming with fish and marine life. Behind him stood Maya and Timothy, whistling and encouraging Zane to dive into the water. It was hot, and a dry breeze was blowing starboard, ruffling the white canvas awnings that covered the aft section of the sailboat.

Elise Germain was there as well. She was wearing a light white cotton dress, and was seated at a table under the awning, sipping a cappuccino. She held her sunglasses in one hand, admiring Zane's nakedness, as he balanced out on the plank above the water. He looked back and winked, flexing his beautiful body for their benefit, and then dove out into the abyss, plunging down into the clear cool waters below. Down he went, diving and swimming deeper and deeper, ever deeper, until he was amongst rich sensual masses of fish and coral. Everywhere he looked there were coral and reeds, it was so rich, so colourful, so vibrant, like the kind of coral one found in aquariums, or videos from what the Great Barrier Reef looked like before the oceans started to die. He was mesmerized by the natural beauty, letting the brilliantly coloured reeds wrap themselves around his body, holding him and stroking his naked skin.

He looked up and saw Timothy and Maya dive in. They were waving at him from the surface, signalling to him to swim up to join them. Zane suddenly realized he had been down for some time, and needed to get air, he was about to swim for the surface, when he realized he couldn't, his body was ensnared in the corals and the reeds. He struggled, trying to pull himself free from their sensual embrace, but they refused to release him. He was trapped, and he was running out of air. He thrashed around, fighting, churning, tearing, his

222

desperate movements shredding his bare skin against the sharp edges of the colourful reef. All around him pieces of his flesh and blood filled the water, turning it a murky brown colour, as his vision filled with red and white stars from the lack of oxygen. It was no use, he was done for. He looked up and saw Timothy and Maya, they were still signalling to him, this time more and more frantically, as they realized his predicament, but seemed unable to help him. Zane struggled weakly, and then in desperation he opened his mouth and took a deep breath.

He jumped up in bed, covered in sweat, gasping for air. He looked around. He was in his room. The light shades were up and the mid-March sunlight was streaming in.

"Oh my god," he groaned out loud, "a dream, it was just a fucking dream."

"Dr. Fischer, you had a rather agitated sleep and your heart rate was quite accelerated prior to awakening. I took the liberty of opening the blackout shades and venting with treated outside air to increase oxygen levels."

"Thanks EVO."

The dream was perturbing, it seemed as if it were some terrible manifestation of his sense of entrapment and lack of control, being entangled in a project that had appeared so glamorous at the outset, but was rapidly transforming into something more ominous and foreboding.

Rubbing his eyes, he dragged himself out of bed to grab a quick shower, remembering it was laundry day just as EVO sent him a reminder. Annoyed, he tugged at the sweaty bed sheets, dumping them and a pile of dirty clothes into a laundry box outside his front door, to be retrieved and processed by the floor's laundry bot.

An hour later he was on the SkyTrain, on his way to meet Maya at the Fraser Riverside Walk.

Date Saturday March 8th, 2121

Zane ambled leisurely from the SkyTrain station towards the Fraser Riverside Walk, relishing in the glorious late Saturday morning sunshine. The March sky was a bright cloudless blue, and everywhere he looked there were hints of spring in the air. People were smiling, trees were covered in cherry blossoms, and the sun's rays had a warmth to them that called for one to lose some layers and show a bit of skin. He and Maya loved the river walk for their regular weekend strolls, its southern exposure lined with coffee shops, parks, and patios, and there were multiple connections to the SkyTrain and light rail network running its entire length.

A tap on his shoulder snapped him out of his dreamy state, and he turned around to see Maya standing in front of him with a big smile.

"Hey handsome, I saw you walking out of the station and ran to catch up," she huffed, a bit out of breath.

"Ha, nothing like being chased after by a beautiful woman on a gorgeous day!"

"Oh my Zane, so playful, look what a bit of spring can do to you! I'm curious what you'll be like when it really starts to warm up," she giggled.

"I turn into a Bengalese tiger!" he growled, laughing.

He gave her a big hug, as they walked into their favourite café to pick up two pre-ordered coffees to go, before heading off for a long afternoon meander along the riverside.

"So what you get up to last night handsome?" Maya asked.

"Ah, not too much, basically just attempted to have an early night. I really needed to catch up on sleep after all the crap we had to work through at the office yesterday."

"What's going on at work now?" she asked, "can you tell me?"

"Ah it's kind of classified at this point still."

"Zane, you and some Syllabus people, as well as a bunch of government experts were all over the major US news feeds last week. I even watched you take a grilling from that Californian Libertarian Senator, so don't tell me it's classified."

"Yeah you have a point. Well I can't be too specific, but we are undergoing a restructuring to better prepare ourselves for the last part of this project, the so-called consultative phase, where we have to promote the President's plan before it goes to a vote in Congress."

"Got it, sounds like a lot of work. I bet you are anxious for this to start to wrap up."

"It's my job to handle these sorts of things, but let's say this project is a few notches of stress beyond my level of tolerance. I'll be very happy to move onto something lower key."

"Any ideas as to when the American President will send this healthcare legislation to Congress?"

"Can't say exactly when; however, I can tell you I'll be very busy at work now that the President's Climate Infrastructure and Rehabilitation Act cleared Congress yesterday. I'm expecting to be part of the whole consultative phase, which means criss-crossing America to promote the bill in front of the public and local politicians. That is going to be extremely draining…"

He paused, suddenly feeling very tired, "God Maya, I'm really needing a holiday right now. I even had this dream last night, where I was on holiday with you, Timothy, and one of my firm's clients on some sail boat in the Mediterranean. We were out swimming, the sea was blue and flat like glass, there was the smell of figs, rosemary, and lavender; the air had a magical mid-summer texture to it."

"Oh my, sounds lovely!" Maya smiled.

"It was, until I got caught in layers upon layers of coral and weeds, and ended up drowning."

"Euuh, well at least it was just a dream," she said, as she stopped and wrapped her arms around him, holding him close to her. Her cheek was against his neck and her hands slid up his back, running over his ears and through his thick mat of dark curly hair. After a minute she gently released him from her embrace, her eyes staring intensely into his, tears rolling slowly down her cheeks.

"Hmm, what's up? Do you have something to tell me…" he tailed off timidly.

"I do," she smiled.

"What is it?" he asked curiously.

"You don't know Zane?"

"Don't know what? Ah, is it something I should be aware of?" he asked.

"It's happened Zane."

"What's happened?"

"Oh my, you really have no idea!" she laughed, wiping the tears from her cheeks. "Zane, our number was called a couple of days after we submitted our lottery application; there's been successful fertilization."

He looked at her stunned, his mouth wide open in bewilderment, unable to utter a word in response. Blindly ignoring his confused reaction, she wrapped her arms around him and hugged him tightly, her head pressed against his shoulder. My god, he was really going to have a child, this after swearing his entire life to never impose the suffering of the human condition upon an offspring. Had he made a mistake offering to help her? Had he broken his principles to maintain a relationship with a beautiful woman? Regardless, it was too late to turn back now, after this much investment, there was no way the Reproduction Bureau would consent to having the gestation aborted.

Elise Germain

Date - Monday March 10th, 2121

That Monday, while the rest of the group was dealing with restructuring and moving, Zane and Antonio had a productive time huddled with their small teams in Sean's conference room, getting to know each other while fleshing out their strategy for Phase Three. Their teams were closely knit, no surprise given both Zane and Antonio formed the foundation of Syllabus' scientific liaison with the US Administration. Zane's staff consisted of an economist and an actuary from Tel Aviv, and an Indian born data specialist from New Zealand, while Antonio's support was all American, including a geneticist, a Medicare economist, and a library scientist who straddled both of their teams.

It was a pleasant change having Antonio just as a colleague and not as a project manager. Being relieved of project management had brought his level of intensity down a few notches and suddenly it was once again possible for them have a more relaxed and open working relationship. The two of them collaborated well together, creating a dynamic that provided welcome relief from the intensity of hashing out their plans for the public consultation phase.

Those plans were developed using Zane's updated data analysis and modelling, directing them to focus on simple studies comparing quality of life for naturally conceived people versus genetically engineered people in the United States. This was the simplest way to show the public how genetic engineering was dividing America into two very different types of people. Their two teams decided to focus on presenting outcomes in cancers, neurodegenerative diseases, and pandemics, while avoiding fertility and IVF, which they knew would only provide fodder for religious extremists and white supremacists. They also ran budget simulations on the data, showing how the current situation was costing Americans trillions more than it would under the President's plan.

At around 18:45 Zane wrapped things up for the day, leaving his office early for his meeting with Elise Germain. As he walked to the elevators, he looked around the floor, observing that most of the meeting rooms, technology facilities, and work cubicles were now in place, occupied with junior consultants plugged like mindless drones into SyNet. He knew for them the work day had many more hours to go, where company needs always took priority for anyone serious about their career.

He sighed softly to himself, as he stepped into the elevator and punched in the override code, ensuring the lift would travel non-stop to the lobby. A couple of minutes later he was outside the building, seated on a bench at the agreed meeting point facing onto Memorial Plaza. The plaza was nearly empty, the rush hour crowd largely dissipated, affording Zane a clear view of its magnificent checkered black and grey surface. From where he was sitting, he could hear the dancing water fountains in the centre of plaza, which formed part of the memorial to the thousands of people who lost their lives to the terrible earthquake of July 23rd 2043.

It was hard to believe it had only been four days since the dinner on Thursday night in Washington. So many things had changed – a different project manager, a major restructuring, a new office, and dozens of additional employees. Friday night was even more

230

surreal, with the visit from Timothy and the terrible dream that followed. Then on Saturday, the news from Maya that he was still trying to comprehend.

Someone tapped him on the shoulder. He looked up and saw a short slender man standing before him, dressed in a black suit and a wool peak cap.

"Dr. Fischer, please follow me," the man said in a flat monotone.

Zane stood up and followed him across Memorial Plaza, past the main SkyTrain Station entrance. They arrived at the curb and were met by a small black vehicle. The side door slid open and they stepped inside, as it closed behind them. The vehicle remained stationary beside the curb for a couple of minutes and Zane wondered what was going on. Suddenly he heard a beep, and then felt a light shock in his arm, which rippled from his wrist into his head. He closed his eyes in mild discomfort, reopening them a moment later to see that he was disconnected from EVO and the Internet, just like what happened with Timothy on Friday night.

The man said, "we are now offline from the Internet. Your EVO has been deactivated and will remain so until the end of your meeting."

The vehicle pulled away from the curb, joining the traffic travelling westbound on Broadway Avenue. The late rush hour traffic was heavy, as trucks, cars, and service vehicles crawled at a slow steady speed, all controlled by the city's AI transit management network. They inched along Broadway, as it curved northwards, becoming Burrard Street, the city's most westerly north-south arterial. Burrard connected the long densely populated Broadway Uptown district with Salish City's Downtown, via the famous old Burrard Bridge, which along with The Lion's Gate, was one of only two the bridges to have survived the terrible 2043 earthquake.

The car squeezed over into the far-left lane just before Burrard Bridge, turning west onto Kitsilano Road, towards the city's most exclusive addresses scattered about parts of the forested Point Grey peninsula. They sat in silence, the man staring vacantly ahead, while Zane gazed in awe out the windows at the empty dimly lit roadway, trying to comprehend the world before his eyes. The sensation was disconcerting, it was the first time he had ever seen the outside world without augmented digital reality - there were no street signs, no advertising, and no digital billboards. Curiously even the physical streetscape looked subtly different, just enough to catch his attention. He stared outside, trying to understand what was missing, before coming to the icy realization that the version of the world everyone saw through their eyes, was really a digitally enhanced optical illusion, air-brushed by EVO and its retina lenses.

Zane guessed it must be about eight in the evening, as the mid-March sun slowly dipped below the horizon. This part of the city was almost uninhabited, turned into a vast regional park after the 2043 earthquake and fires wiped out most of the neighbourhoods that had existed here at the time. It was an area for the rich, a segment of the city's elite who preferred large isolated private mansions to the sumptuous glitzy penthouses of Downtown Salish City.

The car suddenly slowed down, turning past an open gate into a secluded tree-lined private drive. It followed the narrow winding

232

path, and about a minute later came to a stop in the middle of a smartly arranged gravel courtyard, framed with lush exotic vegetation and early blossoming spring flowers.

"Sir, we have arrived at our destination. We may exit the vehicle here."

Zane and the slender man stepped out of the car and walked up the stairs into the front lobby.

"May I take your coat sir."

"Yes please, thank you."

"Sir, you may proceed to your left and take a seat in the room at the end of the hallway."

"Are there any lights?"

"Don't worry sir, they will turn on as you make your way down the corridor."

Zane walked slowly down the passageway, his steps muffled by the thick carpeted floors. As he walked, the lights in the ceiling switched on one by one, illuminating perfectly placed pieces of artwork hanging from the eggshell white walls. He must have passed about a dozen closed doors before he arrived at the end, pausing to look back at the lobby, which was cloaked in darkness.

A moment later he stood in a large well-furnished sitting room adorned with stained-glass windows and silk drapes. The floors were covered in layers of plush pastel coloured Persian rugs, and a chandelier hung from the ceiling, its soft yellow light texturing the walls, book cabinets, and furnishings in gentle shadows. In the centre of the room was an antique coffee table placed between two large leather armchairs, and on the far wall stood a large glass liquor cabinet filled with crystal glasses and a selection of spirits, chocolates, and liqueurs. There was a gentle tip-tap of a clock, one of those rare antique standing clocks. It stood beside the liquor cabinet, and the time on its face showed just before eight-fifteen.

Never in his life had he seen such opulence. It was evident Elise Germain occupied a tier of society far beyond anything he had ever imagined possible, perhaps even beyond that of his billionaire friend Timothy. He felt so terribly insignificant standing in the middle of the sumptuously decorated study, wondering more than ever why Germain had the remotest interest in meeting a mere mortal like himself. If she wished an audience with Syllabus, why not meet Jared Berg, or for that matter the company CEO?

"Dr. Fischer, so glad you could make it."

Zane jumped in surprise, turning around to see Elise Germain walk through the doorway behind him.

"Would you care for a drink?"

"Yes please."

"What would you like? I have almost unlimited options," she smiled.

"Do you have any gin and tonic?"

"I do, Bombay and Schweppes."

"Perfect."

"Very good."

She walked to the cabinet and pulled out two crystal glasses and some bottles of alcohol. As she was preparing the drinks, the man in the black suit appeared carrying a tray containing a wooden cylinder and some sliced lemons. He placed it on the cabinet and left the room.

"What do you think of my assistant? He's very good, isn't he?"

"Yes, very thorough and polite," Zane replied.

"He's a customized AI droid, built and designed by Alpha Systems in Ontario; he's so real you wouldn't even know, it's almost eerie how we can make machines like that. I had him customized to be exactly like my favourite house servant who died several years ago in a traffic accident. Alpha Systems acquired his entire digital history and downloaded it to the droid's operating system, so it acts and sounds just like I remember him. He is so perfect, that to be honest there are times I even think it's him."

"Remarkable! I would have never known he wasn't human." Zane replied, incredulous.

Germain opened the wooden cylinder and took out several ice cubes, dropping them into each glass. She asked, "care from some slices of frozen lemon? They're from my garden."

"Yes please doctor."

"Zane, I think we can do away with calling each other doctor," she said as she finished preparing his drink. She handed him his glass and then poured herself a dark cherry coloured liqueur over ice, "Drambuie, my favourite."

"So welcome to my humble abode, my Vancouver home," she smiled.

He nodded politely at the reference to Salish City's former name.

"Zane before we get started, you should know we are completely offline here in case you haven't noticed. This house and compound are protected from the prying eyes and ears of the Internet using some remarkable technology that costs Zelion a lot of money and government licencing fees to maintain - part of the benefits of being CEO of a strategically important company. Have you ever experienced being offline like this before?"

"Never, this is quite novel for me," he lied.

"It takes getting used to. For example, EVO and much of the Internet dependent AI in the compound do not function properly when blocking is activated. Just in case you're wondering, it's all entirely legal, after all we do thankfully live in a liberal society, and not a totalitarian one. The important thing is I have to be very discreet about its use because it is not something the 'everyday man' has access to."

Germain looked at Zane and raised her glass with a smile, "to our success, to the success of the President's healthcare initiative."

They took a sip of their drinks, Germain motioning to Zane to take a seat in one of the two large leather armchairs placed around the coffee table in the middle of the room.

"Zane, I want to say I was very impressed with your testimony in Congress, you've done remarkably well. Those Libertarian Congressmen are like packs of ravenous wolves, especially the Senator from California, John Smith!"

"Well to be honest it's been a steep learning curve. At the start it was quite intimidating; however, with time I've become more accustomed to the whole process," he lied, knowing full well how much he hated being in a public position.

Germain continued, "well just make sure you don't get too comfortable, it's only going to get harder from here on in. Libertarians, the insurance industry, religious extremists, pseudo-scientists, and enemy states are going to do everything they can stop this legislation. We must fight this greed, ignorance, and corruption, to ensure all Americans get the same benefits that have allowed the rest of the developed world to experience such dramatic gains in lifespan and quality of life. We are at a critical junction - if the President succeeds, it would be most significant transformation of American healthcare in generations, putting all of us on a much better footing to confront the challenges of the 22nd Century."

She paused a moment, "tell me Zane, what do you think? Do you believe genetic technology is a human right? If so, will universal access resolve America's socio-economic crisis? Or do you believe additional measures are required to prevent their further decline?"

Germain picked up her glass and stared at him with her penetrating blue eyes. Besides the tick-tock of the clock, the room was dead quiet, not a sound, not a creak. He was confused, what did she want from him? Surely she knew he could not answer her without being in breach of his employment contract. Was this a trap to compromise his position? Yes he could say he believed universal access to genetic technology was a human right, after all that was central to this project; however, he could not go any further than that."

Zane was about to speak, when Germain interrupted him. "Zane, I understand you have contractual obligations, so I will save you the exercise of inventing a meaningless response. As Canadians we benefit from universal access to genetic medicine and technologies, so I believe it immoral that in America access is restricted based on wealth and privilege. America's arrangement is unsustainable and will lead to a wealthy genetically engineered class controlling an impoverish majority. This elite, as it is already starting to do, will use every means it can to reinforce its position, including emulating the Totalitarian Bloc's use of Engineered Virtual Organisms to monitor and manipulate its citizens."

She took a sip of her drink and then continued. "These Engineered Virtual Organisms, or EVO are an important part of my firm's business; nevertheless, I have long opposed their development. I believe genetically engineering the human body is one thing, but cybernetically enhancing it is another. Unfortunately, because of the financial rewards in a corporatist system, there is nothing I can do to stop my industry's race to develop more sophisticated iterations of EVO. All I can do is encourage America to open up genetic technologies to all its

238

citizens, before the elite and their use of EVO tip the country into a dark and unpredictable future."

There was a moment of silence and then she resumed with a lighter air, "Zane let's put the serious conversation aside for a moment. How about some marijuana to relax? Grown on this property by my gardeners, none of that synthetic garbage the government sells."

Feeling a sense of relief, he leaned back in his seat and watched as Germain opened the wooden box on the coffee table, revealing six perfectly rolled joints, a sealed glass vessel containing fresh leaves, and an aluminium cased vaporization device.

"Do you mind if we smoke instead of vapourizing? Nobody smokes anymore, they've lost contact with the beauty of the plant, the leaves, the aroma."

Without waiting for his answer, she picked up the lighter from the box, lit one of the rolls, and took a deep inhale, slowly exhaling a large plume of smoke that wafted up to the ceiling. After a few moments of silence she took another hit, and then passed the joint to Zane. He put it to his lips, taking a deep breath, and almost immediately started coughing as the sweet acrid smoke scratched his throat. He tried a second hit, this time holding it in his lungs for a few moments, before releasing a giant plume that mingled with the smoky haze clouding the air in the room.

He handed the joint back to Germain and she put it out, placing it on the ceramic ashtray on the coffee table. He took another swig of his drink and slumped lazily back into the chair. The marijuana was smooth, it's effects almost immediate.

"It's good isn't it, apart from the initial smoke?"

"Yeah, very much so. I feel it already," he mumbled.

Germain got up and walked across the room to one of the bookshelves.

"Zane, I know you are aware of the financial stakes for my industry surrounding this legislation. If it passes Congress, we will finally have access to a vast new market of nearly 500 million Americans. An enormous business opportunity; however, for fear of being accused of impropriety and corruption, none of us can get directly involved in the political process. This has meant that ever since this government took office, CEO's and senior people in my industry have had to minimize contact with high-level members of the US Administration and its strategic partners, which includes senior management at Syllabus."

Zane's interest peaked, curious to see where Germain was heading with the conversation. He couldn't help but think she was being slightly disingenuous when claiming she was minimizing contact with senior individuals involved in the gentech project. He need only think back to last Thursday night's dinner in Washington, where she and Robert Dumas, the CEO of MediGen openly spoke with Jared Berg, Marko Ivanovic, Antonio Rubio, and himself about the gentech legislation and what the US Administration and Syllabus were doing. It probably explained why Berg was so furious with Miko Tanaka for not reserving the entire restaurant to ensure maximum discretion, and possibly was part of the reason why Marko was fired. Regardless, Zane thought it would have been wiser on Berg's part to not have had the dinner, or at least not in Washington.

"Zane, this is where you come in: senior enough to have influence, but still sufficiently junior to not raise suspicion. So what am I asking you to do? All I need from you is to ensure the public engagement phase of this project generates sufficient support for this legislation to pass Congress on the best terms for my industry. If that happens, I can guarantee you a full directorship at my company, with exciting responsibilities developing this new American market for Zelion."

Zane was flabbergasted, Germain wasn't just offering him a job, she was asking him to put her company and her industry's interests ahead of those of the US Administration and the American public. He knew if he did so, it would put him in breach of his contract with Syllabus, leading to his dismissal should it ever be discovered. Before he could even formulate an answer, Germain started speaking again, deftly changing the topic of conversation.

"Do you read Zane?"

"Yes I do."

"I mean read Zane. Not EVO's bullshit osmotic novels and endless short form rubbish. I'm referring to books, paper books."

He blushed, "no I don't. I just don't have the time, and paper books are too expensive, too hard to find, and take up too much room in my forty-two square metre apartment. They are the joys of the rich Dr. Germain."

"Ah, indeed they are," she sighed wistfully, as she pulled a book from the shelf.

"This particular book, one of my personal favourites, was written in the early 20th Century, a period of intense transformation. Europe, the centre of the world at the time, was in the process of shifting from rule by monarchs to universal suffrage. Society was changing faster than the blink of an eye, all the social norms which had governed human interaction for generations went out the window. Despite the best efforts of the elite and the powerful, change could not be stopped, it could only be constrained for a short while, only to build up in intensity and explode in waves of protest and violence. Young people in Europe showed no respect for older generations, they were hungry for change, they demanded self-determination, universal suffrage, nation states, independence."

She opened to the front of the book and gave it to Zane, taking a seat. "Turn to page fourteen and read the next couple of pages."

Zane took the book, and without looking at the author's name, read the paragraphs on the few pages before him. As he read, the only sound was that of the tic-toc of the clock, and Germain's breathing from across the coffee table. The text was striking, it was as if it had been written today and not nearly two hundred years earlier, during the horrors of the Second World War.

"Zane, what you have in your hands is Stephan Zweig's *Die Welt von Gestern*', written by one of the giants of 20th Century literature. In that particular text he discusses a period of incredible scientific enlightenment and advancement in human civilization, much like ours. The advent of Western science and technology, the accessibility of it to the masses, the rise of human rights and self-awareness. The decline of common diseases and ailments, and a dramatic improvement in quality of life and standard of living."

"He explains how because of the Industrial Revolution, Europe and America suddenly had access to technology that in the past was unimaginable, even to kings and queens. Such technology – plumbing, electricity, automobiles, telephones, and washing machines were not just accessible to the monarchs and the industrialists, the industrial revolution also made them available to the new bourgeoisie of Europe's growing cities."

"It all came to a crash at the start of the 20th Century, as the masses of Europe, with such technology, prosperity, and opportunity at their feet, ignorantly threw it all to the wind, and revolted against the systems in place, ushering in an era of misery, death, and destruction. Why did they do it? Why were they so taken up with the 'isms' of the time - communism, nationalism, fascism, and socialism - that they were willing to risk total annihilation? They did it because they were raging against a powerful elite of aristocrats and powerful industrialists who through divinity and wealth refused to yield to demands for more equality, democracy, and self-determination. For the masses, who believed they had little to lose, going down the dark abyss of violence, war, and revolution was a price worth paying to end a thousand years of rule by absolute monarchs who owned it all. What they didn't bet on, was the monarchs being replaced by new tyrants, who employed the mechanization of the Industrial Revolution to commit murder on a scale never before imagined."

Zane hung onto every word Germain uttered, the marijuana enhancing his senses, his vision crystal clear without the distractions of the virtual world.

Germain looked at him and smiled, "it's intense isn't it? Especially being offline, free of the virtual distractions."

"It is intense, I've never smoked it before..."

"...just like I'm sure you've never been offline before."

In a moment of carelessness, Zane nearly let his secret out, but was cut off as Germain continued. "Zweig committed suicide in the middle of World War Two, convinced the barbarians would win. In the end they didn't that time; nevertheless, they returned in the early 21st Century, in the form of vested interests and big oil money, selling a catchy populist idea that climate change was a hoax concocted by scientists and intellectuals to ruin economic growth. It wasn't long before they took power in America, Brazil, Indonesia, India, and Russia, and once in control, led us sleep-walking into a full-blown climate and ecological crisis, which could only end with the collapse of human civilization."

"Ultimately civilization was saved by four very distinct events. The first one was a unified liberal E.U., which moved to quickly modernise and remove carbon from their infrastructure, and assist non-aligned states to do the same. The second was the decision by China's totalitarian government to apply brute force to eliminate carbon from its economy and those of its smaller trading partners. The third was the mega thrust earthquake of 2043, which transformed human settlement on the Pacific Coast of North America into dense and energy efficient cities built for

244

earthquakes and climate change. The final event was a terrifying result of how climate change was making us behave in dangerous and irrational ways. The Small Nuclear War fought between India and Pakistan over the Kashmir used just twenty hydrogen bombs; however, they were sufficient to destroy civilization on the entire Indian sub-continent, exterminating nearly a half-billion people, wiping out the economies of India and Pakistan, and crushing Sri Lanka, Bangladesh, Burma, Iran, and Afghanistan in the aftermath. An ironic footnote to that war: it instantly extinguished carbon emissions from that part of the world, sparing us a degree of additional warming."

The air in the room was still and humid. Germain stood up walked back to the cabinet, filling her glass with more liqueur, while preparing another gin and tonic for Zane. Taking a seat, she passed Zane his glass and then reached over and lit another joint, inhaling deeply, before passing it to Zane.

He took another two deep puffs and started to feel the room spin, his heart accelerating and a light sheen of sweat forming on his back.

"Do you mind if we open a window?" he asked.

"Of course not."

Germain stood up and walked to one the large bay windows. She drew open the curtains and swung out one of the windows, letting a gentle ocean breeze drift into the smoke-filled room. He could hear the sound of the sea and the calls of some sea birds. It was a sound he rarely heard, after all there were never any birds by his apartment, just drones, thousands of them delivering parcels, a constant hum of rotors and electric motors.

"Zane, our evening is nearly done. I wish to conclude our time together with some final words of reflection."

He looked up at her, as she stood in the middle of the room.

"The weeks ahead will not be easy, expect your data analysis and your credibility to be contested at every juncture. Our enemies will say your analysis is flawed, fake, skewed, a hoax. They will say you have vested interests, that you're being paid to lie by big foreign gentech firms like mine. As they get more desperate, they may even resort to violence. Through the coming storm you must fight back with facts and reason, standing up for every American to have access to a technology that should be publicly accessible. Zane if our side fails, then just as in *Die Welt von Gestern'*, we may well see the beginning of a new and terrible cycle of tyranny and revolt."

Germain walked past Zane and out the door, leaving him alone in the room, seated in the leather chair with his drink in hand. The clock continued its relentless tic-toc, as the smoke slowly dissipated, replaced with fresh spring sea air drifting in through the window. He sat patiently, reflecting in the silence. He agreed with Germain, America's healthcare system had to change, it needed to universalize access to 22nd Century medicine before it was too late. The problem was those fighting for change were largely disingenuous regarding their intentions, many of them with ulterior motives to use the healthcare legislation for financial gain and to push their own nebulous agendas. How tragic it was that neither side of the healthcare debate had the interests of the

American public at heart, instead they were both blinded by their own greed and self-interest.

The droid in the black suit appeared at the doorway.

"Sir, I hope you enjoyed your evening. If you may, please follow me."

Zane stood up and followed him down the long hallway, the lights turning on as they walked towards the front foyer. He wondered, looking at the back of robot, if the machine had a conscious. Did it think? Was it sentient? Did it feel pain and suffering like the deceased human being it was designed to replace? Improbable for now, given how primitive AI still was; however, he had no doubt it was a real possibility in a not too distant future.

They arrived at the front entrance and the droid disappeared momentarily, returning with Zane's coat. He helped Zane put it on, and then led him down the steps to the same black vehicle parked in the courtyard.

"Sir, the car will take you directly to Memorial Plaza. In twenty minutes the blocking system in the vehicle will deactivate, reconnecting you and your EVO to the Internet. Have a good evening."

Date - Tuesday March 11th, 2121

Tuesday morning Zane walked out of the SkyTrain station at Memorial Plaza, a familiar cup of coffee in hand from his favourite coffee shop, his mind still analyzing yesterday evening, churning the events over and over in his head. Elise Germain, billionaire, CEO of one of the world's largest genetic technology firms. Did she really offer him job last night as a director, in exchange for putting her company and her industry's interests ahead of those of Syllabus, the US Administration, and the American public, or did he misunderstand what she meant? Ultimately it didn't matter, if the contents of the meeting leaked, he knew they could be used against him, potentially leading to accusations of impropriety, dismissal, and potential criminal charges for corruption. It was an error in judgement to have met her last night, and he swore to never make such a mistake again.

His thoughts were interrupted when he saw a large number of people gathered in the rain at the far end of Memorial Plaza. They were clustered near the entrance to Syllabus Tower, holding drenched American flags and shouting at one another, while lightly armed police officers attempted to keep them apart and push them away from the building doors. As Zane approached the tower, he was corralled aside with other people, where he was searched and then asked to finish or dispose of his coffee. Trying not to burn his tongue, he finished the hot drink as fast as he could and then was escorted past the crowd into the building.

"Man, what the hell is going on downstairs?" Zane asked Leyla, as he dropped into her new office at the southwest corner of Floor 100.

"Oh it's a circus Zane, three main groups protesting Syllabus and its involvement in the gentech legislation. One thinks Syllabus is part of a global conspiracy to turn Americans into genetically engineered robots, another thinks the legislation is a government plot to implement a tax hike to fund a giant socialist project, while the third is actually in favour of the project, but thinks it should be an American consulting firm doing the implementation, not us."

Robbie breezed in through the door, holding a large mug of coffee in one hand and a croissant in the other.

"Hey guys!" he grinned, taking a small bite of the end of his croissant, some flakes of it falling onto his tight black t-shirt. "I don't know about you, but I took a cab in this morning and got dropped off underground. I didn't want to deal with protestors given the shit load of work we have to get through this week."

"Yeah good idea, I think it's going to be an ongoing thing these protests," Zane replied.

"Well you guys could come in earlier like I do. Protestors are lazy, there was no one here when I arrived at 6:45 in the morning," Leyla quipped, swivelling in her chair to look at Robbie standing by the front door.

"Yeah, but Leyla my dear neither Robbie nor I own a luxury three-bedroom apartment a block away from work."

"True, I guess that's a minor detail I forgot about …Oh a message from Sean to meet him in his meeting room right away. You guys get that?"

"Yeah," they answered, "I guess we should head over there."

They filed out of the room, stopping along the way for coffee and the complimentary morning croissants set in a basket beside the coffee machine.

"Hey everyone, welcome to Syllabus, Floor 100, where never have so few been hated by so many," Sean dryly joked, as everyone took their seats.

"As you all know from the news this weekend, the Climate Infrastructure and Rehabilitation Act, CIRA as it's better known, passed Congress and was signed into law. This wonderful news means our project is now front and centre, with all the media and political attention that comes with it. Given Syllabus' very visible role, it should be of no surprise we have a not so small crowd gathered outside our front door this morning. We can expect these crowds to be a fixture, especially with warm sunny spring days on their way."

"So without further delay, I have the following information to give you from security services. They are asking all of us to activate our security monitoring applications inside EVO, so they can alert us in the unlikely event of an incident nearby, or in the building. I am also asking all of you to avoid using public transportation to come to work, instead Syllabus will pay for all of you to use authorized cab services, which will drive you directly into the secure underground drop off area in the building. This will be protocol for the remainder of this project."

"In the unlikely situation there is an incident, I will lock down access to the floor and provide you with further instructions as I get them from building security services."

"Any questions?"

"This cab thing, does it include me?" Leyla asked, "I mean I only live a block away from here."

"Leyla it does. I know it's an inconvenience, but the last thing we want is you being tracked home by a group of protestors."

Zane anxiously raised his hand, "Sean I live far from here, forcing me to commute by cab will take hours! Can the company provide me temporary accommodation near the office?"

"Yes I've got that covered! For your information, on the same floor as the company fitness facilities, there are two dozen small serviced apartments, which I can vouch are of an excellent standard, having been staying in one since my arrival. These suites are at your disposal should you need one. Would any of you like me to reserve one for you?"

Out of the team, only Zane and Antonio raised their hands – no surprise, given everyone else either lived near work, or were more than pleased to enjoy free door to door cab service.

"Great, I will reserve two apartments, blocking them off from tonight through to the end of the project."

"Just curious, what about our support staff? What do we tell them?" Anita asked.

"I'll deal with that. My plan is to send out a broadcast message asking them to be vigilant when entering and exiting the building. They are not considered to be of high asset value like yourselves, so Syllabus will not be offering them transport and company accommodation. "

After the meeting Zane, Antonio, Miko, and Sean stayed behind to review revised security arrangements for their public engagements in the United States during phase three of the project. Under the new plan, the US Department of Internal Security was now in charge of all security, and had instructed all accommodation be in premium, high security hotels.

"Hey Antonio, you got a moment to chat a bit more?" Zane asked, as the two of them left Sean's meeting room.

"I do, how about we head over to my office?"

Antonio's office was still disorganized. None of the company art was on the walls, a wall calendar and a map were still on the floor, and scattered about the room were several piles of gadgets and paper books on human and animal genetics.

"Sorry about the state of things in here, I've had my hands a bit full lately!"

"Ah no problem, my office isn't much better," Zane laughed, as they both sat down.

"I'm guessing you want to chat about what's going on," Antonio said, as he leaned back with his arms behind his head.

"Yeah I do, how did you guess?" Zane joked.

"Not too hard to figure it out," Antonio smiled. "So what exactly is on your mind?"

"Antonio, you and I are the only two in this office facing the public, everyone else is back-end support, sheltered from the storm we are going to confront in the weeks ahead."

"True, but wouldn't you rather be on the frontlines than stuck here as a glorified secretary? Zane, we get all the fame, the excitement, and the glory!"

"Ah yes, the fame, the excitement and the glory! Along with the bonus of maybe being knocked off by some nut case libertarian!" Zane laughed, rocking his chair slowly back and forth.

"Zane it comes with job. I can think of a few cases where employees of a client sent me menacing threats because they didn't like the restructuring we were implementing. People hate change, they fear disruption, and the bigger it is, the more determined the resistance."

Zane ran his hands through his curly hair, "Antonio, the deeper we get into this, the more I'm convinced the President shouldn't have gone for the centralized Medicare option. Americans have a deep distrust for what government and experts can offer, and I think this plan is a step too far for them. I wish I could have convinced her to take a more moderate approach by including some private insurers and private clinics, but I didn't want to put our contract at risk, because I had a feeling her mind was made up even before my presentation to her in December."

"You made a wise move, the last thing we wanted was to risk losing the contract, especially one of this size and prestige." Antonio paused a moment before adding," Management consulting is a delicate balance between pushing for the change we believe will have the best outcome, and accepting what the client wants. Once the client makes their choice, our job is to adapt and implement it, putting our personal opinions aside."

There was a knock at Antonio's office door, as Robbie leaned in through doorway.

"Sorry to interrupt you guys. Leyla, Anita, and I wanted you to check out an example of some of the AI and communications tools we've been working on, give you an idea of what they are capable of doing."

Zane and Antonio got up and followed Robbie over to Anita's area of the floor, where she and Leyla were discussing their new EVO integrated application, which had gone live that morning in selected target markets."

"Hey you two! Bet you guys are looking forward to going the US!" Anita joked.

"Oh, I'd rather not talk about it," Zane replied.

"Ah yes, Zane's not too happy about meeting 'ordinary Americans', but he'll soon find out they're not all that bad!" Antonio laughed. "Anyways, what you guys got to show us?"

"A shaper application," Anita answered.

"Hmmm, what is a 'shaper application'?" Antonio asked, raising his eyebrows in obvious curiosity.

Anita smiled, enjoying the attention, "well in the context of this project, a 'shaper' is a viral propaganda bot, which bonds to a user's EVO when they interact with a friend who already has the bot. Once installed, using meta data, it instantly learns your opinions and politics surrounding gentech, and then adapts all kinds of pertinent content displayed in your news to synchronize with your opinions. This is called the baiting process, designed to reinforce and agree with your opinions, to reduce the probability you will try delete it when you discover it's bonded to your EVO."

"And how does the shaper get installed in the first place?" Zane asked.

"Well this is where your research came in very handy Zane. What we did was use your data analysis to identify Americans who are strong supporters of gentech, and then have the President's campaigners contact them, asking them to install the shaper on their EVO, giving it access to their social networks. Once accepted, the shaper burrows into their social networks, sending itself to contacts in swing states who identify as slightly in favour, slightly against, or undecided about gentech."

"Amazing..." Zane said in disbelief.

Anita went on to explain the shaper was engineered to then imperceptibly shape the content the user receives to gradually shift their opinions on genetic medicine and technology. It was a fast learner, retreating to offer less provocative content whenever it detected resistance, and advancing more aggressive content when it detected acceptance. It was designed to be ruthless, constantly learning about you to keep you engaged, and never losing sight of changing your opinions as fast as possible.

Date - Friday March 11th, 2121 to March 31st, 2121

For most of the rest of March, Zane's world shrank to nothingness, his social life evaporating as he spent nearly all of his waking hours slaving away on Floor 100. The long days meant commuting home to Lougheed City was impossible, and he ended up taking Sean's offer, temporarily relocating to one of the tiny apartments the company maintained on the leisure and sports floor of the tower. Living at work came with plenty of benefits: unlimited free meals, free gym access, a housekeeping service, and an easy commute. It was so easy, he probably would have never left the building if it weren't for Maya insisting he spend a few nights with her at her place.

In the second week of March, Steve McNeill flew out from Washington for a week, bringing with him his team of scientists and specialists, as well as security experts from the FBI. His visit was intended for them to put together the public engagement phase of the project; however, conflict immediately arose between Syllabus and McNeill and his experts. The Syllabus team, led by Zane, Antonio, and Miko wanted to set up a broad public consultation program, running several thousand focus groups led by local medical experts, as well as a dozen large public town halls run by Syllabus in conjunction with the US Administration. They believed this was the most effective way to build public support; however, McNeill and the US Administration disagreed, they were adamant there was not enough time to run the focus groups, and wanted to only do the townhalls in very large formats, using a small number of experts that included Antonio and Zane.

McNeill and the US Administration were unrelenting, they had a tight timeline and wanted the public engagement phase completed by mid-May to get the legislation through Congress before the summer recess. Ultimately the two sides were unable to come to a compromise, forcing Jared Berg to get involved and order Zane, Antonio, Miko, and the rest of the staff to follow McNeill's instructions and put the Syllabus agenda aside. They had no choice but to listen, and reluctantly cancelled the public focus groups and proceeded to organize the large format townhalls to McNeill's specifications.

Within days of McNeill departing, Miko finalized and released the approved schedule. They were to start in Burlington, Vermont, then move down the East Coast to New York, before moving to Seattle after a long weekend. From Seattle they were to spend two weeks travelling down the West Coast, ending in Orange County, California. From there, they had a few more stops in Texas, Florida and the South, before ending in suburban Washington in late May, in time for the President to send the legislation to Congress.

With the travel schedule finalized, Zane contacted Timothy to see if the offer to fly in his airship was still on the table, and if so would he be open to flying back together from New York to Seattle. Timothy immediately replied, thrilled to hear from Zane after so many weeks of radio silence. It was agreed to meet in New York after Zane's townhall, while Timothy would use the opportunity to get to the city for some long delayed business meetings he had been meaning to have with lenders. With everything confirmed, Zane informed Miko he would be making his own way to Seattle from New York City.

It all seemed to be quickly coalescing together, when suddenly everything took a dramatic turn one late morning on the last day of March. It was around nine in the morning, and Zane had just arrived at the building after having spent Saturday and Sunday night at Maya's. He was in the elevator travelling from the underground cab drop off to his company apartment, when the fire alarms suddenly sounded through the entire 101 floor tower. The lift immediately decelerated, the doors opening on the twenty-ninth floor offices of some financial services company. He stepped out of the elevator, and was instantly swept up in an anxious crowd shuffling for the fire exits and the long slow descent to Memorial Plaza.

Upon exiting to street level, he could see the plaza, shopping centre, and SkyTrain station were all closed to the public; furthermore, there were dozens of police and fire personnel positioned at every major entry point, blocking the movement of people in and out of the public space. Concerned there may be a security threat, Zane decided not linger in the shadow of the tower, and instead made his way through the throngs of people to a corner just near the entry to the shopping centre, where he was able to locate a small piece of concrete to sit on and watch the growing crowd.

As he sat down and the adrenaline of the moment dissipated, he suddenly noticed his EVO had gone completely offline, making it impossible to contact his team and determine the cause of all the chaos. In listening to the conversations around him, he soon realized everybody was encountering the same problem, which meant it was probably a general Internet shut down, something he had never before experienced. With the blackout and lack of information, people around him started wondering if the cause was a cyber-attack, a fire in the building, or maybe even a security threat. Zane could sense some people around him were worried there was a security issue and were wondering why the police were not reactivating the Internet to transmit emergency information through EVO. As if to allay their concerns, messages suddenly started broadcasting from loud speakers, asking everyone to remain calm and not exit the security perimetre.

The messages seemed to relax the crowd, and soon enough his attention shifted to observing how people were reacting to being unplugged from EVO and the Internet. There were all kinds of reactions; however, he got the most amusement observing people his age and younger, who probably had never been offline in their lives. They were like infants, curiously and comically grasping at a novel world they had never before encountered. As for older people, the reactions were quite different, mostly consisting of exclamations of surprise, confusion, and delight, as they rediscovered seeing, feeling, and hearing the world as they had known it before the era of permanent augmented reality.

After a while Zane tired of watching the people around him, his head starting to buzz from the noise of the crowd and the constant announcements from the loudspeakers. He decided it was worth trying to see if he could escape to one of the side streets, where there would almost certainly be more room to stretch out. He left the patch of grass and pushed his way through the crowd toward one of the exits, but was abruptly stopped by a large burly police officer who told him it was prohibited to exit the plaza. When he asked why, the officer explained that outside the security perimetre the Internet was still working, which meant anyone who exited the security zone risked being run over by a drone or vehicle if their EVO did not reactivate properly.

Frustrated, he turned back into the crowd, and was just about to consider trying to search for his colleagues when the Internet suddenly reactivated. Immediately there was total confusion and pandemonium, which then lasted about an hour as the Internet service surged on and off, overloaded by a tsunami of data that had accumulated in cyberspace and was now being dumped onto the thousands of people jammed into the plaza. Finally, about an hour later, he was able to locate his colleagues who had only just exited the building and were standing exhausted at the lobby doors.

"My god I can't believe we just descended a hundred flights of stairs!! I thought we were never going to reach the bottom!" Anita gasped, out of breath.

"Yeah, my legs are finished!" Miko added.

"Zane, do you know what the hell is going on? The Internet is off in the building and EVO still isn't working for me," Anita asked.

"Well I don't know much more than you guys, it's been the same down here in the plaza – no EVO, no Internet, no information. The police had us all corralled inside the plaza for the past few hours, not allowing anyone out for fear someone may get run over by a -"

Leyla cut in, "ah guys my EVO is back on and I have a stable Internet connection. It seems there were several major domestic terror attacks in the US related to gentech, one on a private hospital facility just outside Houston, another at a government Medicare clinic in Seattle, and several others that are still ongoing. In Seattle it seems a passerby tossed an explosive device into a

Medicare clinic; however, luckily it didn't detonate. The perpetrator was caught by local police and has also been identified as having connections to right-wing religious fundamentalism."

"Holy fuck, do you guys see the information on the Houston attack?" Robbie exclaimed anxiously.

Zane's EVO was already on the news update, images of injured people, body parts, rubble, and first responders filling his retina screen. He could see what had happened, that several gunmen had entered the reproductive technologies wing of a private hospital and opened fire on everyone inside, before blowing themselves up using explosive vests. There were hundreds of injured and many dead, and it was already confirmed the terrorists were anti-gentech religious extremists, who believed Americans needed to stop the "apocalypse" and take arms against the President's plan to impose human genetic technology on the country.

Zane sat alone in the cab, stuck in traffic somewhere on the freeway between Salish City and Burquitlam. A heavy evening rain was cascading down the windows, blurring whatever he could see through the glass and turning the street lights into blotches of white and yellow light. It felt strange to be going back to his apartment, he hadn't been there since the security protocols had been put in place back on March 11th; however, after all the day's chaos he desperately felt he needed to put space between himself and Syllabus, even if just for one night.

His screen lit up, it was a call from Maya.

"Hey you!"

"Hey! Just hang on, the cab has hologram functionality, let me put your call on there."

A moment later Maya's hologram appeared seated on the bench in front of him.

"Much better! Can you see me?" he asked.

"Yeah I can, it's perfect! It's like you're sitting on my sofa right here in the living room!" She giggled.

"Well I'm definitely not in your living room! I'm stuck in traffic somewhere between Salish City and Burquitlam, going at about half a kilometre an hour!"

"Oh, poor you! You know you could have come over again tonight!"

"No, after all that happened today I felt I needed to go home to something familiar, even if my condominium is about as sterile as a hotel room," he laughed.

"Gotcha, that's okay," she smiled.

"Zane, I just want to say you're special to me. I feel so fortunate for our random meeting on that mountain in Squamish, it forever changed my life…"

He smiled at her and was about to reply, when she asked, "do you want to see something pretty amazing?"

Zane smiled, "sure, especially if it helps me forget about the world's problems."

"Well I think you'll like what I've got to show you then!"

Suddenly a hologram image popped up in the middle of the cab just to the left of Maya. Zane jumped in surprise, wondering what it was. The image was cylindrical in shape, and had a tiny barely humanoid form suspended in some sort of clear liquid.

"What do you think Dr. Fischer?" Maya asked, smiling.

"Oh my god, it's…"

"It is!

He reached out with his hand and touched the hologram before him, his fingers pointing at the large head and at what seemed to be a tiny beating heart. Maya did the same thing, their hands connecting over the tiny image floating in the middle of the cab.

"Amazing…" he mumbled.

"It is, isn't it? Another life, made from you and I," Maya whispered.

For a couple of minutes he sat watching the floating form suspended in the middle of the cab, then suddenly the image faded and Maya waved at him.

"I've got to get going Zane, I have a late evening department call in a few minutes and then I need to pack for my meetings in Bologna and Paris. I'll be back in Salish City in ten days, hopefully we can see each other then."

"I'll probably be down in America by then, but I'm sure we can find time to chat, even for just a few minutes."

"For sure! Please be safe Zane. Today's events should serve as a wake-up call."

He smiled, wanting to say he cared for her, but instead said, "thanks, I promise to be safe…you take care too."

She blew him a kiss and her hologram image vanished.

He leaned back in the seat and closed his eyes, overcome with emotion. Maya truly seemed to care for him, not just as someone to hang out with and enjoy sex, or to reproduce with and have a baby, but as someone she actually loved. He wondered if it was possible. Could they "love" each other? Or was he foolishly imagining it? After all, in the 22nd Century nobody was supposed to love anyone other than themselves. Up until now every human transaction he had experienced in his life was constructed to optimize self-worth, pleasure, vanity, and status. Surely this one was no different? Or was it? Was she, as someone who had lived a different kind of life, capable of loving someone with no conditions and no demands? It was hard for him to comprehend, his societal conditioning so ingrained into his being.

Tired and anxious, he opened his eyes to see where they were, only to discover he was still stuck in traffic somewhere on the freeway. Frustrated, his thoughts drifted from Maya back to the terror attacks and the chaotic evacuation of the Syllabus Tower. The day's chaos had brought everything into focus. No longer was it possible to look at the project through the detached filtered lenses of mathematical models and data analyses, suddenly it was visceral, violent, and terrifyingly human.

The reaction at Syllabus to the attacks was swift and decisive. As soon as everyone was back in the building after the evacuation, Jared Berg and Sean Chan sent out an urgent message for a general meeting to discuss new security protocols for the entire company and in particular for Floor 100. In the meeting the two of them explained that as soon as they heard about the threats, Syllabus and the local police took the precaution to evacuate the entire area, affecting not just Floor 100 and Syllabus, but also all the other companies in the building, as well as the adjacent shopping centre, City Hall, and the Chinese Imperial Bank of Canada building. The police pushed for the evacuation because videos from some of the attacks showed terrorists calling on fanatics to strike other organizations involved in the gentech legislation. They explained that for foreseeable future, the Salish City police department would install a concrete perimetre around the tower, and anything and everyone entering would have to go through a pre-clearance check in order to gain access.

He sighed despondently, looking out the cab window at Burquitlam's vast sea of skyscrapers gleaming around him, filling the sky with bright flickering lights. The rain had let up a bit, and the cloud cover had lifted slightly, making it possible to see some of the tops of the buildings. He could tell from the rumbling trains and commuter rail that the cab was approaching the enormous urban rail hub at Lougheed City, which meant it wouldn't be much longer before he arrived home. Home, whatever that meant in the 22nd Century, stuck in a tiny glass and concrete box, dozens and dozens of floors above the ground.

He rubbed his eyes, feeling terribly conflicted about his job. The more he worked on this project, the harder it was to completely agree with either side of the gentech debate raging in America. On one hand he agreed with the President, Steve McNeill, and Elise Germain, who contended everyone should have access to genetic medicine, including the right to have a genetically engineered child, just like the baby he and Maya had conceived. Yet on the other hand he wondered about the consequences of such decisions. Was it right that in Canada there were no more naturally conceived children? Was it right that every Canadian was forced to use genetic engineering and artificial intelligence? Or that mothers used gestation pods to create their offspring, never becoming pregnant and never forming a biological bond with their offspring?

Was this technology dangerous, unnatural, and ungodly, as so many opponents to the President's legislation claimed? Did it need to be stopped, protecting ordinary Americans from a technology they had not yet been exposed to? Was there reason to the madness behind the religious zealots who were violently trying to stop the march of human ingenuity into the lives of ordinary Americans? In its rush to escape the human condition, were humans setting themselves up for some unknown and terrifying reckoning that was still lurking below the horizon? Or was scientific intervention in the genetic code simply a natural continuation of evolution, where humans were finally masters of their own destiny? The naysayers in America were right on at least one point: the clock could not be rewound if in the future it were discovered human genetic intervention was a mistake.

"Dr. Fischer."

Zane jumped, *"yes EVO."*

"As you can see, you have reached the Lougheed City exit; however, the Internet has informed me there has been severe flooding at the base of the exit ramp, and traffic is stopped until the water can be cleared. It is possible you will be stuck here for another couple of hours."

"Oh no! Should I get out and walk?"

"Under Syllabus' emergency security protocol you are not allowed to walk outside without authorization. If you exit the vehicle I will be required to inform Syllabus and you could be sanctioned."

Zane sighed, he felt trapped like an animal in a cage at a zoo. Frustrated, he reached into his shoulder bag and pulled out a small vial of sleep capsules, popping three into his mouth. In an instant they dissolved on his tongue, leaving a sweet citrus flavour on his pallet.

"EVO, set an alarm for when the cab is within two minutes of the destination."

"Alarm set."

Within a couple of minutes the passenger cabin in the cab started to slowly twist and turn, forming a dizzying tunnel of billions of pulsating multicoloured points of light, flashing in and out of focus. He started to accelerate down the tunnel, faster, and faster, and faster, and then suddenly a miniscule point of brilliant white light appeared way off in the distance, seemingly billions of kilometres ahead. Relentlessly, in a steadily growing crescendo of white noise, the point of light grew, consuming the collage of colours like a merciless cancer steadily destroying every living vibrant cell in its path. Then abruptly, just as the white light filled his entire view, he found himself sitting beside Maya in a silent, brightly lit, white, porcelain-tiled hospital ward.

The two of them were seated on a bench holding each other excitedly, as a nurse entered the room, carrying a newly born baby wrapped in a freshly pressed down blanket. The nurse had a distant sombre look on his face, as he slowly approached them with their child in his arms, placing the tiny package in a cradle in front of them. They thanked him and then looked down at the child before them, gently folding back the covers of the blanket to reveal its face. Immediately they both screamed in terror, as in an instant their excitement turned to horror, their child a twisted and deformed monster with a large unsightly head and a contorted hideous face. The elephant child resembled neither of them, it was as if it were the result of a genetic experiment gone terribly wrong.

Zane was mortified, looking down at them from one of the windows were Jared Berg, Steve McNeill, and Senator John Smith. His gaze darted nervously to the other windows, which were filled with the faces of all of his colleagues, and other random people. Everyone was pointing their fingers at him, laughing hysterically and shouting insults. He lowered his eyes in shame, turning to look at Maya, but she had fled with the nurse, and instead Elise Germain was seated beside him, angrily shaking the hideous child in the air. Zane snatched the deformed infant from her hands and ran out the room, turning down the hallway, running vainly in search of an exit, but only finding endless blue doors and white lit hallways, which all seemed to lead to nowhere.

Date – Tuesday, April 1ˢᵗ, 2121

He woke up the following morning to a ringing alert, with dozens of urgent messages from Syllabus. Zane activated his retina receptor and looked at the communications cascading across his view. There were messages from the CEO, as well as several from Sean Chan. A scandal had broken.

"EVO, turn on the news now!"

"What news would you like to watch?"

"Network, US, major"

"Searching, activating."

"Hi Marsha, wow who would have imagined this story this morning, my God. Yesterday a series of deadly domestic terror attacks across the US, and now this today. All adding to the tension and uncertainty surrounding the President's genetic technologies legislation."

"To explain to those just joining us now, a man by the name of Marko Ivanovic has just accused Secretary of Health Steve McNeill of secretly receiving millions of universal dollars in bribes from Syllabus Corporation, the giant Canadian global strategic consultancy responsible for developing and implementing the President's Medicare funded gentech plan."

"Ivanovic and McNeill were business partners in a Washington based human genetic engineering lobbying business that they sold to Syllabus last year. The two went their separate ways, with McNeill taking a job in the President's campaign, while Ivanovic was hired into Syllabus as a director. Ivanovic claims the bribes were paid by Syllabus to secure the contract to develop the President's

genetic medicine and technologies plan, shortly after her campaign won the Presidential election in November."

Oh man, this is not good, Zane thought, as he stood staring at the screen.

"*We can confirm that Secretary McNeill has denied the accusations, and has requested the FBI initiate an immediate investigation into the claims. The White House has made a statement that the claims are lies.*"

"*The CEO of Syllabus has also ordered an immediate investigation into the allegations, and the vice president of strategic development, Jared Berg has made an early morning statement confirming Marko Ivanovic was fired in early March for making threats against the company and some of its staff. Mr. Berg also stated neither he, nor the company, had made any special payments to Secretary McNeill in order to obtain consulting work for the gentech bill. Berg has stated he and Syllabus will be cooperating with the FBI in their investigation.*"

His EVO suddenly flashed a call alert, it was his VP, Jared Berg. Zane dropped the news and took the call.

"Zane, you've seen the news, right?"

"I have yes, I don't know what to say. What is this all abou-"

Berg cut Zane off, "no time to chat about this now. I need you to get to the office immediately, and take a helicopter if there's too much traffic."

"What about you sir? Your name is mentioned in this, it's all over the news…"

"I'm cooperating with the FBI and the RCMP, not your concern. Okay Zane, I can't talk any longer, I need to call each of your colleagues, and I've got my hands full. I'll see you at Syllabus in a couple of hours."

The call dropped and Zane immediately got himself ready for work, turning the news back on to listen to the chatter of the journalists as they speculated about what all this meant. Various Libertarian and Republican pundits on the network insinuated the scandal surely went further than just McNeill, and wondered if the President may have been influenced as well. Social Democratic commentators argued back, saying everything was speculative, there was no proof of wrong doing, and the timing of leak was highly suspicious.

Through the glass panes of the boardroom, everything on Floor 100 looked like business as usual; however, everyone knew it was far from the case, the entire project unhinged following the allegations of bribery and the terrorist attacks. Inside the boardroom Zane, Antonio, Leyla, Anita, Miko, Robbie, Sean, and a few others sat huddled around the table, listening intensely as Jared Berg explained by hologram from his office upstairs, how Syllabus was responding to Marko's accusations. Firstly, he said Syllabus had already filed a lawsuit against Marko Ivanovic for breach of contract, slander, and damages. Secondly, there were already plans to publicly release full details of the purchase of Ivanovic and McNeill's consulting company once approved by the CEO and the vice-president of finance.

"I know this is all very disconcerting," Jared said, continuing in a calm and measured tone, "but at this point we must not get distracted by this attack. It is a ploy to throw us and the US Administration into disarray, just as we start the public engagement process."

"There is one more thing…" Berg paused to grab everyone's attention "We have an ace up our sleeve…"

"Oh, what is that?" everyone asked, leaning anxiously forward into the table.

The white screen behind Berg's hologram suddenly filled with a high-resolution clip of Marko and the company CEO in a virtual meeting. They appeared to be in a heated discussion about Jared Berg and the project, with Marko arguing Berg should be fired for incompetence and the CEO should make him vice-president given his experience in gentech. The conversation got more

274

charged, and the incriminating part came at the end, as it sounded like Marko was threatening to sabotage the project if he didn't get what he wanted.

"Wow, that is certainly an ace," Robbie said, as everyone seemed to breathe a sigh of relief.

Zane turned to face Antonio and asked," Antonio, this may be awkward, but is there anything you are allowed to tell us? After all you were involved in this from quite early on."

Antonio hesitated, looking to Jared before talking. "Jared brought me into the project at the end of September last year because of my expertise in gentech. At that point it had been a few weeks since the President had been confirmed as the Social Democratic nominee at their convention in Dallas in August of 2120, and they were on the hunt for expertise to prepare them for taking power should they win the election in November. Steve McNeill, their gentech and health care specialist, approached Syllabus and two of our competitors to prepare proposals for their campaign on the gentech file. We wrapped up our proposal in early October, and were selected by McNeill and their campaign a couple of weeks later to proceed with phase one, should they win the election."

"As soon as we won the contract, our CEO, Jared, and Marko decided I should run it in phase one. If we were selected for phase two, I would hand over management to Sean Chan, so I could then focus entirely on the technical aspects of the file. I accepted their offer, on the condition I could retain my existing team, which explains why all of you were strongly encouraged to stay with me following the end of the last project in early November."

Antonio finished talking, and there was brief silence.

"Sounds pretty standard to me. Jared, so now what? Are we going to release those recordings and hope he either disappears, or public opinion decides he's a sleaze bag?"

"Not quite Zane. Our first step is to try to get Marko to sign a new non-disclosure agreement, threatening to release the recordings if he doesn't cooperate. If he refuses, then we'll make everything public. Regardless, our objective is to keep the public engagement phase on track, sticking with Secretary McNeill's timeline."

Sean looked over at Berg to see if he was done. Berg gave him an affirmative nod, waved goodbye to everyone, and then his hologram vanished.

"Alright everyone, what we need to do now is keep working as business as usual. Jared and Syllabus' senior management will deal with this crisis, and we'll see how things unfold from there. Miko, how many people are expected at the first public consult in Vermont this coming Monday?"

"Well Sean, as directed by Steve McNeill, I have reluctantly organized the townhall to take place at the Sanders Convention Centre in Burlington, seating capacity 5,500." Miko replied, shaking her head in obvious frustration at the absurd size of the event. "I'll be flying out tomorrow with some of my operations management team to work with the local operations and the FBI to get everything ready."

"Zane, Antonio, how you guys feeling about Burlington?" Sean asked.

Zane answered, "mixed feelings – as we've said on a few occasions it would be much better to be doing small focus groups than trying to interact with stadium-sized crowds. That said, Burlington will be a positive crowd, there's high support for a public plan across New England given gentech is already covered by Medicare at the state level in Massachusetts, Vermont, Maine, and New Hampshire."

"Miko, the next stop is New York, correct?" Sean asked.

"No, first Philadelphia and Detroit, then New York on April 10th, then we have a long weekend break, before the next round in Seattle, followed by San Francisco, and Los Angeles. The West Coast will be more challenging than Burlington, New York, and Philadelphia, lots of Libertarians and Republicans there, so we should expect opposition in the crowd. After that it's over to Houston, Nashville, Oklahoma City, St Louis, Tallahassee, Atlanta, Charlotte, and then the last stop is in suburban Washington D.C. in mid-May. A total of fifteen cities over four weeks, each venue with between 5,000 and 10,000 capacity, which means we have to be ready for big and unpredictable crowds!"

"It's going to be challenging, I really hope they'll listen to us early on and change the format to smaller focus groups. The messaging on this could very easily get out of control," Leyla said, shaking her head in agreement with Miko.

Zane quickly jumped in before the discussion took a different direction. "Ah, Miko already knows, but just so all you guys are aware, I'll be making my own way from New York to Seattle right after the townhall ends."

"Ah yes, I noted that. Zane will be taking the weekend to fly out of New York to Seattle with his friend Timothy Klein."

"Timothy Klein! My, is he paying for a weekend get-away for Zaney?" Leyla winked.

"Ah, I'm joining him for the weekend on his airship."

The room went silent, as everyone looked incredulously at Zane.

"Airship? What? Since when did Timothy have one of those?" Leyla asked.

"He's had it a couple of weeks, it's his newest toy, negative carbon emissions…"

Zane's answer was meant to provoke some humour, and it did exactly that. The entire room burst into laughter, ending the meeting on a bright and positive note.

A View From Above

Date - Thursday April 10th, 2121

It was just after noon, the New York townhall had wrapped up, and Zane dashed off the stage, leaving Antonio, Steve McNeill, and the other panelists to handle questions from the news media. He went into the staging room, grabbed his luggage, and took the elevator up to the rooftop of the convention centre, where the elevator doors opened onto an enclosed glass waiting area. There he was greeted by a droid and led to a seat to wait for his drone transport to arrive.

A few minutes later a helicopter landed on the rooftop helipad, its rotors slowing down, and the passenger door sliding open. Zane stood up and followed the droid through a door onto the helipad, where he was quickly guided to his seat at the back of the chopper. He buckled in, as the passenger door closed and the chopper's rotors accelerated, lifting them slowly from the helipad. In moments, New York's breathtaking skyline unveiled itself in the windows around him, as the drone accelerated into the sky, hurtling east from Manhattan towards Queens.

Zane took a deep breath, as he leaned back into his seat and looked out the window at the sea of skyscrapers. What a crazy morning it had been, the townhall had gone as well as he could have hoped; however, just like in Burlington, the New York media and audience strongly criticized the format, arguing Syllabus and the Department of Health should have run smaller and more accessible public events for phase three, not a monster-sized townhall. He couldn't agree more with the media's assessment; however, the problem was that Steve McNeill still stubbornly wanted stick with the same schedule and format, ignoring all efforts by Zane, Antonio, and their team to convince him to delay the mid-May vote in Congress to allow for more public engagement.

Undoubtedly the situation was going to get more challenging in the days ahead. They were leaving friendly territory, and Zane was worried about the states on the West Coast and in the South, where the President's plan faced an angry coalition of voters who were either Republican, or had a deep Libertarian distrust of government intervention in their private lives. He sighed, perhaps a dose of really bad townhalls on the West Coast wouldn't be so bad. Maybe there was an outside chance they would change the Health Secretary's mind; however, Zane doubted it, McNeill was a stubborn fool driven by a timeline and an ideology incompatible with any compromise. The more the project evolved, the more Zane, Antonio, and the rest of the team wondered why McNeill had even bothered to hire Syllabus to begin with, it just seemed they were getting in the way of his agenda. Zane increasingly believed Syllabus was just there to give the process an element of professionalism, and as Timothy had warned, a perfect scapegoat should the gentech legislation fail to pass Congress.

There was one other question, which remained unresolved, and that was what had happened to Marko Ivanovic. After the urgent and panicked meeting with Jared Berg and the team back on April 1st, the whole scandal had gone strangely quiet. All Zane knew was Syllabus and Ivanovic had signed a non-disclosure agreement, and the matter was now closed; nonetheless, this didn't stop public rumours from the Libertarians that Ivanovic had been bribed to keep quiet. Libertarian media channels were now aggressively pushing conspiracies that Jared Berg and Syllabus had bribed

McNeill, Ivanovic, and the President to secure the lucrative consulting deal. Was this true? He had no idea, and he certainly wasn't going risk his career trying to find out.

He gazed out the window, taking in the view of the Empire State building, the Liberty Tower, and the new United Nations complex on the banks of the Hudson River. New York City was a marvel, a modern-day Venice built entirely below 22nd Century sea levels. The city was fighting an endless battle against the rising seas, using a complex network of tidal management systems to keep the water out. Those systems were strained to their limit, and were slated to receive a massive upgrade under the President's new climate infrastructure act.

The minutes melted by as he watched the city unfold beneath him like a giant glass, steel, and concrete carpet stretching off into the horizon. Before he knew it, the skyline of Manhattan and Brooklyn had receded in the distance and they were approaching the gargantuan Kennedy Airship Station, which stretched from the edge of Kennedy Airport towards Long Beach City, perched on the Atlantic seaboard. A couple of minutes later the chopper touched down beside a group of other parked drones on the edge of the airship station.

Zane hopped from the helicopter, walking to a waiting surface transport drone. A minute later he was gliding across the vast airfield, passing row upon row of giant zeppelins. It was an unbelievable sight to see, there must have been at least a thousand of them parked on the airfield, in all sorts of shapes and sizes. Some of them were smaller and designed for private use, while others were huge and were clearly intended to serve the luxury tourism and travel market. Aside from the airships, there were also dozens of other service vehicles and drones buzzing around the airfield, ferrying passengers, crew, and materials between the terminal buildings and the airships.

The surface transporter pulled into platform 242, where Timothy was standing waiting in front of his airship, sporting a big friendly grin on his face.

"Zane, you made it, so good to see you again my friend!", he exclaimed, as Zane jumped from the transporter onto the tarmac.

"Woah, this thing is amazing, it's like a spaceship!" Zane exclaimed, as they walked up the boarding ramp into a minimalist half-oval shaped front cabin with large wrap-around floor to ceiling windows. The space was divided in two, with the bridge and pilot area at the front, and a kitchen and lounge area at the back. Behind the lounge was a short corridor, which led to what appeared to be a bathroom and one or two other rooms at the back.

Wasting no time, Timothy took Zane's bag and tucked it into a cabinet in the utility room down the short corridor, he then walked back to the front door and slid it shut into a locked air-tight position. With everything in place, they took their seats up front at the bridge, where Timothy went through his departure checklist on the glass computer screens spanning the bridge deck. About ten minutes later there was a metallic clunk, as the retention cables holding them in place released and they slowly drifted off the ground. Once they were about twenty metres off the tarmac, the ultralight polymer wings flexed outwards and the ship's twin electric propellers engaged, pushing them down into their seats as

282

they accelerated into the sky under the remote guidance of air traffic control.

"Sunglasses?" Timothy asked, passing Zane a pair to filter out the bright afternoon sunlight.

"Thanks, I forgot to bring a pair of my own." Zane replied, sliding them onto his face.

"We're going to be under remote guidance for the next few hours as we navigate through New York's crowded airspace. Standard procedure to avoid anything messy from happening. Oh, and there's one more thing."

"What's that?" Zane asked, just as his EVO and Internet connection abruptly shut off.

"We won't have any Internet connectivity in the sky. Up here everything non-essential to navigation can stay offline, it's a safety loophole still available to pilots that's been around since the early days of the Internet, when digital distractions from devices were responsible for some pretty gruesome air disasters."

Timothy grinned, as he added, "it's all the reason why many rich people like me become pilots and buy expensive private aircraft like these. This is about the only way to be disconnected without having to pay huge licence fees to the Internet Police for authorized signal blockers."

There was a beeping sound and Timothy's attention was diverted from Zane back to the bridge deck interface. While Timothy was focused on the computer panel, Zane swiveled around in his seat to glance at the cabin. It really did look like a spaceship, especially the bridge, with all the sleek curved glass instrumentation panels running along the wide floor to ceiling windows. The kitchen and lounge area were also futuristic, with a small cooking area, glass table and chairs, and two translucent sofas. He also noticed the floor of the entire cabin was transparent, offering remarkable views to the airfield below.

"Sorry about that Zane, I just had to release some additional navigational controls to the remote pilot. Anyway, we're all good now until I can switch to manual navigation, which won't be for at least a couple of hours. Since I don't have to pilot for now, how about I give you the low down on how this puppy works!"

Zane nodded enthusiastically as Timothy continued, "you may not have noticed when boarding, but the entire vessel's exterior and wings are wrapped in photovoltaic cells, which are critical to powering nearly everything onboard. The ship itself is divided into two components - the cabin and wings, which are constructed from a carbon fiber titanium mold, and the balloon, which is made from an advanced fire-resistant self-healing elastic polymer. Everything inside is ultralight, even the furniture and the beds are hollow - essentially just super comfortable air-mattresses."

"Fancy that, Mr. Timothy Klein, the billionaire, sleeping on an air-mattress!" Zane laughed, as he leaned back in his seat with his hands behind his head.

"Oh my friend, you wait and see, the furniture is truly out of this world!" Timothy replied, with a big grin on his face.

It had been a half an hour since lift off and with each passing moment more and more of New York was revealed through the windows and the floor below them. From the bridge they had a sweeping view of Kennedy Airport, the Manhattan skyline, and the Statue of Liberty gleaming in the sunlight in the distance. Eventually, at around five kilometres in altitude, the thrusters on the wings gently rotated ninety degrees into a horizontal position, and the ship stopped rising and changed trajectory, accelerating towards the northwest of the city in a broad westerly arc.

A few minutes later Timothy released his seatbelt, "Zane, we'll still be under remote guidance for at least the next ninety minutes, but we're clear to unbuckle and take a walk around."

Timothy led him on a tour around the living quarters located down the short corridor in the other half of the cabin. They consisted of an enclosed engineering room, a fully equipped bathroom with transparent floors and walls, and a compact master bedroom at the back of the vessel with a double bed and two small side tables. As Timothy walked Zane around, he explained how the balloon above the cabin was in fact comprised of dozens of compartments, which were filled with either pure Helium or ambient air. Stored in multiple high-pressure storage tanks located at the front and rear of the aircraft, the Helium was pumped in and out of the balloon chambers to allow the airship to change altitude. When the ship needed to ascend, air was released from the compartments and then replaced with Helium gas. When the ship needed to descend, the Helium gas was extracted back into the high-pressure storage tanks, allowing air to subsequently fill the vacant balloon chambers. On the ground, just a few chambers were filled with Helium, providing enough lift so the ship didn't tip over.

"So, what's our top speed?" Zane asked.

"Those electric thrusters out on the wings can push us up to 180 kilometres per hour, which means we could cross the continent in about twenty-four hours if we went non-stop. Also, I didn't mention this, but we can get some serious altitude, theoretically up to ninety kilometres above the surface of the earth - not quite space, but still a good view of the curvature of the earth below!"

"Incredible, I definitely hope we'll have the time to do that!" Zane replied excitedly.

"We'll see, maybe I can book us a lift window somewhere out in the Midwest. Anyway, on to more important matters! Do you want a drink? I have everything for gin and tonics – your favourite!"

"Sure, sounds lovely, but double me up on the gin please, I need it after today!" Zane joked, as he sat down at the table.

Timothy went into the small kitchen and dug into the fridge and cabinets, pulling out an unopened bottle of gin, some ice cubes, lemon, and tonic water. He mixed the drinks and brought them to the table, taking a seat in the chair opposite Zane. Neither of them said a word, both mesmerized by the constantly changing panorama passing below like some slow-motion film.

"I never get bored of it," Timothy said after a while, getting up to make another round.

"I can see why, it's magical," Zane replied, moving to the sofa to stretch out.

After about a half an hour of total silence, there was a ringing sound from the bridge deck. Timothy got up to see what it was.

"Ah, nothing to worry about, it's just a message from the remote pilot giving me authorization to take manual control if I want to. If you don't mind, I'm going to give it a whirl for a bit. You're welcome to join me up here, or maybe you're more comfortable on that air-filed sofa," Timothy laughed.

"Euhh, you're right and I'm wrong, this sofa is pretty damn comfortable for plastic and air. I think I'll hang out here and take in the view."

Timothy smiled and turned his attention back to the guidance system, leaving Zane to while away the time staring out the windows, watching the landscape pass beneath him. The hours drifted by as they travelled south, passing over New York, Philadelphia, and Washington, and then turning west to cross the Appalachians, from Virginia to North Carolina, and then to West Virginia. Finally, as the sun started to approach the horizon, they were treated to a magnificent springtime sunset over the vast flat expanse of the American heartland, pillars of electrified cumulonimbus clouds meandering like slow lumbering giants amongst the flickering lights of Knoxville, Lexington, Columbus, and other towns, refracting the sticky orange, red, and pink hues of the fading sun. Timothy made a point of ensuring they kept a safe distance from the thunderclouds, for all their beauty, the force they contained could easily tear the airship apart, sending them plummeting to a gruesome and fiery death.

"Okay, I'm feeling a bit peckish. I'm going to hand over control to a remote pilot so we can start preparing some dinner."

Timothy exchanged several messages with the tower at the Lexington Airship Station, and after about twenty minutes they took over piloting the aircraft, freeing him up to leave the bridge and start cooking the evening meal with Zane.

"Timothy it's so quiet, I've never experienced anything like this before, it's almost unnerving."

"Yes it does take some getting used to, being up here liberated from the endless chatter that clutters our lives. I remember my first time on this thing, when I brought it back from the Munich factory. I was supposed to be accompanied by that gorgeous Bavarian sales rep, but she abandoned me at the last minute, leaving me stuck flying back alone. Zane I had never been so terrified in my life. My whole life I've been surrounded by people and technology, and suddenly there I was confronted with crossing an ocean and two continents by myself."

"I remember the first few hours of the journey, they were so hard I nearly turned around to have someone else pilot it home for me. It was as if I were trapped in solitary confinement, forgotten to the outside world, a prisoner to my own devices; nevertheless, the anxiety eventually passed, slowly giving way to openness as I whiled away the time, vacantly watching the world drift by below in total silence. It was magical, I saw the towns and castles of Europe, the endless expanse of the North Atlantic, and the barren moonscape of Greenland, stripped bare of the ice sheets that once covered it, a monument to anthropogenic climate change."

Zane half listened to Timothy ramble on. His wealthy friend had no idea of the real-world problems ordinary people confronted, how they were forced by political and economic systems to do things they didn't necessarily agree with in order to earn a salary to pay things like rent, mortgages, taxes, and food bills. He thought of how much easier his life would be if he could quit this project and not suffer any impact to his career, his reputation, and his income; however, that was impossible, instead this weekend in the sky was like crossing the eye of a hurricane, watching one half of the storm recede in the distance, as the other lurked menacingly below the horizon.

"Zane I think we've got everything we need," Timothy said, as they sat down at the table and dug into the decadent spread of white wine, fruit and vegetables, bagels, cheese, lasagna, and slices of perfect synthetically engineered salmon. After dinner was done, Timothy cleaned up the table and loaded the dishes into the steam cleaner, leaving Zane to stretch out on the sofa and look at the night sky. The view was magical, stars filling the heavens like billions of glimmering shards scattered across a velvet carpet. There were so many of them, infinitely more than he had ever seen in his life.

The night drifted by in silence, Timothy checked the remote navigation one last time and then disappeared to his room, leaving Zane alone, lost in his thoughts. What was in store for him over the next three weeks? Was Syllabus going to be able to convince McNeill and the President to push back the Congressional vote to allow for better public engagement? Or was McNeill going to keep forging ahead with the same plan, ignoring Zane and his colleagues? What would happen if the vote in Congress failed?

Would Syllabus be blamed, and if so, who on his team would be scapegoated? Would he be the next Marko Ivanovic, forced disappear after signing a non-disclosure agreement on some unknown terms? What about Elise Germain, who had been so quiet since their meeting? Would she and other gentech CEO's risk charges of conflict of interest to get involved to try save the legislation? What would that mean for Zane if somehow it were leaked that he had met with her in private, especially if Syllabus fell out favour? So many questions, and no clear answers, just more and more uncertainty.

"Hey Zane, sorry to interrupt."

He looked up and saw Timothy standing in the hallway in his pyjamas, ready for bed.

"No problem, just ruminating about work."

"Gotcha. Listen, if you don't mind I'm going to take the bedroom for myself tonight. I feel like I need a good solid sleep after a busy few days in New York this past week. How about you grab a shower and freshen up while I set up the sofa for you to sleep on."

Zane padded down the short corridor to the bathroom, the door sliding open automatically as he walked into the efficiently designed space - shower stall, washbasin, wall mirror, heated towel racks, and a peculiar looking dry incineration toilet. He stripped naked, tossing his clothes to one side of the heated bathroom floor, as he turned to briefly admire his image in the floor to ceiling mirror. He stepped into the shower stall and the water instantly turned on, cascading in an aerated wash cycle of hot water and thick suds of fragrant lavender and mint soap. He closed his eyes, soaking in the luxuriant aroma and steam surrounding him, losing track of time and space. With a soft click, the shower switched from wash to extended rinse, and he opened his eyes to see the bathroom had plunged into darkness, giving him a spectacular view of the stars and distant flickering city lights clearly visible through the transparent surfaces of the ceiling, floor, and exterior wall. Dumbfounded, he stood in silence under the steady stream of hot water, staring at the constellations surrounding him, while vaguely attempting to identify one or two of them. It was futile, without EVO everything before him was a nebulous mystery.

"Hey Zane, you still awake in there, or did you drown under all that water?" Timothy laughed, tapping on the bathroom door.

"Ah yeah, god this bathroom is out of this fucking world." Zane gasped, as he shut off the water and wrapped himself in a warm fluffy towel hanging on one of the heating racks.

"Decent shower hey? Not bad for five thousand metres up in the sky. You can thank the balloon surface area for collecting and condensing all that water for you to enjoy!" Timothy winked, as he led Zane back to the lounge and dining area.

"I'll be sure to send it a thank you card tomorrow," Zane laughed.

"Well here's your bedroom my friend, sorry about the improvised state of things. The cabin windows will go completely dark when the sun starts to rise, so don't worry about being woken up by sunrise. I suspect we should be in the American Midwest by early morning, assuming good winds and no unexpected flight path changes from the autopilot network."

They said their goodnights and Timothy walked across the lounge and down the hallway to his bedroom, the door sliding closed behind him. Zane pulled off his towel and draped it on a chair, sliding naked under the duvet, his head coming to rest on the cool satin covered pillows. The lights dimmed and the cabin went completely dark, stars filling the sky beyond the edge of the balloon's convex surface. He sighed in awe, his life suddenly seemed so meaningless and ephemeral when contemplating the infinite expanse of the heavens above. He was nothing but a speck of matter in the river of time. In just two hundred years every physical trace of his existence would have vanished, and yet the same sky that had graced this planet for millions of years would still be there, just as it was when the first humans walked the savannas of Africa.

"Hey mister, you sleep well?"

"Euhh…" Zane groggily rubbed his eyes as he stretched out on the sofa, "I did, probably one of the best nights I've ever had."

Timothy smiled and he walked over to the bridge to deactivate the window dimming. In moments the cabin started to brighten, revealing bright blue skies and brilliant sunshine.

"So here's the update. We're just east of Kansas City, travelling about 80 kilometres an hour in a southwesterly direction. We've also just been given some pretty amazing news…"

"Amazing news? What's that?" Zane asked expectantly.

"We have been cleared to do a vertical lift up to sixty-six kilometres altitude at 15:00 Mountain Time - just confirmed this morning from Amarillo, New Mexico."

"Sixty-six kilometres? Timothy, that's unbelievable, how did you get that? Aren't altitudes about fifty kilometres restricted to weather and research balloons, or am I wrong?"

"You are kind of right about the altitude restrictions; however, sometimes they feel nice and make an exception. I guess we lucked out!"

"Well, I have no complaints about that! So what's the plan now, Captain Timothy Klein?" Zane winked.

Timothy laughed, "well there isn't much to see around here, so rather than waste time, we'll hit the throttle and aim to be at our assigned coordinates a bit early."

"Sounds good!" Zane replied, as Timothy headed over to the bridge deck to communicate the instructions with the remote pilot, leaving Zane to stretch out on the sofa under the covers. After a couple of minutes there was a soft noise as the wings rotated slightly and the propellers turned faster, accelerating the ship to the southwest at a new and higher altitude. Timothy looked over the panels one more time and then went over to the kitchen to pour a cup of coffee.

"Well we're on remote pilot, all the way to the lift site. Care for a cup Zane?"

"No I'm fine, just enjoying the lie in for the moment, but I'll get there eventually."

Timothy finished in the kitchen and took a seat at the table, sipping his coffee.

"While you were sleeping I was listening to NPR on the old-fashioned airwaves this morning. It seems the White House is facing pressure from moderate Republicans over the gentech legislation. This morning their Congressional caucus asked the Administration to delay the Congressional vote by a month to permit broader public engagement. They argue there is widespread fear and confusion about the legislation, which Libertarians, right-wing Republicans, and extremist are exploiting to sow public discontent."

Zane laughed, as he got out of bed and slipped on some clothes, "wow, taken right out of my own mouth, it's what my colleagues and I have been repeating to the damn US Administration for weeks. The White House is so obsessed with their schedule, they don't realize they're doing more harm than good to their cause."

"Zane, if the White House doesn't change tack, it would seem to me this legislation may never pass Congress. Don't you think it would be opportune to consider exiting this project now?"

"I would, but I think resigning at this juncture would cause irreparable harm to my reputation and great embarrassment for the White House and Syllabus. So while I'm disappointed the Americans are ignoring my advice, I'm going to keep my contractual obligations and hope to avoid being scapegoated if this thing falls apart."

"When does the contract end?"

"On May 15th, when the public engagement phase ends."

"Will the Americans retain you or Syllabus for work after that?"

"If the legislation passes they could offer us the contract to implement it; however, I'm pretty sure they'll go the patriotic route and pick a domestic consulting partner."

Timothy sighed, "well it's almost over thank god, I just hope security is tight at the public engagement meetings you're doing."

"Trust me I think about it all the time, the last thing I want is to be a statistic in an American domestic problem. Besides, I also have an exciting new side project I'd like to see through, and it doesn't involve Ponzi schemes," Zane winked mischievously.

"New side project? What would that be," Timothy asked curiously, rocking back in his chair.

"Well, you're the first to know…"

"Know what?"

"Maya and I applied for the Reproduction Lottery, and…"

"Woah! Zane, you're having a kid with this Maya chick? Crazy, when did this happen?"

"About two months ago."

"Man, you've kept it a secret from me that long! Am I really the first to find out? What about your parents, don't they know yet?"

Zane shrugged, "Timothy, why would I tell them? You know, they live self-centred lives in Aotearoa and couldn't give a shit about what I do."

"Yeah I guess they're still mourning that you decided to do consulting instead of academia," Timothy replied dryly. "So what's next? Has the Reproduction Bureau indicated where the infant will be assigned after birth?"

"We haven't gotten that far, after all we're only two months in; however, since Maya is a full professor, I imagine they will place it at one of the crèches on her campus, which would also give us decent visitor access."

"Hopefully that comes through, the university's crèches are excellent and have a reputation for the highest placement rate to the top state boarding schools."

There was a sudden loud roar, and then a sonic boom. Zane and Timothy jumped in surprise, clutching at the kitchen counter as a jet came hurtling past, shaking the airship.

"Wow, that was fucking close! Sounded like a military jet! I damn hope those lunatics know we're here." Timothy yelled angrily, as he dove over to the bridge to send a message to the nearest control tower.

"Me too, I sure don't fancy getting shredded and plunging to earth in a burning mass of plastic!"

"Pheww! Air traffic control has apologized, apparently it was a test pilot who decided to have some fun and has just been reprimanded and called back to base."

"What a douche bag! Those jets exceed fifteen times the speed of sound - it would be impossible to avoid a collision if he messed up!" Zane exclaimed, still shaking with adrenaline.

"Well we're good, the airspace is clear and let's hope it won't happen again. Now how about we clean up your bed and make this place look like a living room again?"

The jitters from the air incident soon faded, as they finished cleaning up and setting the table for something to eat. After brunch, the rest of the day was decidedly less eventful, drifting for hours across the giant expanse of the American Midwest, watching the lush irrigated agricultural land fade into brush, scrub, and finally the vast deserts of Colorado, Arizona, and New Mexico. By mid-afternoon they reached their assigned lift position, parking at about four thousand metres altitude above the honey coloured, desert landscape of Navajo, New Mexico. While they waited for authorization from Amarillo, Timothy methodically went through a checklist with the ship's computers, verifying all the airlocks were sealed and everything was secure for a high-altitude lift.

When he was done, he led Zane to the engineering room, which was separated from the rest of the vessel by a sliding airlock door and divided into two compartments. The first compartment was filled with instrumentation and touch screens, which Timothy explained were used to run the ship's life support and power management systems, as well as the distribution of helium between the storage tanks and the balloon chambers. It also had storage cabinets, some of which contained high-pressure fire-resistant spacesuits, air tight helmets, jet packs, parachutes, flotation vests, and air tanks.

Timothy grabbed some undergarments and a pair of spacesuits from the cabinets and passed them over to Zane. He then picked up two helmets and led Zane past the second sliding airlock door into the second compartment. This compartment was completely sealed off from the rest of the ship and had two airtight hatches, one in the ceiling giving access to the balloon, and the other in the floor providing an emergency exit the outside. On the walls there were several parachutes, air tanks, fire extinguishers, a vacuum sealed life raft, and survival packs. Standing in the middle of the compartment, they dropped everything into a pile on the glass floor, stripped out of their clothes, and pulled on the comfortable undergarments, spacesuits, and helmets.

Once they were fully kitted out, Timothy connected them to a couple of air hoses and instruments to check everything was fully operational. He and Zane then unplugged, took their helmets off, and returned to the bridge, where they reconnected to portable oxygen tanks located on the side of their seats, and hung their helmets onto clips on the bridge panel in front of them. As Timothy explained, the suits were required in the event of a rapid loss of air pressure. Should the vessel completely fail, they would put on their helmets, activate the oxygen supply, don parachutes, and evacuate via the second engineering compartment airlock located in the floor.

About ten minutes after taking their seats, the screen lit up with the lift authorization from Amarillo air traffic control. Timothy accepted the authorization and then tapped some instructions into the glass control panel in front of them. Almost immediately the ship started to slowly ascend, accompanied with a constant soft hissing noise, which Timothy explained was Helium being pumped from the compression tanks into the balloon, giving the ship more buoyancy. Over the next two hours they ascended into the heavens, the details of the landscapes below becoming more difficult to discern. After a few of hours of ascent, the ship gradually decelerated, eventually coming to rest at sixty-six kilometres above the planet's surface.

From their position they had a majestical view of the Earth below, its curved surface tinted in hues of green, blue, pink, and brown, with puffs of wispy white clouds interspersed with the silver contrails of speeding jets. Above through the glass cabin extending past the lip of the balloon, they could see the sliver reflection of the new moon, as well as the first stars making their appearance in the early evening sky. Kilometres beyond, into the void, were dozens of flickering lights from distant orbiting satellites and space stations - the launch pads for transport to Lunar and Martian bases.

After an hour the spring sky faded to black, the final traces of sunlight evaporating below the horizon, revealing other numerous oddly lit manned and unmanned balloons floating around them like solitary medusas in a frigid lifeless sea. Far above them the heavens came to life, billions of stars from the Milky Way and beyond filling the sky like diamonds spilt across a blackened carpet. Alone up there it felt as if they were suspended in time, their only connection to the Earth being the distant flickering lights of towns and cities scattered far below on the surface.

Timothy interrupted Zane's thoughts, "that bright light cluster down there to the north-west is Las Vegas. We're actually moving in a west-north-west trajectory, so we will pass over the city in about an hour, as we begin our descent."

After about forty-five minutes, the bridge's control panel blinked, and the ship began to slowly descend, drifting gently over the vast darkened expanse of the Grand Canyon, The Hoover Dam, and finally the brilliant flashing lights of Las Vegas. About three hours' later they were stationary at an elevation of five thousand metres, just near the dry dusty foothills of the Sierra Nevada Mountains and the start of the Continental Divide.

Standing in the engineering room, Timothy and Zane removed their suits and undergarments and got back into their regular clothes. Timothy then took a few minutes to stow the equipment, while Zane went to the kitchen to prepare a light dinner.

"An experience like that sure makes me wish I had of been a cosmonaut instead of a mathematician at a consulting firm." Zane said, as they sat together finishing dinner at the kitchen table.

"Well it wouldn't pay nearly as well, but it would sure be a lot more exciting."

Zane laughed dryly, "Timothy you forget, I've got no shortage of excitement doing what I'm doing right now…"

They laughed, then Timothy said, "Zane, it's not too late for you to change careers. You're young enough with the right training to make a shift, not like me. I'm too old and wouldn't last a day in a space training camp."

"Timothy, don't be ridiculous, you're in amazing shape, and you have better genetic composition than I do!"

"Thanks mister, genetic composition aside, that ship has sailed. Anyway, I'm glad you enjoyed this. You know you're always welcome to join me whenever you want. In fact we should do it as soon as your project wraps up. Where is your last public engagement event?"

"It's a big townhall on May 15th in Arlington, Virginia."

"Hmm, I'll see if I can arrange my schedule and meet you there. If not, we can meet in Salish City and do something a bit more fantastical than this. We can take this thing far, really far, maybe across the Pacific Ocean to the South Pacific, or down to Chile and the Atacama Desert, where we can do lifts as high as we like."

Timothy looked up from the table to the clock on the wall, "eleven fifteen already! We should get to bed so we can make an early start tomorrow."

He stood up and began clearing the table, "Zane you're welcome to join me in my room, or we can set up the sofa again for you. We're going to camp here overnight and first thing in the morning we'll head due west to the California coast, and then make our way north along the coastline. We should arrive in Seattle by early evening, unless we run into turbulence."

While Timothy was cleaning up the kitchen, Zane went to the bathroom to quickly shower and freshen up. When he was done, he went to Timothy's room, stripped naked, and slid under the cool covers at the far end of the bed, which was located under the curved glass exterior of the cabin. As he lay there, he could see the lights of Las Vegas flickering and gleaming far in the distance, while up above in the darkness, the sky shimmered with endless twinkling stars and orbiting satellites.

A few minutes later Timothy came into the room and climbed in beside Zane, wrapping his big arms around his friend. They lay together in silence, before Zane rolled over and kissed him on the lips. Timothy smiled and grabbed Zane tighter, as they started kissing passionately, their naked bodies slowly grinding against each other as they rolled around under the covers. After a few minutes Timothy pushed Zane into a corner of the bed, pinning his sweaty body down, and wrestling him onto his side. Zane playfully tried to resist, but his friend was much stronger and more determined, and it wasn't long before he felt Timothy enter him, just slightly at first, and then deeper and harder, until he was completely inside. At first Zane felt a feeling of intense raw discomfort; however, it soon faded away, and before long he was completely overcome by waves of intense pleasure. Timothy was in complete control, Zane could offer no resistance as his friend reached around and grabbed him, sending them both hurtling headlong towards the edge. Minutes later it all came to a writhing, sweaty climax, as they both collapsed exhausted and entangled in a corner of the bed.

They kissed each other gently for a few minutes afterwards, looking at each other in the eyes, the bedroom ever so slightly illuminated in a soft blue by the starlight and the sliver of the new moon. They both smiled, and then Timothy gave Zane a gentle nudge, directing him to the bathroom to shower, while he fixed up the bed. By the time Zane returned to the bedroom, Timothy was already sound asleep, his deep breath filling the air like the sound of small waves lapping the edge of a sandy shore. Zane slid gently under the covers, giving his friend a kiss on the forehead, before rolling over to the far side of the bed. Just a few minutes later he drifted off into subconsciousness, lulled asleep by the sound of Timothy's deep breathing, and the serenity of the world surrounding him.

"Zane, Zane, wake up, we gotta get out of bed!" Timothy shouted.

He rolled over groggily, suddenly grabbing onto the bedsheets as the ship abruptly rolled and he was tossed off the bed and onto the floor in a heap. Timothy was already scrambling out of the room on his hands and knees, making his way to the engineering room. Alarms were ringing, and the glass dimming had deactivated, letting in a piercing desert light into the cabin. Zane had no idea what time it was and what was going on, all he could do was blindly follow Timothy to engineering to grab spacesuits, parachutes, and helmets.

In the engineering room they donned the same equipment from their space lift the day before, and then scrambled on all fours to the bridge, strapping themselves into their seats. Zane looked first at the flashing navigation panel, and then outside at the giant towers of dust blowing across the vast desolate landscape, in waves so high he could hear the particles scratching along the sides of the cabin. As the ship nauseatingly tossed and shuddered, he realized they were trapped in turbulence from powerful thermals gusting from the mountains into the continent.

He looked back down at the panels and saw the ship's autopilot had already jumped into action. They had gained three kilometres in altitude and were rising faster and faster to escape to safer and more stable air. For the next thirty minutes the two of them sat strapped in their bridge seats, savagely tossed around like helpless ragdolls as the ship battled the elements. Zane struggled to stay focused on the horizon, wondering how much more the vessel could handle, expecting at any moment to hear an evacuation order from the ship's computers.

Yet as suddenly as it began, the winds abruptly dropped, and they came to a gradual rest at just over fifteen kilometres above the Nevada landscape. Timothy let out a deep sigh of relief and deactivated the autopilot, sending several messages to the Las Vegas control tower, before setting a course northwest straight over Death Valley towards San Francisco.

"God, I'm amazed neither of us vomited during that lovely rollercoaster ride," Timothy muttered, a bit whiter than normal in the face.

"Stomachs of steel!" Zane joked, his head still hurting from the experience.

Timothy smiled weakly," we'll see, mine is feeling a bit tender at the moment, hopefully it will pass."

"Hmm...So what's the plan now? I'm guessing that episode threw our schedule off a bit."

"Yeah, we're going to need to make some good time to compensate for that emergency vertical lift; nevertheless, I think we should still be good for a late evening arrival in Seattle, especially if we get to travel at this altitude for a few hundred kilometres."

They spent the next couple of hours straightening out the cabin and putting everything away that had fallen out of place. By the time they sat down to a late morning breakfast, they had already crossed California to the coast and were sweeping over the Bay Area at an altitude of twelve thousand metres. The city of love was barely visible in the distance below. Zane would have liked to have had a closer view, but their trajectory was restricted in the crowded airspace above America's most magnificent and powerful metropolis, home to the technology barons and their perfect genetically engineered offspring. It wasn't long before San Francisco faded into the distance, and over the next several hours they gradually descended to an altitude of two thousand metres, crossing from California into Oregon and the Cascadia region.

They headed north, hugging the coastline, travelling at about 180 kilometres an hour over breathtaking swaths of wild empty beaches interspersed with cliffsides cascading into the dark blue waters of the North Pacific Ocean. The land was practically devoid of urban settlements, America's bitter social conflict between genetically engineered and naturally conceived seeming so remote.

Towards the evening, as they headed inland towards Seattle, the skies began to turn a dark grey, and a steady rain was falling by the time they landed at Tacoma Airship Station. The silence of the weekend abruptly ended within moments of touching down and releasing the airlocks, as the Internet reconnected and EVO turned on, releasing a flood of information and urgent updates onto his retina screens. He gave Timothy a farewell hug, and before he knew it he was slumped in the back of a cab on his way to a hotel in downtown Seattle.

Governor McRae

Date - Thursday May 8th, 2121

Zane stared despondently out the tinted glass. They were in a driverless minivan heading west on an elevated freeway to the Gulf Coast. Outside the air was oppressively hot and sticky, building steadily for the cathartic release of an evening thunderstorm. All around them were the Florida Everglades, the giant dying river of brine flowing slowly from the north of the state down to the Gulf of Mexico. The Everglades had long since been in decline, and were now mostly saline, diluted by sea waters washing deeper and deeper inland past what were once extensive banks of offshore mangrove islands. Levees had been built over the years to try protect the exposed coast, but the force of ever more powerful hurricanes and higher sea levels made that futile. Florida was drowning, and Governor McRae had only that on his mind.

Zane struggled to keep his eyelids open as he gazed out window at the sea of reeds, ignoring the conversation in the front part of the vehicle cabin. He was exhausted. He, Antonio, and the rest of the specialists on the panel had been travelling America for nearly a month since the public engagement process started in New England in early April. The results of the process were already playing out just as his mathematical models had forecasted, and there was little cause for optimism. Just as Zane and his team had warned, the public engagements were too few, too large and too cumbersome to sway public opinion in their favour, and had only given more opportunities for the opposition to derail the legislation. Yet despite all the clamouring for a new strategy from many Social Democrats, moderate Republicans, and the gentech

307

industry, the White House remained fixated with their legislative timeline, ordering Syllabus to leave future public engagements unchanged.

Up until now, the worst of the public meetings had been in the California, where Senator John Smith and his supporters had sown his home turf with anger and suspicion. The senator's presence was everywhere, in the hostility of the audiences, in the local media's ceaseless personal attacks on the panel's participants, and in the violent street marches against human genetic technologies. It was similar in Seattle, where the huge townhall and Syllabus' strategic advertising buys did little to dent the growing narrative that the President's plan was a dual conspiracy by industry and government to sterilize the naturally conceived, and steal genetic technology from the city's wealthy genetically engineered class.

Syllabus and government media campaigns were a bit more successful in thwarting the conspiracy narratives in the Central States, which meant they faced marginally more receptive audiences in Houston, Nashville, and Oklahoma City; however, they were abruptly stonewalled in St Louis, where the public meeting was cancelled after graffiti was found warning of a bomb attack by anti-gentech extremists if the meeting went ahead. Efforts to hold a smaller alternate public consultation in Kansas City were shelved by the governors of Missouri and Kansas, after violent street protests between various groups in favour and opposed to genetic technology caused damage to parts of the city centre. In the end Zane and the rest of the experts left both cities empty handed, arriving a day earlier in Tallahassee to make good with Governor of Florida.

"Gentlemen, I really want to thank you all for coming on down to Florida, always an honour to have visitors from out of state, especially when they're here on business for the President. Gotta love us, we're a big state, a Republican state, and yes, sometimes a Libertarian one - though I do my darndest to keep those miserly bastards out of office."

Zane looked up at the governor, politely laughing with everyone at his joke.

"I know you're all here to talk to me and my fellow citizens about reproduction, gestation pods, and super humans. It seems that's all you White House types have on your minds these days. Well the President did get me the climate money I needed here to fix my state's drowning cities, so I owe it to her to do everything I can to deliver the Congressional votes she needs for this gentech thing of hers. But boys, dammit you people in D.C. really have no idea of the stink'n mess we have down here. I find it just a bit funny how you're all so worried about making perfect little babies, when so many of our cities are drowning under seawater."

They arrived at the coast, turning into a parking in front of a small government building. The limousine pulled into an empty stall and the doors slid open. Zane started sweating as soon as he stepped out of the vehicle, his shirt clinging to his sticky skin, as the perspiration ran down his face and back. The limousine doors closed behind them, and most of the occupants followed the governor into the building to use the washroom facilities.

While he waited, Zane ambled over to the exterior of the building, where could find some shade from the oppressive sun. The air was buzzing with insects, and he swatted in vain as they hummed around his face, landing on his ears, eyes, and lips. Nailed to the exterior wall of the building was a large information panel that talked about the history of the area. He learnt the submerged community in front of him was known as Marco Island, a vast real estate scheme conceived in the middle of the 20th Century, which collapsed a hundred years later when flooding became so frequent, that insurance companies refused coverage and the state government ceased maintaining infrastructure and services.

Antonio appeared at his side, "fools, they should never have built anything like that out here, but the local politicians were on the take, and everyone wanted a piece of the Sunshine State."

"Yes it's hard to imagine anything like this getting approved today," Zane replied, slapping at a mosquito that had landed in his ear.

The governor and the rest of the occupants of the van appeared from the building. McNeill waved to Zane and Antonio, signalling to join them. They followed the group down a narrow elevated walkway to a helicopter pad, where there was a large black tinted drone parked silently on the platform.

"Okay everyone, all aboard the chopper! We're going to a floating sea platform in the Gulf of Mexico, where we'll take a fun little boat trip down to Miami. For those of you struggling with our Florida springtime heat, I promise lots of AC in the chopper, and there should be plenty a breeze to make it tolerable once we're on the boat out on the water."

The doors slid open and everyone stepped inside. Within moments the electric powered rotors were roaring, propelling them into the sky above the remnants of Marco Island. From his window at the back of the drone, Zane could see the damage climate change had inflicted on the coastline below. Traces of mangrove islands remained, as well as some partially submerged levees and dilapidated crumbling hotels and office parks. A couple of minutes later Marco Island faded from view, the helicopter was soon far out to sea above the gleaming blue expanse of the Gulf of Mexico.

The flight lasted just ten minutes, the electric powered helicopter coming to rest on a floating metal pad in the middle of the sea. Moments later they were on a driverless electric hovercraft, roaring towards Miami. In just thirty minutes the skyline of the city appeared, glassy skyscrapers reflecting the hot sticky sunlight. The boat made a wide arc, as it approached the outer reaches of the city, eventually decelerating to a near crawl as it entered the downtown core.

Everything was underwater.

"Gentleman this is what we're facing in Florida. We're the fourth most populous state in the country, and losing population like you can't believe. Everyone wants out, now that the ship is sinking. All these buildings were built with big money, most of that money was made by very rich people who made their fortunes in the old carbon economy – cars, planes, oil, plastics, mining, forestry, cattle farming - the same carbon economy that has caused us to go underwater."

"The sea came in, just as the scientists said it would. First just with hurricanes, then with high tides, then all the time. Finally the streets were always under water, the sewers just leaked everywhere, and the place became uninhabitable. Apocalypse."

Everyone looked up at the towers around them. Antonio was the most impressed, after all he was Latin American, and had some connection with the mythology of Miami, Latin America's gateway to America.

"I see there are lots of drones flying about. Whose are they?" Antonio asked.

"Ah most of those are US military, making sure no one comes in here. These towers are dangerous, a few of them have become unstable and could disintegrate without warning. Like the one that collapsed over there."

They turned their heads and looked at the enormous mountain of rubble rising out of the water.

The governor continued, "there are also a lot of private surveillance drones flying around here, keeping an eye on assets, though to be honest, there ain't much they can do. The top floors of some of these buildings, the more stable ones, are also occupied by very wealthy people involved in all sorts of shady activities, so they have their drones keeping an eye on things."

"How the hell do people live up there without services and in this heat?" Antonio asked.

"Oh, they have service drones bringing water, batteries, solar power, AC units, and food supplies from outside."

"Amazing…" Antonio muttered.

"What about the stability of the buildings?" One of Steve McNeill's aides asked.

"Ah, every now and then those bastards float cement-laden barges in and pump concrete into the foundations to keep them upright. They also have their own submersibles checking on the stability of the towers. We tolerate it because it keeps the infrastructure upright, and up until now we didn't have the money to do a controlled demolition around here."

Zane asked, "aren't those residents vulnerable to crime and disease?"

"Not in the slightest! For extra security, they've filled the lower floor stairwells and elevator shafts with concrete to stop looters from ever getting up there, and they also have drones watching everywhere, just like they're watching us now. As for disease, it's a problem down here, but up there it's squeaky clean and well sprayed for mosquitoes."

"Secretary McNeill, what do you think?"

The Health Secretary looked at the governor, "I think this is fucking nuts, if you ask me."

"Hahaha, that about sums it up, which is why it's my priority to deal with what we have going on down here as soon as possible."

Antonio asked, "sir, just who exactly is living in those penthouses?"

"Very rich folks, drug money, AI billionaires, mostly some serious Libertarians who don't want anyone messing with their money."

"Oh, are we in danger here?" one of Zane's co-panelists asked.

"Most definitely not ladies and gentlemen. They may be watching us, but they know they'll have the full force of the US military hitting them in seconds if they try take out the Governor of Florida and the Federal Secretary of Health."

"Mr. Governor sir, just how deep is the water level here," asked another one of McNeill's aides.

"Hmm, it varies from about three feet at low tide, to about ten feet at high tide. You've got to be careful boating around here, very easy to run aground. Part of the reason why we're in a hovercraft and going so slowly."

The governor tapped McNeill on the shoulder and pointed straight ahead. "Secretary McNeill, you see that flag up there, at the top of the white tower straight ahead of us?"

"Yes I do," McNeill replied.

"Well, in that penthouse lives one of Florida's wealthiest men. A billionaire real estate mogul in his nineties, who moved his assets out of the state well before everything went sour. Most of the people who held on here were left with nothing when the City of Miami went bankrupt. He bought this whole tower out, costing him five hundred universal dollars for an asset that should have been worth a billion. Unbelievable!"

The governor eyed the skipper, giving her a hand signal to get moving.

"Okay people, this place is fascinating, but we don't want to be here after sunset. Time for us to turn around and get back to Tallahassee for dinner, so you folks can get a good night's sleep before your big gentech townhall tomorrow. I think you're expecting about five or six thousand people in the convention centre. Should be lots of fun…"

Zane grimaced, imagining Florida was going to be the worst of them all, worse than Seattle, and in all probability the governor was not going to be helpful.

The Tallahassee Convention Centre was packed beyond capacity for Florida's only public engagement event on the President's gentech legislation, with crowds filling the lobby and overflow rooms. The Sunshine State had two principal socio-economic demographics, and it was the older, wealthier, conservative one who was clearly in the majority that morning. The rest were hardly to be found; they were the disenfranchised low-income majority who were dependent on Florida's antiquated Medicare system for healthcare.

At around ten, Governor McRae leapt energetically to the stage to introduce the panelists, basking in the roar of an appreciative crowd. It was easy to understand why he was so popular, he was tall, handsome, slightly overweight, and had the irresistible folksy charm of a Southern Baptist minister, who knew how to sweep a congregation off its feet.

"Okay folks, thanks for coming today! Please accept my sincerest apologies for the lack of space, the organizers of these meetings were only able to provide us one townhall in Florida, so we'll have to make do with what we got. Anyway, we have the honour to have before us some mighty fine out of town experts from industry, academia, and government to take your questions about the President's big healthcare initiative, called the Human Genetic Technologies Act."

There were soma catcalls and jeering from the audience, and the governor had to stop and wave to get everyone to quieten down.

"Now as we all know, the President, she is a good friend of mine, we worked hard together to get the climate bill through Congress, which was so important for our lovely state. The President is now asking for our support to update Medicare, so we should give her people some of our hospitality and lend them a patient ear. I've been told this bill will update Medicare to include all kinds of genetic technologies, so all our fellow citizens can access them, not just those folks with big money or private insurance."

Once again the audience grew agitated, clearly not pleased with what he had just said. Rather than try calm them down, the governor just gazed about the hall, letting the crowd blow off some steam. After a couple of minutes, he abruptly spun on his heels and strutted across the stage, slowly rolling his head and shoulders, whilst pointing his fingers in the air, as a Kay-Li mix came blasting out the auditorium speakers. The hall instantly erupted in a roar of approval, rising to their feet to cheer and stomp along to the man they had come to see.

The governors' eyes met Steve, Antonio, and Zane's as if to say, "watch me, this is how it's done", and then, as quickly as it began, the music stopped and the crowd took a seat.

"Folks," he continued, "as we all know, our healthcare system has been nationalized for some time now, not like in the bad old days when our grandparents had to have private insurance to visit the doctor or go to hospital. Yet times have been a changing, and most medication and treatments are not using pharmaceuticals, they're using genetic medicine and technology, which are not covered by Medicare. You only get to access these amazing treatments if you're rich, have pretty darn good private insurance from work, or invested in a private insurance plan for retirement."

The governor rambled on for about twenty minutes, saying very little, and especially avoiding explicitly throwing his support behind the Human Genetic Technologies Act. It was clear Zane and the other speakers were once again going to be stuck with the dirty work, trying to explain to these self-interested conservative Republican and Libertarian voters that it was in their nation's interests to have the other eighty percent of their population covered by a Medicare plan that included modern medicine. Judging from the audience, it was going to be an experience on par with San Francisco.

When the governor was finally done sweet talking his audience, Steve McNeill took to the podium to dryly explain a bit about the Human Genetic Technologies legislation. When he was done, he awkwardly handed over to Zane and the other panelists to briefly present the medical technologies and why they needed to be added to Medicare. Afterwards the governor took over to moderate a ninety-minute question and response period, where various members of the audience had been pre-selected to ask random questions.

The first one to ask a question was a bespectacled elderly white man, with a strong New York accent. "Secretary McNeill, my concern is you experts claim genetic technologies are safe, but really, we've only been using them for about seventy years in humans at this level. If you're an evolutionist, that is a speck in time compared to the work of nature. If you're a creationist, who believes we are all works of God, are we not messing with God's divine creation?"

McNeill nodded, "thank you for your question. Yes your concern is completely legitimate; however, I will say this, humans have been playing with nature since the beginning of time, always with an element of unknown. Take for example genetically modified foods, vaccines, EVO implants, artificial intelligence, driverless cars, deep sea exploration, and Lunar and Martian mining – these are all technologies we now take for granted, which all use the same scientific principles to bring tremendous benefits to our lives."

"The fact is science and technology have consistently improved our quality of life and standard of living, it is simply undeniable. Imagine the world without plumbing? Or no electricity? The choice we now confront is whether to open the new technological wave - genetic technologies, to all Americans, both rich and poor, or continue to leave it accessible only to the rich. If we stay with the status quo, the data shows those who don't have access will be left further behind. Is that morally acceptable? What would God say about that? What are the consequences if we let this continue for just another generation or two? Will we be locking out seventy or eighty percent of our fellow Americans from living a healthier, happier, and longer life? How will America be able to compete with other developed countries who offer these genetic technologies to all of their citizens?"

A part from a few random insults shouted out at McNeill, the room was mostly quiet, as people absorbed what he had just said. The governor signalled to the next pre-selected question, which came from a short black woman wearing a bright blue t-shirt with "I love Florida!" splayed in neon letters above some colourful beach scene.

"Thank you Secretary McNeill and Governor McRae, as well as your panelists for coming down here today to talk to all of us. I just wanted to say I'm in favour of genetic technologies because I see us in America being left behind by the rest of the world if we don't offer it to everyone! Our country has become so divided between the genetically engineered elite and everyone else, this is not sustainable! If we continuing doing nothing, we'll see more violent protests, more inequality, and it won't be long before this country will cease to function as a democracy!!! We need to stand up and fight for our right to have this…"

The mic was silenced, it was evident the woman was not going to ask her question, and had instead decided to use the moment to ramble on about her personal point of view and waste valuable question time. Zane cringed, it was here where the shortcomings of McNeill's large townhalls were clearly visible. In a small focus group that woman would have had the chance to speak her mind, and the elderly white man with the glasses would have easily been refuted; however here, in a hall of thousands of people, it was impossible to control the crowd dynamic.

A young overweight man about Zane's age took the microphone. He was wearing a yellow baseball cap, loose fitting pants, and a t-shirt with a logo from some local sports organization.

He shouted angrily, his face glowing bright red, "I'm a Christian and I have a fundamental concern about what we are doing with God's work! God made us who we are, what gives us a right to meddle in his creation, especially using taxpayers' hard-earned money?"

MacNeill was about to answer, when the governor waived him off and took the microphone. "You know young man, you raise a valid point, and to be honest this has always been a concern I've had with genetic technologies all along. Now I'm not genetically engineered, and I'm sure most of us here aren't," the room roared in approval, breaking into loud cheering and jeering that lasted for a couple of minutes.

Once the noise stopped, the governor continued, looking straight at the crowd, "we are all creatures of God, and whether we believe in Creation or Evolution, we can all agree it is a risky thing for us to be meddling with something as complex and beautiful as a human being. I believe rather than making genetic technologies accessible to all, we can solve the problem by banning the elite from making these fancy genetically engineered babies, and if we catch them doing it, we just lock them up!"

There was a roar of applause in the hall, as the crowd jumped to their feet, shouting and chanting the governor's name. McNeill leaned over to Zane and Antonio, covering the microphones, "we've lost this one, the governor's gone rogue, probably for the perfect presidential campaign sound bite…"

Antonio and Zane had just arranged their luggage and were about to take their seats, when McNeill came over and asked Zane if could take the window beside him. He nodded in surprise, letting the Health Secretary slide past and sit down in the window seat. It was the first time in the public engagement process they had sat together on a flight, McNeill either preferring to sit alone or occasionally with his aides in a separate cabin at the rear of the government jet's spacious interior.

The lights dimmed and the aircraft started to taxi slowly from the terminal. Zane turned to look out the window, awkwardly making eye contact with McNeill. He smiled politely, and was about to look away when McNeill shook his head and started talking, opening up to Zane in a flood of regret and frustration. As he spoke, he admitted the townhall format he had chosen was a disaster, a missed opportunity. He acknowledged he had rushed the process, and should have listened to Syllabus to slowly and steadily build broad public support. With the format he had imposed, the agenda was too easily hijacked by conservative groups, as they divided and picked the electorate off one by one, convincing Americans the technology was unethical, dangerous, elitist, expensive for taxpayers, and an unfair subsidy for the poor.

As Zane listened, he couldn't help but feel sorry for the Health Secretary. Sitting beside him on the plane was a defeated and exhausted man, watching a life dream slip from his reach, just at the moment when it should have been on the verge of becoming reality. McNeill was a shadow of the man he had been six months ago. The vigour, the energy, the fire, and the charm were gone, replaced by a tired unassuming individual who had lost his sense of purpose. There was nothing Zane could say to make him feel any better. The time to change tack had long passed, with just ten days remaining before the public engagement process ended, adding more townhalls to push the vote out later would only show the Administration lacked confidence in the bill's support.

"Zane I'm worried, I never imagined it would go sideways like this. I've been so committed that I never believed people could be brainwashed into believing genetic medicine was not a human right. The opposition is picking this bill apart, using public fear over genetically engineered babies to ignore all the other benefits of modern medicine that are not accessible to most Americans. The Congressional vote is going to be close, I just hope we can keep enough moderate Republicans on our side after what happened with Florida Governor McRae today."

"What will the White House do if the votes in Congress don't add up?"

"Zane I don't know, I don't have a back-up plan. This is my career, my dream. I spent my whole life working to make this technology accessible to everyone in this country. I can't imagine us failing, after we've gotten so close! Why in America do we let people suffer from cancer, when in other developed countries people practically never get the disease?"

"Secretary McNeill, America is a complicated place with many divergent interests, where a small organized minority can use fear to pit a disorganized majority against itself. Fear is a powerful motivator, and I worry we didn't give the time in the public engagement process to adequately address people's concerns about the technologies we were offering them. Hopefully I'm wrong, but only time will tell."

McNeill shook his head despondently, "I fear you are right Zane."

There was a moment of silence, filled by hum of the jet's engines, before McNeill added, "we may not have the chance to speak like this again before it's all over, so I want to take the opportunity to apologize for not listening to you and your team. I hope everything works out, but if it doesn't, I will surely take the fall for the Administration, something I will willingly do. I hope you and your team do not get blamed for this. It would be unfair, after all it is my fault, and only I should suffer the consequences."

McNeill looked away from Zane to his window, as the Airbus' electric engines began to spin faster and faster, and then they started to accelerate, hurtling down the runway into the Florida night sky.

The Rally

Date - Thursday, May 15, 2121

Zane sat on the sofa gazing out his hotel window at the late afternoon sky and the scene on the National Mall below. From his vantage point he was able to watch the hundreds of construction workers assembling stages and screens for the President's giant gentech rally on Friday, the final effort to mobilize support before Monday's Congressional vote.

In Zane's opinion the rally was a waste of time because the legislation had no chance of passing Congress. Its supporting coalition had collapsed, and it was too late to do anything about it. The Administration was only running the vote to show how close they were to being able to pass it, and then use the result to mobilize their base for the 2022 mid-term elections. How absurd it was, if only they had listened to his team and properly engaged the public, then they would be looking at a winning vote, instead of having to mobilise for another election over the issue.

Zane got up and poured himself another large glass of gin and tonic, taking a seat on the balcony to get some outdoor air. It was hot and unpleasantly humid, the East Coast sweltering under the first long heat wave of the year. Yet despite the weather it still felt good to be outside and alone, after so many weeks of being trapped indoors in front of large aggressive crowds. He felt he could finally breath, even though he knew things were about to get very complicated. Soon after the vote in Congress he expected both Syllabus and the Administration to begin blaming each other, and then passing the fault down the chain of command to selected scapegoats. He expected to be one of them, ousted like Marko

Ivanovic and labelled as an incompetent who had pushed the wrong implementation strategy.

Once fired, would he be employable? Certainly not at Stanford or at one of Syllabus' competitors, but maybe as a professor or lecturer in some pathetic second tier university, or as an employee in a small shabby consulting firm in Salish City. He sighed and took a swig of his drink. Whether he was fired or not, this failed plan to reform American healthcare was going to have his name on it, and it was going to take a long time for his reputation to recover from such a mess.

He wondered what Maya was going to do. She was an immigrant in a prominent faculty position who didn't need the distraction of being partnered with someone implicated in one of the biggest legislative failures in recent American history. More than likely their relationship was finished, to be ended with a short text message wishing him the best of luck in the future. The only connection that would remain of their time together would be the child they conceived, deposited in a state operated boarding school, to be visited from time to time.

Zane took another swig of his gin, his thoughts drifting to Elise Germain. It seemed like years had passed since their meeting in her house in Salish City back in March. Once the plans for phase three were announced, she had faded from the scene, politely declining invitations to appear in the public eye, and pulling Zelion back from the spotlight. Almost certainly she recognized the flawed strategy for the public engagement and made the wise decision protect herself and her company from the fallout. He imagined her disappointment, and laughed dryly as he stared at his empty glass, wondering if the promise of a directorship was still open to him.

He felt tipsy as he got up and stumbled back into the hotel suite, his clothes sticky with sweat and humidity from sitting outside. He stripped down to his underwear and stood looking at himself in the mirror. The past four months on this project had taken its toll, he had lost muscle mass, and the definition in his body had faded, after weeks and weeks of little exercise and countless unhealthy meals in restaurants and hotel cafeterias.

"EVO!" he slurred aloud at the computer.

"Yes Zane."

"Put on something energizing, I'm going to try do some exercise."

A couple of seconds later some random high energy music blared out of the hotel room speakers. Zane dropped to the floor and started doing push-ups and sit-ups, so many that he soon lost count, his mind clouded in a fog of exercise, booze, and loud music. After what seemed an eternity, he collapsed out of breath onto his back on the bed, feeling nauseous and exhausted as he stared vacantly at the ceiling.

What should he do with the rest of the day? He had no obligations to be anywhere that evening and the hotel room was his for the weekend if he wanted it, paid for on the company expense account. There was no rush to be back in Salish City, he wasn't due there until Tuesday for the debrief to be conducted by Sean Chan and Jared Berg, assuming he wasn't fired beforehand.

"God, I can't lay here all day like this," he muttered out loud, "I need to get outside and escape, get away from this madness."

Suddenly, in a burst of energy, he jumped up, pulled on his sweaty clothes and work shoes, went to the bathroom to wash his face and fix his hair, and barged out the hotel room to the elevators. A few seconds later the elevator doors opened onto a brightly lit, white, marble-floored lobby, populated with the usual collection of beautiful genetically engineered professionals who patronized these sorts of establishments. They were all flawless: ideal height, optimal weight, and perfectly symmetrical faces. Avoiding making eye contact, Zane breezed past the staff and hotel guests, his steps barely audible above the sound of the Bach Concerto Brandenburg Number Three coming from the Steinway Piano at the far side of the lobby. The concierge smiled and opened the front door for him, wishing him a pleasant afternoon. Zane ignored him, quickly disappearing into the crowd of passersby on the sidewalk in front of the hotel.

About fifteen minutes later he flopped into a seat on a train for Edgewood, a popular upscale neighbourhood for Washington's elite, with views across the city. As the metro stops ticked by one after the other, it was impossible not to notice how the types of people on the train changed depending on where they were in the city. Sometimes they looked like the guests in his hotel, while other times his kind were more of a rarity, outnumbered by degenerates, the kinds of people one rarely saw in pure genetically engineered societies such as Canada.

Immersed in the ever-changing human scenery passing before him, he was suddenly snapped back to attention when EVO alerted him his Edgewood stop was coming up. He was just about to get up and shuffle past the other passengers, when his eyes fell upon the name of a station two stops further down the line on the metro map. He hesitated, wondering whether he should exit at Edgewood, or continue to General Public Hospital. The train glided into Edgewood Station and EVO sent another alert for him to move to the doors and prepare to disembark. He ignored it and stayed seated, watching as the doors closed and the train pulled out of the station.

Two stops later Zane stood up and exited the train, taking the escalator down from the platform to street below. As soon as he reached the station exit he was hit by a wall of sticky clammy heat, his clothes instantly becoming wet with a mixture of sweat and humidity. He looked up above the station entrance and saw a large screen with news and a thermometre, which read forty-one-degrees centigrade, with a forty-nine-degree humidex.

He looked around, getting his bearings as EVO quickly computed the fastest and safest route to General Public Hospital, instructing him to exit the station to the right and follow the road for one kilometre to his destination. He walked out the doors onto the sidewalk and was immediately struck by two things. The first thing was the state of the infrastructure – most of it were run down and covered in graffiti, with only some of the street level shops open - a far cry from the polished aesthetics of Central Washington. Even the exterior of the metro station was a shabby mess, with unintelligible graffiti covering the exposed rebar and cracked concrete walls. The sidewalk in front of the station was equally unappealing: narrow, with a high curb that dropped abruptly into the wide congested main arterial road. The second thing he observed was the physical diversity of people loitering around the station entrance. They were dressed in urban and street attire, and came in the sorts of shapes and sizes one rarely saw in the central business districts of America's most desirable cities.

Feeling conspicuous, he decided to waste no more time and hurried past the loiterers down the wide street towards the hospital. About ten minutes later he arrived in front of a vast imposing complex on the main road. The building was about eight stories tall, and its entire façade was constructed out of preformed unpainted grey concrete, with very few windows. The were some people idling around on the sidewalk, as well as a number of others seated on the stairs in front of the entrance. He walked past them, climbing the half-dozen stairs to the front doors.

Once inside, he was immediately struck by the smell of old concrete and chlorine bleach. The lobby was uninspiring and institutional, the floors paved in cracked dark green tiles and the walls painted in a tired greyish powder blue, which appeared even more fatigued in the flickering neon light. Everywhere he looked there were people milling around. Most of them had the usual ailments, such as broken bones, cuts, and bruises; however, there were many who seemed to be suffering from sicknesses he had never seen in Canada, and had difficulty identifying.

This was the eighty percent, the majority of Americans who had no private health insurance and were stuck with a decrepit Medicare system without genetic medical treatments. These people had been mostly invisible to him throughout this project, the forgotten and silent majority. They were the statistics, the numbers, and the data points in graphs and tables, presented through studies to Congress to be debated without any conclusion. They lived lives incomprehensible to the twenty percent of Americans who had access to gentech through their private fortunes and the private health plans. These people, the eighty percent, lived trapped in a genetic Apartheid.

"Excuse me sir, can you spare some change?"

Zane snapped out of his thoughts and looked down at a small frail man holding a box with some lose paper bills in it. Zane was about to say he had no money and then realized he had a roll of bills in his pocket. He fished some of them out and dropped a couple into the box.

"Thank you sir! You lost, what yah looking for?"

"I'm looking for…Ah I found it, thanks man."

Zane gently pushed past the man and crossed the lobby, following a series of directions posted on the walls. He eventually arrived in an enormous room, with rows upon rows of people splayed out in chairs attached to IV lines and medical instruments. It was the cancer ward, everyone in there being treated using chemotherapy drugs, the antiquated medications that killed fast growing cancer cells, but caused horrible side effects. He was shocked, it was something he had never seen with his own eyes, after all, cancer had largely been eliminated in Canada and most developed countries through the use of state funded genetic engineering and genetic medicine.

As he walked the room, the shock gradually turned to anger and frustration. Anger at America's selfishness and lack of political will to fix a situation that left most of its citizens to suffer so unnecessarily, and frustration that there was nothing he could have done to have made a difference. The reality was the

President's plan was doomed from the outset, not just because it was poorly conceived or the public was inadequately consulted, but because much of America was too ignorant and ideologically opposed to even consider providing genetic treatments to all of its citizens.

"Sir, are you a doctor?" A man asked.

"No…ah…I'm not. Sorry." Zane stuttered.

"Oh, you look like one. Can you help me anyway? It appears my IV treatment line has become blocked. Can you call a nurse?"

"Ah yes of course," Zane answered, stooping over to look at the man's IV connector tube.

Zane stood up and saw a nurse nearby.

"Nurse, can you please fix this man's IV line, it has malfunctioned."

The nurse looked at them. He was about to say something, but his attention quickly went to the man, who was obviously in a bit of discomfort.

Realizing he was out of place, Zane took one more look around and then left the room in search of his next destination. Within steps of leaving the cancer ward he entered a maze of endless long grey hallways, all of them seeming to lead everywhere, except where he wanted to go. After about fifteen minutes of walking, he began wondering if what he was hoping to see simply did not exist at this hospital. He was just about to give up and follow the arrows back to the lobby, when he spotted a sign, which read "Psychiatric Medicine – sixth floor'.

He quickly located a lift and took it to the sixth floor. A short ride later, the elevator doors opened onto a quiet windowless hallway, with a large panel that had a list of departments on the floor. He found the directions to the psychiatric section, and began walking quickly through the maze of grey corridors, passing fewer and fewer people as he went. After about ten minutes he suddenly stumbled upon a barrier set up in the middle of the corridor, with a sign that read, "closed for maintenance, entry strictly prohibited".

"Shit! Now what?" he muttered out loud. He debated turning around to try access the ward from another floor, but ultimately decided to take a risk and see if he could cut through construction zone to save the hassle. Turning around to make sure no one and no cameras were about, he hopped over the barrier and scurried down the hall, following it as it turned left, right, and left again, abruptly arriving at the intersection of two unsigned corridors, one that went to the left, and the other continuing straight ahead, with a windowed grey door at the end. He walked up to the door and looked through glass. There on the wall facing him was a sign that read, "Psychiatric Wing, Geriatric Medicine".

He pulled at the door handle, but it was locked and wouldn't budge. All he could do was look through the glass at the scene on the other side. There were a number of very old people wandering around aimlessly in hospital gowns like zombies - disoriented, disheveled, and staring vacantly into space. Some of them were shaking uncontrollably, victims of some horrid neurodegenerative illness that had robbed them of their dignity. An old woman seated on a bench facing the door caught his eye, she was small and frail, and was staring intently at Zane through the glass. She seemed so innocent, vulnerable, and terribly alone. He waved at her, and she waved back. He began to cry, something he had not done since the day Maya told him they were going to have a child.

How could it be so many people had to suffer like this? How could it be in a country with so much wealth, so many had to suffer so terribly? Wasn't America supposed to be a light unto the world, a land of hope and prosperity? No, that was rhetorical bullshit, the proof was before his eyes. America may have invented many of the medicines to prevent these diseases, but it was determined to keep them inaccessible for the majority of its citizens.

"Excuse me sir, are you here visiting a patient?"

Zane jumped, turning around to see a security guard standing beside him. He had been so engrossed in his thoughts and looking at the woman, that he had not heard the guard approach him from the other corridor.

"Ah…Yes I was actually, but I'm finished with my visit."

"Very good sir, but you shouldn't be in this area, it's actually closed to the public as it's about to undergo renovations."

"Oh, I didn't see that," he lied, "I just took the elevators from a lower floor and followed the signs."

"Hmm, I will have to speak to building maintenance, as this area is definitely off limits. You are the first person I've seen here in at least a couple of shifts." The guard was about to continue, when an alarm sounded.

"Sir, nothing serious, probably just one of the patients tampering with the fire alarms. Happens all the time. If you can please go back in the direction you came from. I would escort you out, but I have to attend to this first."

Zane nodded, as the guard turned around and hurried away in the opposite direction, leaving him standing alone in the middle of the empty hallway. He looked through glass one last time to see if he could find the woman, but she had vanished. Wasting no time, he quickly walked back to the elevators, hoping not to run into any other security guards. The fire alarm, which had been ringing all this time, abruptly went silent just as he arrived at the entry to the construction zone. He was about to hop the barrier when his eyes caught an emergency exit sign to his left, indicating a door to a staircase leading to the floors below. Thinking it may be a shortcut, he pulled it open and descended the dusty poorly lit staircase to the next floor. The door on that floor was locked, and try as hard as he could he was unable to get it to open. He returned to the sixth floor, but that door was also locked from the outside and there was no way to open it. Slightly annoyed, he tried the doors on all the remaining floors, but those were also all locked off. Concerned he may be trapped in the staircase, he was just about to send a message to security via his EVO, when he spotted one last door on what seemed to be the ground floor.

Anxiously, Zane threw all his weight at it and was thrown off balance as it unexpectedly flung open, sending him stumbling to the ground. The door slammed shut behind him, as he regained his balance and realized he was standing not inside the hospital, but in fact alone in an abandoned parking lot at the back of the complex. Annoyed, he turned around and grabbed the door handle, tugging at it repeatedly to try get back inside the building, but it was stubbornly locked. Dammit he thought, now what? So foolish of me to take a shortcut, after all this isn't Salish City, it's fucking inner city D.C!

EVO interjected, "*Zane, I urgently recommend walking north through the parking lot and turning around the side of the building to access the main street. It will take you five minutes. This is not a safe area to be in. I will order a cab to pick you up at the corner.*"

"*Yes, please, I will go to the street now, get a cab —*"

"Hey man, what you doing out here man?"

Zane spun around, thinking it was a security guard. Instead what he saw were three tough medium built young white men standing beside a large dumpster in the parking lot, not far from where he was. Two of them were dressed in loose-fitting knee length shorts, matching basketball shirts, and dark coloured skull caps that covered the tops of their heads. The third one wore glasses, had a small backpack over his shoulders, and was in tight-fitting urban trousers with no shirt on, his defined torso covered in what looked to be tattoos, though it was difficult to see in the poor early evening light.

"Hey man you locked out? Looks like you can't get back inside! You knows those doors don't open from the outside man!"

Zane realized he was in trouble, these guys knew he was locked out of the building, and could surely see he wasn't from the neighbourhood. Trying not to sound intimidated, he replied, "ah yeah, I'm trying to get back inside, just-"

He was cut off by the guy without the shirt. "Hey you don't sound like you belong here!" Where you from pretty boy?"

One of the other two men added," yeah, look at him, he looks like one of those rich gentech boys from the city. Looks like he made a wrong turn and ended up on our turf!"

Sweating profusely from the heat and humidity, Zane stared at the three young men, his back pressed up against the locked door, hoping desperately someone would magically open it from the inside. He should never have taken the short cut, in fact he should never have even left the hotel room that afternoon, or at the very least followed his original plan and gone to Edgewood for the evening.

"Yo man, are you gonna answer my question? Where you from man?" The shirtless guy with the glasses shouted.

Trembling, he replied, "I'm not from here, I'm a guest researcher from Canada."

"Ah, a brainy Canadian, eh! Hahaha! Okay, we'll treat you nice, I mean you people are all so nice up there."

They laughed, clearly enjoying playing with him.

"What you got on you bro'? Bet you got a fancy device implant with access to a big fucking foreign bank account!" One of them shouted.

Zane didn't know what to do. He could strike first, maybe hit the shirtless guy who seemed to be the ringleader, and hopefully that would scare them, especially since he was a lot bigger and taller; however, he was outnumbered and didn't know where to run afterwards. Suddenly one of the men reached into the dumpster and pulled out a bottle and threw it at Zane's head. He ducked, but was drenched with a sticky liquid as the container shattered against the door behind him.

EVO whispered, *"Zane, a cab is waiting, it appears you are in a difficult situation. I will initiate a security call and implement safety mode."*

He decided he had no choice, he had to strike first and then make a run for the cab, hoping it would be where EVO said it was; however, before he could act the three men charged at him, knocking him to the ground. He felt a sharp pain as his head smacked against the pavement, his vision blurred.

"Grab his head man! Quick, get the scanner before his EVO goes offline! Fuck yeah, do it!"

"Look at the light fucker, look!"

Zane tried to look away, but then felt a blow to his stomach as his body was pinned down against the asphalt. He felt something clip around his wrist, where his EVO implant was installed, and then a bright blue light hit his eyes, leaving him blinded and disoriented.

"You got a lock on it man?"

"Yeah, I got it, this fucker's got money man. Fuck yeah! We've got forty thousand out of his account."

"Zane, emergency call executed, going into shutdown to protect essential identity information."

There were a few more blows to his stomach and his head, and then he blacked out.

He woke up coughing and sputtering. He was in a deep pool of water, and a heavy rain was falling on his face. He struggled up, lifting himself to his elbows, and then to a seated position. He was in a flooded parking lot, it was dark, and there was no one around. As he came to, he realized what had happened, he'd been assaulted, mugged, and his EVO had deactivated – certainly to prevent the theft becoming more serious. There was no way to reactivate the device, which meant he was offline, injured, and lost somewhere on the wrong side of Washington D.C.

Stumbling to his knees and then to his feet, he quickly realized how lucky he was to have come to when he did, the parking lot was already covered calf deep in flood water, and with just a few more minutes of unconsciousness he would have certainly drowned. He stood disoriented in the humid sticky downpour for a moment, before deciding he needed to get to the main street as fast possible, or else risk being assaulted again. Wading across the parking lot, he headed for the only way out - a dark alleyway between the hospital complex and what appeared to be an abandoned brick warehouse building.

He arrived at entrance and peered down into the poorly lit alleyway, trembling in fear as to what may be in there. Realizing he had no choice, he pulled himself together and shuffled into the darkness. As he walked he looked anxiously about, catching glimpses of layers of graffiti and exposed electrical wires visible on the dripping façades of the buildings on either side of him. The alley was only about forty or fifty metres long, but it seemed like an eternity as it jogged left and right before finally dumping him out onto an empty flooded street. Standing in the knee-deep water, he reached into his pockets and sighed in relief as he found a soggy clump of loose bills, which hopefully would be enough to catch the train, assuming he could find a station.

He stumbled along in the downpour, following the deserted flooded road for about a kilometre, until eventually reaching the intersection of a busy nameless street. He decided to follow the busy street to the left, comforted by the presence of passing cars and the possibility of finding a metro station to get him out of wherever he was. Zane wondered how awful he must look. Horrid, he imagined. He didn't care, all that mattered was finding a way out of this terrible nightmare he had stumbled into. He trudged along, doused repeatedly with waves of filthy street water from the constant traffic speeding by in the darkness. Zane had no idea how long he'd been walking, when suddenly his eyes caught the faint unmistakable sign of a flashing metro station a good kilometre down the street. He sighed with relief, and began walking as fast as his could to get to the station.

The rain was just coming to a stop by the time he arrived at the station entrance. It was packed with commuters, and there was no sign of a human or droid attendant at the pay gates, which meant he had to determine out how to access the metro system using real money and without the safe and familiar assistance of EVO. Throngs of people mindlessly pushed past him to the trains, not a soul showing the slightest interest in wanting to help or ask what was wrong. Never had he felt so alone and so fragile as he did in that moment.

"May I help you sir?"

Zane looked over and saw a mobile automated droid attendant standing beside him. "Ah yes," he sputtered. "I'm trying to figure out how to pay with bills. We don't have these where I come from."

"Understood. Let me do this operation for you sir. What is your destination?"

"I'm going to the station at the National Mall, my hotel is just near there."

"Very good sir, that will cost eighteen universal dollars. Please beware there is peak pricing in effect for your route at the moment."

Zane pulled out the damp clump of bills from his pocket, holding them in his shaking bloodied hands. God I must look unsightly, he thought, but at least it doesn't matter to the droid, all it cares about is its programmed functions.

"Sir, it will be faster if you give me the bills, I will be able to help you count what you need."

"No, I'm good, here's a twenty."

"Sir your token, as well as two dollars change. Thank you, and have a nice day."

He took the change and the token and walked to the gates, dropping the token into the slot. The glass gates slid open and he joined the masses of people climbing the stairs to the metro. How curious they call it a metro, he thought, especially when most the system is built above ground! A packed train pulled into the station just as he reached the top of the stairs, and he was pushed into the car by throngs of other riders crushing inside. He winced in pain, realizing his abdomen and back were badly bruised. The train was packed like sardines, and the air conditioning was battling to keep the temperature at a tolerable sticky thirty degrees.

After over an hour he arrived at his destination, stumbling out the train and joining the crowd of people pushing slowly up the stairs to the exit. He suddenly realized why there were so many people heading for the National Mall, they were all going to the giant pro-gentech rally.

Just at the top of the stairs he found himself beside a bank of public toilets. He slipped a note into the reader and the door slid open. Once inside the door slammed shut behind him, leaving him standing in front of a cracked mirror.

"Oh man Zane, what the hell happened? You look like shit! Fuck, you look like you've been to hell and back," he groaned out loud.

His face was badly bruised, his nose was clearly broken, he was missing a front tooth, and his shirt was ripped and bloodied. Wasting no time, he slowly pulled his shirt off and turned the faucets on, lathering his face and torso with soap to give himself

342

as much of a scrub as he possibly could. Hopefully he could get himself looking decent enough so the hotel security would be more cooperative in letting him enter the building. Without a doubt they were going to have lots of questions for him, given he had no ID, no money, and no connectivity to the Internet. Once he'd finished washing himself, he turned the faucets off and painfully put his shirt back on, taking a last look at himself in the mirror.

He exited the toilet, joining the crowd as it inched towards the station exits. After what seemed to take hours, he finally made it outside into the stiflingly hot early morning sunshine, arriving at a vantage point with a view towards the White House and onto a National Mall covered with hundreds of thousands of protestors. The crowd was of a scale he had never witnessed before; however, just as imposing were the numbers of D.C., Virginia, and Maryland state troopers lining the street on both sides of the metro station exits. There were thousands of them, and their massive presence was enforced by something he'd never seen before: dozens of imposing two-metre tall humanoid military class drones. The droids were all in sleep mode, and none of them appeared to be carrying any arms; however, Zane knew they could be activated at the push of a button to diffuse any situation where it would be too dangerous to send in human security enforcement.

"EVO, direct me to the hotel."

Silence.

Shit, no EVO, and there are at least a million people between me and my hotel, wherever it may be, he thought. How was he ever going to find his way there if he didn't remember where it was, and even what it was called?

He started walking aimlessly down the street, mingling with what seemed to be a very agitated crowd on the street in front of the mall. As he wandered around he saw protestors carrying state and national flags, as well as all kinds of messages in favour of genetic medicine. There were people his age calling for full public access on the grounds of social justice. There were others with emotional stories of loved ones who desperately needed the technology to overcome a fatal illness. Others carried signs with dark warning of genetic Apartheid, social exclusion, and imminent authoritarianism if the technology were not made accessible through Medicare. To his surprise, there were also many religious protestors with signs arguing that god had given humanity this new technology with the duty to use it for good and for social justice.

Zane had walked about four hundred metres from the station, when all of a sudden there was a loud explosion from up the street, followed by more smaller blasts, and the sound of gunfire. Screams erupted from the crowd on the street and further up the mall, and before he had an idea of what may be happening, a torrent of people came pushing down the avenue, colliding with his part of the crowd. Under the crush of people, he struggled to stay on his feet, and saw several protestors around him fall and get trodden by the stampeding crowd. Swept up in the wave, Zane pushed and struggled his way towards the side of the mass, in the hope he could reach the front doors of any building before being carried by the crowd towards the fences protecting the White House South Lawns.

In the passing moments he realized his efforts were futile, there was no chance he was going to make it to the edge of the crowd, what he needed to do was stay on his feet to avoid getting crushed by the stampeding masses of panicked protestors. Suddenly there were more blasts, and the air was littered with the sounds rattling of gunfire, which grew louder and more persistent. The crowd roared in a collective agony, while above their heads the sky filled with hundreds of surveillance and media drones, witnesses to the chaos and carnage suddenly unfolding below.

As he surfed the crowd forward, Zane looked above the hundreds of heads before him and realized his section was being swept towards the White House security perimetre, a barrier consisting of barbed wire and large electrified fences. He could see the people at the front of the crowd were trying to push back, to avoid being squashed, shredded, and electrocuted against the fence; however, their efforts were futile, the force of the crowd was too great for them to resist. As he was pushed towards the fences, the shrieks of pain and wretched cries grew ever louder, and he wondered if he would be next, or if ultimately the layers of corpses would be sufficient to save him from being shredded on the wires.

All of sudden from the crowd behind him, there was an eruption of loud squealing noises like the blood curdling screams of thousands of pigs trapped in a 20th Century slaughterhouse. He turned his head away from the carnage in front of him to see what it was. What he saw was a battlefield, with hundreds of thousands of people stampeding across the National Mall under a dense haze of drones, humidity, and smoke. Lurching through the crowd were those terrifying humanoid military class droids, dozens of them, two-metre tall giants, swinging their metallic limbs, grabbing and tossing people around like flailing rag dolls of broken flesh.

Those drones were closing in on Zane's part of the crowd, squeezing them like a *pâté* against the White House electrified perimetre. Realizing the new impending peril, the enormous seething mass of bodies around him erupted in a terrified frenzy. In the upheaval he fought to stay on his feet, gasping for air, while batting away arms, faces, and shoulders to avoid being crushed.

In the pandemonium, images of Maya, Timothy, his parents, and a loveless childhood flashed before his eyes. He saw the unborn child he and Maya had conceived, floating peacefully in a pod located in some vast industrial complex on the outskirts of an anonymous city - yet to be born, to live, to breath, to suffer, and to die. He remembered the countless stars visible in the heavens above Timothy's airship, stoically indifferent to the fleeting painful human condition he was forced endure. Agonizingly trapped in a dying and tumultuous crowd through chance and misfortune, he realized his life had been nothing but a meaningless and perfunctory existence, programmed like an automat to seek pleasure, vanity, comfort, and status. What was the point of it all? Why had he even lived? For all the marvels of genetic engineering and artificial intelligence, there was still no answer, and there probably never would be.

The sounds of gunfire and screaming grew louder as he was pushed closer and closer to the razor-sharp electrified fences. Suddenly, when he was just metres from the wires, he felt a cold metallic hand on his back. He shivered and turned around, his sweaty blood smeared face encountering the cold penetrating gaze of an emotionless machine.

Zane gasped weakly, and then it was over.

"Well Joseph, today was a dark day here in Washington D.C."

"Following a month of disastrous townhalls led by the Administration and its consulting partner Syllabus Corporation, today's rally was supposed to empower grass-roots supporters of the President's Human Genetic Technologies bill prior to the Congressional vote on Monday. Instead the event turned into a scene of unprecedented carnage after a group of religious and right-wing extremists charged onto the Mall, firing guns and explosives at the police and the general public, setting off a stampede of hundreds of thousands in the direction of the White House South Lawn."

"In the hope of stopping the stampede, security forces initiated their dormant droid defence system; however, the system malfunctioned, and over a period of two hours many of the machines went on a killing rampage, murdering untold numbers of people."

"Terrible, truly horrific…Mary, any idea as to the numbers of dead and injured?"

"Yes Joseph, police are talking about as many as four thousand dead, and maybe twenty thousand injured. Most of the fatalities did not occur at the initial extremist attack site, rather it was around the White House security perimetre that the damage was greatest, for it was there that people were crushed between the razor-sharp electrified security fences and the masses of stampeding protestors. It was also in that area where the droid units malfunctioned and inflicted their greatest toll on the protestors."

"Thanks Mary, truly horrific, may god be with the injured and those who have perished today."

Date - Monday May 19th, 2121

Dressed in black, the President stood on the lawn of the Rose Garden in front of dozens of cameras. A Commander-in-Chief with nerves of steel in the face of the terrible events that had occurred two days earlier, just a mile away. She was accompanied by her Vice-President, and apart from the Secretary of Health, her entire cabinet stood in a group behind her.

"Ladies and gentlemen, my fellow Americans. Two days ago, across this lawn, our nation bore witness to the worst domestic terror attack in our history. Tens of thousands of people were injured and many thousands killed by domestic terrorists. These extremists were determined to use violence in an act of political rage against our government's just and fair plan to include genetic medicine in our national Medicare program."

"The terrorists came well prepared to inflict maximum carnage against ordinary Americans. They hacked into the police force's droid and drone network and then set the machines upon a path of unimaginable destruction. Using Presidential Order, I have instructed the Secretary of Surveillance and Public Order to conduct a thorough criminal investigation into this matter, with a decision to be made on the future use of droid technology by our domestic police forces."

"These terrorists struck at a moment when millions of Americans of all ages, classes, and backgrounds took the streets of our nation's capital to peacefully protest for what they believed to be right and to be just. I hear their voices; their dreams will not be silenced and they will not be forgotten."

"In the interests of the country, I and my cabinet have elected to temporarily suspend today's joint Congressional vote on the Human Genetic Technologies Act. This suspension is effective immediately, and will remain in place until further notice."

"God bless those who have fallen here, and god bless America."

About the Author

An African-Canadian writer, musician, and entrepreneur based in Vancouver and Sevilla, Glen Albert Phillips was educated at HEC Montréal and ESADE Barcelona in International Business, and at the University of Victoria in Environmental Management and Chemistry.

Besides English, he speaks Spanish, French, Portuguese, Hebrew, and Italian acquired from many years of travelling and working in numerous countries.

Glen is currently working on completing his third novel, a work of science fiction based on his experiences and observations from travelling in an increasingly turbulent world.

Glen has also produced a compilation of photography and poetry, some of which have guitar accompaniment.

www.ingramcontent.com/pod-product-compliance
Lightning Source LLC
Chambersburg PA
CBHW020840020726
47497CB00005B/1182